First Do No Harm

by

Peter Sykes

Peter Sykes served as a consultant surgeon for 25 years, later becoming the medical director of an NHS Trust. In 1998 he led the group that became the 'UK Medical Management Team of the Year'. During the final three years of his career, he was involved at a national level in the control of quality of surgical services.

He is now retired, and when not writing, spends his time gardening, golfing, enjoying the company of his grandchildren and occasionally grumbling that *'things ain't what they used to be'.*

****

Peter's first novel **'The First Cut'** was published in 2011. It described Paul Lambert's medical misadventures as he was thrown, bewildered and unprepared, onto a busy surgical ward as a newly qualified doctor.

This was followed in 2013 by **'Behind the Screens'** which tells real-life tales at a time when care and compassion ruled supreme in British hospitals. Some of the stories are humorous, some sad, others poignant, but all are very 'human'. The novel also follows Paul's chequered love life and unveils some of the 'high jinks' that doctors get up to when off-duty.

Foreword

The election called by Edward Heath in February 1974 was fought against a background of a miner's strike, a three day working week and ministerial advice to save hot water by taking a bath with a friend! The salaries of staff working for the NHS had not kept pace with sharply rising inflation and hospital budgets had been cut as austerity measures were imposed to correct the burgeoning national debt. Labour won four more seats than the Conservatives but did not obtain an overall majority. Nonetheless Harold Wilson decided to 'go it alone' with a minority government. Mrs Barbara Castle, the left wing MP for Blackburn, was given cabinet responsibility for health.

Nurses felt underpaid and undervalued and had observed how industrial action by the ancillary workers had won them a large pay rise. Many younger members of the profession, unhappy with the results of their Royal College's negotiation with the Government, had joined the more militant National Union of Public Employees (NUPE) or the Confederation of Health Service Employees (CoHSE) both of whom were actively recruiting. The same was true for radiographers and physiotherapists.

The Junior Hospital Doctors were furious that overtime was paid at a rate less than a third of base rate and then only if their consultant was prepared to sign their claims form – which many weren't!

The Hospital Consultants were concerned that their pay had been eroded by inflation and also wanted a new contract which allowed them greater clinical freedom. Their greatest anxiety however was the Labour Party's pledge to remove 'pay beds'. These 'pay beds' enabled consultants to treat their lucrative private patients in NHS hospitals. The 'pay beds' had been the concession that had overcome the doctor's resistance to the creation of the NHS in 1948. The British Medical Association (BMA) had declined to negotiate the doctor's terms and conditions of service with Aneurin Bevan, the Health Minister, fearful that they would simply become salaried civil servants. There were many stormy meetings and a prolonged acrimonious power struggle ensued. Bevan referred to the BMA as a *'small body of politically poisoned people'*. The BMA chairman spoke of Bevan as the *'medical fuhrer'*. Bevan finally managed to win the doctor's support by offering concessions, including access to 'pay beds'. Later he was to describe it as *'stuffing their mouths with gold!'* Mrs Castle however believed passionately that private practice had no place within the National Health Service and vowed that they should be removed.

The stage was set for a battle royal in which the patients would become the main casualties and the reputation of all combatants would the tarnished.

Disclaimer

This book is a novel set against the political disputes that beset the National Health Service between 1974 and 1976. All the national political characters are real. I have portrayed their actions and beliefs as faithfully as I can after extensive research of archive material.

The City General Hospital characters are not real. Similarly the clinical events described are fictitious.

This book is dedicated to healthcare workers everywhere. May care and compassion be their constant companions.

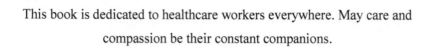

All author royalties from the sale of this book will be shared equally between East Cheshire Hospice, Macclesfield and St Ann's Hospice, Stockport.

I wish to thank Sean Butler for designing the book cover. Steve Linnell of Linnell Illustration created the cartoon character and similarly gave his time and expertise free of charge. I am also grateful to Julie Mann, Edward Vickers, Gill Lynch, Danuta Silva, Halina Kwiatkowski, to the many friends who searched for errors of spelling and punctuation in the final manuscript and to my wife Jane for constant support and for providing numerous cups of tea and the occasional gin and tonic.

Above all, I thank the many patients that it has been my privilege to serve for giving me the inspiration to write this book.

The photographs are reproduced by kind permission of the Royal College of Nursing and Solo Syndication; the Emmwood cartoon by courtesy of the Daily Mail.

It may seem a strange principle to enunciate as the very first requirement in a hospital is that it should do no harm.

Florence Nightingale

Chapter One

"*EQUAL PAY FOR WOMEN*" the crowd chanted as they surged onto the stage; "*WE DEMAND EQUALITY.*" Some were dressed as cooks, some as cleaners, others as factory workers. They held aloft banners proclaiming the same message. They were led by a slip of a girl wearing a thin grey cotton shift; she looked to be no more than nineteen. The sash across her chest bore a single word; 'BARBARA'.

The women marched across the boards to a plywood door set in a painted canvas wall. The sign on the door announced that this was the FORD MOTOR COMPANY. Barbara hammered on the door demanding entry.

The audience roared their approval. They all remembered the strike by the women in the sewing room which had halted Ford's production line for three weeks and brought the company to its knees. So did the person being parodied whose intervention had been such a triumph, not just for the women at Dagenham but for women throughout the land. Barbara Castle, now Cabinet Minister with responsibility for Health and Social Services was sitting on the front row of the balcony with her husband and numerous trade union officials.

"Go get 'em, Barbara," a voice shouted from the body of the hall. "Give 'em hell."

Inside the Ford factory, four workmen in dirty overalls were sitting round a table playing cards. The overloaded ashtrays and numerous empty mugs suggested a long unscheduled tea break. No-one moved in response to the clamour outside. The women's leader knocked again, even more vigorously than before.

"You'd better go and see what all the fuss is about," one of the gamblers said to an apprentice who was lounging in an old armchair reading a girlie magazine.

Reluctantly, the lad got to his feet and wandered over to the window.

"It's those bloody women again," he reported.

"Well, tell 'em to piss off." A great roar of laughter from the audience greeted this remark.

"I suppose someone has to," the lad said smiling. He opened the door, gave the women a two fingered salute then slammed the door in their faces.

"That's the way to treat 'em. If they think they can come in here and demand the same pay as us, they can damn well think again. All they do is sit and chat while they stitch a few bits of material together for the car seats. That's not difficult; anyone could do it. It's not like the skilled work we do on the assembly line making the bloody cars."

Outside the factory door, the women turned away looking disheartened. Then one of them cried, "Hey Barbara, we mustn't give up; show them some of your old magic. Let them see that we mean business. Here, take this."

From her bag she produced a wig covered with great curls of flaming red hair which, with great ceremony, she set on her leader's head as carefully and gently as if she were crowning a queen. Subconsciously, up in the balcony, Barbara Castle touched her own hair, conscious that as streaks of grey had appeared, her fiery, ginger locks were not as vivid as they had been in her youth. But that didn't worry her. She delighted in being caricatured; she loved these irreverent reviews that the Trades Union Congress (TUC) put on each year at Transport House. She was relaxed. This was an evening she enjoyed; an evening when she could be amongst friends and put aside all her cares, problems and responsibilities.

On the stage, the women's leader now stood taller and prouder than before. As if by magic her dull grey shift disappeared, replaced by a shining silver breast plate. A sword appeared in her hand. She was Diana the Huntress, Queen Boadicea and Joan of Arc all rolled into one. Boldly she smashed through the door and led her followers into the factory. The men inside cowered before her and in an instant were brutally despatched with mighty blows of her sword. Victorious, she jumped onto the table and turned to face the audience.

"Success," she cried triumphantly. "Equal pay for women has been achieved." Her words, clear and strident, reached every corner of the room. "Now bring on the hospital consultants. They too shall fall beneath my sword. We demand justice for the common man and woman. No longer shall the rich be allowed to buy their way to the front of the queue for a hospital bed." Her voice rose to a final crescendo. "The private beds MUST go. The private beds WILL go!"

This socialist dogma delighted everyone in the hall. They stood and cheered to the rafters as the girl took her bow and left the stage to rapturous applause.

"They really admire the work you do," Barbara's husband said as the ovation finally subsided. "You should be very proud. Introducing the Equal Pay Act was one of the finest things you ever did."

"That's right, "a union official agreed, "and we're all delighted that the 'pay beds' are to be your next target. Where's the fairness in some people being able to avoid the waiting list and go into hospital as and when they please? The National Health Service (NHS) was created for the benefit of all; not just for the privileged few. But a word of warning Barbara; you will need to tread carefully.

The consultants will be a tough nut to crack. However you can rely on strength of the unions. We'll back you every step of the way."

"Tough nut they may be," Barbara replied, delighted to know that she had the unqualified support of the unions, "but crack them I will and I know exactly how to do it. They're desperately keen to win a new contract. I shall grant them that, but my price will be the removal of the pay beds."

"Will you be able to resolve the nurses' dispute as well?" her husband asked, aware that the nurses' anger with the government over their pay claim was also causing unrest.

"Leave the nurses to me," Barbara replied, "I have plans for them as well."

As she spoke there was a curious inflection in her voice and a subtle smile on her lips. The union official was keen to understand the meaning behind her words but didn't get the chance to ask her to explain further. At that moment their conversation was interrupted by a crowd of well wishers, all eager to chat with Barbara about the sketch. Later he went home anxious about her intentions. Abolition of the pay beds would be hugely popular; it would win many extra votes for the Labour Party at the forthcoming election. But he felt that the nurses' dispute needed a softer approach. Nurses were highly regarded; the public thought of them as angels. If Barbara declared war on them, as she clearly intended to do with the hospital consultants, there could be trouble.

Chapter Two

"I may be out when you get home tonight, Paul," Kate said across the breakfast table. "There's a meeting in the hospital this evening that I want to go to."

"So my pretty little wife is planning to go out without me is she?" Paul replied smiling. "I'm not sure that I approve of that!"

"Don't worry. There will be dozens of other nurses there to keep an eye on me; I should be quite safe. Apparently, someone is coming to tell us how the negotiations on our pay claim are progressing."

"Not very well from the sound of it. The government have slapped an embargo on all pay rises. You certainly deserve an increase but I doubt that you're going to get one."

Paul was training to be a surgeon at the City General Hospital and his young wife Kate was a staff nurse on one of the surgical wards. Since their wedding nine months before, they had lived in a flat in the grounds of the hospital and had quickly settled into a comfortably routine.

"Actually, I'm rather afraid that I shall be late home tonight as well," Paul continued. "Today's the day that the new doctors arrive; the day we all hate because we need to supervise them so closely."

"But it's the day all the student nurses love. Another group of handsome young men for them to flutter their eye lashes at!"

"Is that what you did when I first arrived on the ward?"

"Of course; I thought that somewhere deep inside you there might be a little basic potential; some raw material that I could mould into something acceptable, so I grabbed you before anyone else had a chance," Kate replied grinning. She reached for her nurse's cap and gave Paul a quick kiss. "Anyway, I must dash. Sister will kill me if I'm not on the ward by seven forty five. See you tonight. Oh and Paul, treat those new doctors gently. They're bound to be nervous."

After the door closed, Paul sat for a few moments and smiled to himself as he thought about Kate. He blessed the day that they had met. He delighted in her company. She soothed him when he was angry, teased him if he became pompous and lifted him when he was low. He thought she was just perfect. He didn't feel that he was in anyway special himself and found it difficult to understand why Kate had chosen him above all others. Paul was not tall, well built or handsome, and he was very conscious of his own deficiencies. He regarded himself as being a rather dull individual who lacked confidence and was socially inept. He felt that Kate could have had her pick of all the men in the world, yet she truly loved him. He had indeed been extremely fortunate.

Then, waking from his reverie, he glanced at the clock, threw the dirty dishes into the sink, grabbed his white coat and set off for the wards.

*****

Janet and Malcolm, quietly apprehensive of the task that lay ahead, had arranged to walk to the ward together to report for duty on their first morning as doctors. They had moved their belongings into the hospital the night before, though only Malcolm was able to stay overnight. The bedroom that was to be Janet's was still occupied by the outgoing doctor; one of the housemen being required to be on duty in the hospital at all times.

As they left the residency they walked along the short covered passage that led to the main hospital corridor. There they joined the stream of staff heading for the wards; porters in brown overalls pushing the large heated metal trolleys containing the patients' breakfasts, cleaners sporting pink aprons carrying buckets and mops and nurses wearing their smart blue uniforms as they prepared to relieve the night staff. A few were still wiping the sleep from their eyes; one or two were grumbling about their poor wages and irregular hours but most were chattering cheerfully. At the cross roads where the casualty and outpatient staff carried straight on and the managers turned left into the administrative block, the two newly qualified doctors turned right into the surgical corridor then, eschewing the lift since it was always quicker to take the stairs, they reached the corridor leading to the Surgical Five wards. With a nervous glance at each other, they approached Sister's office.

As usual, Paul was on the ward early. His boss Mr Leslie Potts was due to undertake his Monday morning ward round within the hour and he wanted to make sure that he was familiar with all his patients, just as the ward sister wanted everything to be 'spick and span' whenever matron paid a visit. It was a matter of pride for Paul to have all the facts and figures needed by his consultant, at his finger tips. Specifically he needed to be certain that no fresh problems had arisen during the course of the night. The last thing he wanted was for the consultant to identify a clinical problem that he had overlooked.

However, with the new house officers arriving, this was no ordinary day. Fresh out of medical school, they knew little of ward routine, still had to learn how to perform simple practical procedures and had yet to appreciate the foibles, those irritating little idiosyncrasies of the consultants they were to serve. They needed to be watched like hawks for they were likely to make mistakes that could jeopardise patient care. It meant a lot of extra work for Paul and the nursing sisters as they supervised the 'virgin' doctors. Janet and Malcolm would remain in their new posts for six months. Then, just when they were getting settled into the job, they would be replaced by two more complete novices!

As Paul left the office to review Mr Potts' patients, he met the two house officers as they arrived. He was immediately struck by the great contrast between them. He turned to greet them.

"Hello, I'm Paul Lambert, the surgical registrar. You must be our two new house officers."

"Yes, that's right. My name is Janet Smith." The words were sharp and clear, the voice surprisingly confident.

"And you will be working for Mr Potts, I presume," Paul said.

"Yes, that's right. How did you know?"

"I didn't know," Paul said, "it was just a guess."

The truth was that it wasn't a guess at all. He had worked for Mr Potts before and knew his reputation. He had an eye for the ladies. He always appointed the prettiest of the female graduates to be his house officer, irrespective of their academic achievement in the final medical exam or their performance when attached to the surgical unit as a student. Paul noted however that this girl was not in the usual Leslie Potts mould. She was indeed tall and strikingly good-looking, but her hair, though blond, was unfashionably short and tousled. Paul thought that it could have been her crowning glory but no attempt had been made to make it look attractive. With her clear complexion and high cheekbones, she could have been a model but devoid of make-up her face was unsmiling; indeed her expression rather suggested that she found the meeting somewhat disagreeable. It was her eyes though which were her most notable feature. They were strikingly blue and had a directness that seemed to challenge those who met her gaze. And her clothes were severe. For her first day at work, she had chosen an elegantly tailored grey pinstriped suit, a plain white blouse sealed with a brooch at the neck and highly polished black, flat heeled, leather shoes.

Paul turned to her companion, whom he recognised as one of the students who had studied on the unit a couple of years previously.

"So you will be working for Sir William, our senior consultant," he said. "I think you've worked with us before."

"Er yes," he said." I'm Malcolm Chapman."

Hearing the name refreshed Paul's memory. Malcolm had been the brightest student they had taught on the unit for many years. He was academically brilliant. His knowledge of surgical disease had almost been as comprehensive as Paul's. When Paul had been teaching the students, there had been times when he had struggled to answer some of Malcolm's searching questions. Whereas Leslie Potts appointed his house officer, invariably female, entirely on their looks, Sir William appointed his according to their academic record. Paul had little doubt that Malcolm had scored the highest mark in the surgical exam. In appearance, he was somewhat unremarkable, one might almost say insignificant. He was at least six inches shorter than Janet, thick set, with a waistline that hinted at a sedentary lifestyle. His face was round, pale and pasty, and with his stumpy nose and thick lensed glasses, surmounted by untidy short brown hair, he had a rather bookish appearance.

The most notable feature about him however, was his white coat, which would have suited someone of a rather grander stature. It drowned him, almost reaching his ankles. The effect was to make him appear shorter and fatter than he really was. Furthermore, the white coat had been adapted by having four large additional pockets sewn into it. Each pocket bulged with assorted pieces of equipment. A selection of pens of different colours, pencils and a ruler filled his left chest pocket, an assortment of request cards for various blood, urine and x-ray investigations overflowed from another, a third pocket was stuffed with syringes, needles, swabs and sticking plasters and all the other equipment required to take blood samples. A fourth contained a tendon hammer and a tuning fork to enable examination of the nervous system. Other pockets held tools to take temperatures, blood pressures and even gloves and lubricating jelly with which to perform a rectal examination. Paul suppressed a laugh. He couldn't decide if the new houseman looked more like a Michelin man in a white coat, a war time spiv selling rationed goods or a mad professor from a horror movie.

"You've come well-prepared," Paul commented cheerfully, though privately he wondered what Leslie Potts would make of Malcolm's appearance. "Anyway, you're both very welcome. I trust you'll enjoy working with us on the Surgical Five unit. Now though, we had better get down to work. Until the boss arrives, I suggest that you join me and I'll introduce you to some of our patients."

As it happened Mr Potts was late, not an unusual occurrence, and Paul had time to review all the patients on the ward before the consultant appeared. When he finally burst through the door, slightly breathless and with a harassed look on his face, Paul was sitting with the two housemen in the office, explaining what was expected of them in their new jobs. All three rose when the consultant entered.

Of average height but stockily built, Mr Potts was aged between forty-five and fifty. Greying at the temples, his dark hair was well oiled and swept back. He had dark eyes, a furrowed brow and a tight mouth that rarely smiled which gave the impression of a man who did not tolerate fools gladly - nor indeed did he! He held himself straight, like an officer on parade, with his shoulders back and his chest thrust forward. Wearing his immaculate suit he was an impressive, some might say, a daunting figure.

"I must apologise for being a little late," he said brusquely. "One of my patients in the private patients' wing has been misbehaving. It's taken me a little time to sort him out." He turned to his registrar. "Lambert, perhaps you could find a minute later in the day to check up on him. He's an elderly and rather frail chap called Morrison. He's two days post op and is a bit chesty. See that he's managing to clear his chest will you. If he isn't, chase up the physiotherapists for me. Get them to give him an extra treatment and if necessary you could perhaps prescribe a cough bottle for him."

Paul was employed by the NHS and there was nothing in his contract that required him to care for Mr Potts' private patients, nor was he reimbursed for his trouble. Paul knew though that he was expected to do as he was asked and that if he demurred it would count against him when the time came to ask for a reference.

Mr Potts brightened when he noticed the two newcomers.

"You must be our new house officers," he said. He turned to Dr Smith, smiling broadly and placing a hand on her shoulder. "Hello again Janet, I remember you well from the interview we had in my office. It's good to see you again, I'm sure that you and I are going to get along fine. I may call you Janet, mayn't I, or perhaps you prefer Jan?"

There was a pause and Paul saw her stiffen; a slight frown crossed her brow. "I would prefer Miss Smith, or Dr Smith, if it's all the same to you Sir," she said. Her voice was cool, the words precise. As she spoke she took half a stride backwards which left Mr Potts' arm hanging rather awkwardly in the air.

For a moment, Mr Potts looked surprised but quickly regained his composure. "Yes, my dear, of course, if that's what you think is most appropriate." For a second it appeared that the house officer might react to the expression '*my dear*', but she held her tongue.

Paul was fascinated by the way Janet had reacted. He remembered all too clearly, the unprofessional relationship that had developed between Mr Potts and a previous tall, blond and attractive house officer called Elizabeth Webb. He recalled also the scene that he and many other members of staff had witnessed at a social event, when Mr Potts' wife had noticed Elizabeth's easy familiarity towards her husband. How the sparks had flown on that occasion! The pair had kept the hospital grapevine alive with speculation and innuendo for months on end. Perhaps Janet had also heard the story and been forewarned.

The rebuff from Dr Smith appeared to change the consultant's sunny disposition. He turned to the other new houseman, "And you are?"

"M-malcolm Chapman, S-sir. I shall be working for Sir William," Malcolm replied his face reddening.

"What on earth are you wearing boy?" the consultant queried, eyebrows raised to the ceiling.

"M-my white coat, Sir," Malcolm replied.

"I can see that, I'm not a complete fool! But what on earth have you done to it?"

"I've arranged for a few extra p-pockets to be added Sir, so that I can carry all the equipment that I shall need to do my job."

"For heaven's sake, why?"

"It will enable me to be more efficient, S-sir. I shan't have to return to the office every time I need a piece of equipment."

"Well you look like a bloody stuffed rabbit. Go and take it off at once and don't come back onto the ward looking so ridiculous ever again."

"You mean g-go now, Sir?" Malcolm asked.

"Yes, now. Go, go!"

Paul felt sorry for the young man, seeing him treated so roughly and unfairly on his first morning on the ward but knew better than to interfere. He would take Malcolm on one side later, sympathise and explain that he was not the first to have been treated in that fashion by Mr Potts, nor indeed would he be the last.

Malcolm left the ward with his tail between his legs, to reappear twenty minutes later burning with indignation but wearing a more conventional white coat. He was resentful that his enterprise had not been appreciated, and shocked and angry to have been spoken to in that fashion by his consultant, particularly as the reprimand had been witnessed by the whole team. He had studied extremely hard for the final medical school exam. Then, when most of his colleagues had gone to enjoy a well earned holiday, he had done his best to prepare himself for his first job by trailing the outgoing house officer. He had noticed how frequently the medical staff interrupted a patient's treatment by leaving the bedside to fetch some item of equipment that they needed to complete their task. How much better, he had thought, if all these items were on hand; hence his initiative with the extra pockets on his white coat. Although bewildered by the manner in which he had been treated, he was not down hearted. In fact, the episode made him even more determined to demonstrate his worth to the consultant. He vowed that in the months to come he would prove himself to be a hardworking, knowledgeable and resourceful doctor.

*****

The next time that Paul visited the ward, he couldn't fail to notice that a modification had been made to the notes trolley. The trolley was a large wooden box on wheels, the open top being divided by 29 partitions to create a space for each of the patient's notes and x-rays. The spaces were numbered 1 – 30. At each end there was a horizontal bar or handle, akin to that on a pram, allowing the trolley to be pushed round the ward. A white flannel sheet had been hung over each of the horizontal bars, secured at the top by a pair of jubilee clips. On each sheet there were three large pockets. It looked as if Malcolm's white coat had been cut up and draped over the ends of the trolley. Moreover the pockets were stuffed full of the various items that Malcolm had previously carried in his white coat; the investigation cards, instruments, blood bottles, needles and syringes, including of course a pocket with plastic gloves and lubricating gel to enable Sir William to perform the many rectal examinations that he found necessary. Paul immediately saw the value of the trolley, but wondered what Mr Potts' reaction would be to it. He wasn't too long before he found out!

The following day, Mr Potts was only ten minutes late for his ward round. As usual, his juniors were waiting for him in the office, but he merely put his nose round the door.

"Come on, let's get on with this ward round," he said.

Mr Potts always started with the patient furthest from the door, and then worked his way back to the office. This was unusual as most consultants started their round by the ward doors and finished at the far end of the ward. This strategy enabled Mr Potts to dive straight back into the office when he had seen all his patients, thus preventing him from being hijacked by patients' questions as he walked back down the ward.

Eager to get going, the consultant walked briskly down the line of patients and stopped by the end bed, waiting for his staff to catch up with him. Malcolm arrived last, pushing the now rather heavy and cumbersome trolley. Leslie Potts' eye immediately fell upon it.

"What the hell is that?" he demanded.

All eyes turned upon Malcolm. He blinked behind his glasses timidly, but he had anticipated the possibility of an unfavourable comment and had come prepared to stand his ground.

"I know you didn't approve of my white coat, Mr Potts, Sir," he said quietly, "so I've made a modification to the notes trolley instead. I hope you approve of it."

"Well, I don't," snapped Mr Potts. "What on earth is the purpose of it?" he demanded, though the answer to his question was perfectly obvious.

"It's to save t-time on the ward round Sir and for your convenience," Malcolm replied entirely reasonably. "When you require a piece of equipment, we shall already have it to hand and we shan't need to keep you waiting."

"But those drapes will attract germs; all our patients will end up with infections," Leslie Potts said, casting around for a reason to justify his disapproval. "We can't have a mobile bacteria carrier on our wards rounds. Get rid of it."

"But I've thought about that, Sir," countered Malcolm. "The staff in the linen room have made a duplicate set for me, so that we can get these laundered. It won't be any dirtier than the pillows and sheets that the patients are using, or the white coats that we all wear."

Paul and the ward sister shuffled uncomfortably. They thought that Malcolm had shown commendable enterprise. His initiative had much to commend it. Had they been braver, they would have given Malcolm some verbal support but they didn't; they felt that his best plan would be to let the matter drop. They recognised that the consultant had made up his mind and that this exchange would inevitably end up with Malcolm being shouted down.

Mr Potts was not accustomed to having his decisions dissipated by logic or indeed rebutted by the newest and most junior member of his staff. "But it looks like a baby's pram," he blustered. "If we're going to have the damn thing looking like a pram on the ward round, for God's sake give it to Miss Smith, then at least it will be pushed by a woman."

Janet, who already stood an inch or two taller than Mr Potts raised herself to her full height and glared down at him, fixing him with her penetrating gaze. Would she answer him back? Paul silently prayed that she would not. If she did, it would set the tone for an extremely stressful six months.

But Janet's glare melted into a half-smile as she asked, "Do you have a family, Mr Potts?"

"Yes, I do. Why do you ask?"

"Then I do hope Sir, that when your children were babies, you took your fair share of domestic duties; not only washing and feeding them but changing their dirty nappies as well."

There was a prolonged pause and tension like static electricity in the air. Everyone waited on tenterhooks, fearful of how Mr Potts would respond.

Finally, he spoke. "Alright," he said grimly, turning to Malcolm, "this time you win. I will tolerate the trolley on the ward today, but when I do my ward round next week, I would prefer to see the trolley back in its normal state." The words had been spoken as a request but everyone realised that in reality it was a strict instruction.

Chapter Three

"My Bill's got a lump in his groin," the cleaner shouted above the noise of her circular floor polisher. "It's a rupture - at least that's what our local doctor thinks it is. He's got to be seen by one of the specialists here, though God knows when that will be. You can be dead and buried these days before you get to see anyone, the waiting times are so long."

"Let's take a break and have a brew," her friend replied. "Then you can tell me all about it. We've just about finished this waiting room. My back's killing me; it deserves a rest before we clean the corridors."

They were unplugging their machines from the wall when the door burst open and half a dozen nurses walked in.

The cleaner accosted them, irritated by the disturbance. No-one came to the outpatient department in the evening. When all the patients had gone home at the end of the afternoon session, it was theirs to prepare for the next day's clinic.

"Hey, you can't come in here. The departments closed."

"Not tonight it's not," Staff Nurse Claire replied cheerfully. "Tonight we're holding a meeting in here."

"Nobody's said anything to us about a meeting. Who gave you permission? We've cleaned the floor. We'll have to polish it again if you go tramping all over it."

The truth was that no-one had given them permission. The nurses' request to hold a meeting with the representative of the Confederation of Health Service

Employees (CoHSE) in the Nurses Home had been refused by Matron. She might have allowed a meeting with an officer from the Royal College of Nursing (RCN) but certainly not with a union with a reputation for militancy. The hospital's senior manager had similarly declined permission for them to use the hospital's large lecture hall.

The cleaner was used to getting her own way and would have continued to argue her case but, as more and more nurses filed into the hall, she realised she was fighting a lost cause. Some of the nurses were in mufti, others still in uniform having just come off duty.

"Well don't expect us to tidy up after you. We've cleaned it once, we're not going to clean it again!" was her final shot at Claire. She turned to her friend. "Come on. It's time for that cuppa you were talking about."

The vast majority of CoHSE members in the 1970s were hospital ancillary workers; porters, cleaners and kitchen staff. However, the union was keen to extend its sphere of influence by recruiting nurses and was offering support for their claim for better pay. One day, their regional officer, Jimmy Ackroyd, had rung the Nurses Home and found himself talking to Claire, who happened to hold strong views on the remuneration of nurses. He had suggested the meeting. Claire had then discussed the proposal with other nurses, including her best friend Kate, Paul's wife. Frustrated by the lack of progress in the negotiations with the government, they decided that nothing would be lost by listening to what CoHSE had to say.

Jimmy Ackroyd proved to be an accomplished and persuasive speaker, though any nurse expecting a strident call for immediate industrial action was to be disappointed. Jimmy introduced himself as a pathology technician from the Birmingham area. He spoke quietly and calmly, clearly recognising that he was addressing a professional group who, throughout their long and distinguished history, had never previously taken action. He understood that caring people who dedicated themselves to the sick would be averse to doing anything that would harm their patients.

He began by thanking the nurses for their invitation to chat with them, despite the fact that he had suggested the meeting himself! Then he surprised them by describing the work done by his wife, who was a short hand typist working for a well known insurance company. She enjoyed her job he said, the office in which she worked was clean and bright and the people from whom she took dictation were pleasant and obliging. There was a canteen in the building where wholesome food was available at lunchtime, free of charge. His wife's sister, Jimmy continued, worked in a biscuit factory. Her job was to supervise the girls who labelled the biscuit tins. She was also responsible for transporting the tins to the dispatch area. She found the work boring but the hours were regular and her job was secure.

"And do you know," Jimmy said, "that both my wife and sister-in-law get paid more per hour that any staff nurse or junior nursing sister working here at the City General. Yet you nurses have far greater responsibility than they do and your job is much more stressful. Think about the problems you face, the burdens you have to bear. You deal with patients with cancer, you handle medical emergencies and those critically injured in accidents; you care for the dying. And what about the hours you work? My wife doesn't have to work shifts or work through the night as you do. She's at home every weekend with our children. She's always free to take our daughter to Brownies or watch our ten year old son play football. She never has to work through her lunch break. She's not expected to work for an extra hour or two 'til the latest emergency admission is settled into the ward."

Cleverly he had stoked up the nurses' sense of injustice; their anger had been aroused.

"But what can we do about it?" one of them called out. "We can't go on strike."

"That is exactly what the government is relying on," Jimmy replied. "That is why they are able to ignore your claim for a fair wage; that is why the 'gently – gently' approach of the RCN is never going to deliver for you. The government will simply continue to ignore you in the future, just as they have done in the past."

"So what can we do? We could never do anything that would harm our patients. That would be unthinkable."

"You can start by letting the government know that you're angry and that you mean business. You can make your voice heard."

"But surely we must leave that to the RCN. They represent us; they work on our behalf."

"Certainly they should be working for you; they are the biggest group on the negotiating committee. But ask yourself, are they delivering the goods; are you happy with what they have achieved?"

"We don't know yet what they will be able to achieve," a more moderate voice said. "The negotiations are still ongoing. We should wait until we know what the settlement is to be, before we talk of militant action."

"CoHSE are allowed to sit in on the meetings with the Health Department," Jimmy responded, "and I can tell you that the RCN are far too gentle, far too polite. They're never going to win the settlement that you want or give you the level of pay you deserve. The problem is that at the moment, CoHSE don't have much clout at the negotiations, because too few nurses belong to our union. But

I promise you, CoHSE really do get results. Do you remember what we were able to achieve for the hospital porters and cleaners a couple of years ago? They enjoyed a huge pay rise."

Most of the nurses in the hall were student nurses, there were no nursing sisters present, and the majority were impatient with the efforts of the RCN. They did remember the ancillary workers settlement and they felt aggrieved. Many were not afraid to say so.

"No, we're not satisfied with the RCN," declared one.

"Our pay has stayed static while inflation has run wild. We're worse off with every week that passes," another complained.

"So tell us what we can do to make our views heard."

"Here at the City General you are a fairly small group of nurses," Jimmy replied, "but there are at least three other hospitals in this city and many other cities as large as this in the country. You need to get organised. If two or three nurses in each hospital agreed to be local organisers, who knows what you could achieve. You could perhaps start by arranging a little demonstration. The nurses at the Middleton Hospital are arranging a small rally on Saturday week, why don't you join them?"

In fact, Jimmy had yet to approach the nurses at the Middleton but his audience were not to know that! He then called for volunteers to act as local organisers and Claire's was the first of many hands to be raised.

"That's excellent," Jimmy said. "I suggest that those of you who are willing to get involved stay behind after the meeting. I'll tell you how to set up an action group and how to get in touch with other groups in the city. You will find that there's strength in numbers. Talking of which, I have brought some application forms for membership of CoHSE with me. If we had more members we would be so much more effective.

Finally, may I thank you all for coming and I hope to see lots of you at the demonstration on Saturday week. I'll come along as well to give you a helping hand. Together we will really show Mrs Castle that we mean business."

By the end of the meeting there was a sense of purpose and a determination amongst the nurses that had previously been lacking. They had been motivated to be proactive. They would indeed show the Health Minister that they meant business. No longer would they sit back whilst she took advantage of their caring natures and their sense of duty.

Later, Kate expressed her surprise that Claire had volunteered so readily.

"Jimmy's right," Claire answered. "We deserve a proper wage for the hours we work and for the responsibility we carry. As I see it we have a choice, either we put up with our poor pay or we do something about it. We shall gain nothing if we just grumble quietly to each other behind the scenes. I propose to try to improve things."

"You know that the RCN have said that they won't support any nurse who takes industrial action," Kate reminded her.

"I know that, but holding a demonstration in a public area when we are off duty cannot be described as industrial action. So are you going to support me?"

"Of course I will," was Kate's immediate response, "so long as it doesn't mean doing anything that harms patients."

Chapter Four

Barbara Castle took the short stroll to the Treasury in Horse Guards Road enjoying the fresh air and the chance to be out in the bright morning sunshine. The permanent secretary in the Department of Health accompanied her, carrying two large brief cases containing the notes and files that he had prepared for the meeting. After a lifetime spent in the civil service, he recognised the importance of good preparation and the need to have all the facts and figures necessary to support his minister's arguments at his finger tips. He knew that there was a gruelling clash ahead. Arguing with Treasury officials was always tough and today's battle was likely to be tougher than usual. Indeed he had grave doubts of his Minister's ability to win the prize that she so desperately sought. She would need all her energy, enthusiasm and feminine charm to persuade Denis Healey, the Chancellor of the Exchequer, to release the money which she required if she was to achieve her ambition of eliminating the pay beds from NHS hospitals.

Entering the Treasury, Barbara was instantly recognised by the receptionist. She had no need to ask for directions to the main conference room on the first floor. It had been the scene of a number of tremendous battles in the days when she had been Secretary of State for Employment, not least when she had fought for equal pay for the women. She allowed herself a glow of satisfaction at the memory of that tremendous victory.

Denis Healey and Michael Foot, who had succeeded Mrs Castle as Secretary of State for Employment, rose politely as Barbara entered the room.

With a twinkle in her eye, she kissed Denis lightly on the cheek.

"Barbara, I don't get kissed by many members of the Cabinet," he said, a smile on his face.

"I should hope not," Barbara retorted, "all the rest are men; and not particularly good-looking men at that!"

The kiss that she gave Michael Foot was accompanied by an affectionate hug. The two had enjoyed a warm friendship when they had worked together on the left wing of the Labour Party thirty years or so before. But Barbara knew that past friendships would count for nought today. Michael was responsible for the government's incomes policy, a cause in which he believed fervently. Yet she knew that he also supported social justice and there was no justice in failing to pay nurses a fair wage for the work they did for the sick or in being able to jump the queue into a hospital bed. Which side would he be on today she wondered?

"You folk at the Treasury do yourself proud," Barbara commented as she looked around. She walked to the window, admired the fine view of Whitehall then turned to survey the elegant conference room. Despite its dark traditional oak panelling, it was light and airy thanks to its size and high ceiling, from which hung a pair of ornate cut glass chandeliers. Barbara noted the numerous folders and papers that lay strewn across the table. They've been here for some time she thought, no doubt rehearsing the arguments they are going to throw at me. No matter, I've come well prepared. My cause is a just one; I shall fight tooth and nail for the extra money I need.

"Right," said Denis, taking the seat at the head of the table, indicating that as Chancellor, he would chair the meeting. "Let's get down to business. Barbara, you asked for this meeting, so you'd better start by telling us what's on your mind."

Barbara sat at the opposite end of the table. Fired up and ready for the skirmish that she knew was imminent, she wanted to be able to see and judge the expressions on everyone's face as the meeting progressed.

"I want to share with you some of the problems we are facing in my department," Barbara began, speaking directly to Denis. She spoke freely and confidently, ignoring the copious briefing notes that her secretary had placed on the table in front of her.

"We've come into power after years of austerity under Ted Heath's Tory government. As you know, he imposed vicious cuts on the Health Service. He stifled development and left many of our healthcare workers with pay packets that simply don't match inflation. Most of them are Labour supporters; the very people who voted for us and put us back into office. We have a moral responsibility to invest in the NHS. We need to restore the wages of the staff, invest in new technology and, most important of all, we need to eliminate the pay beds."

"So essentially you're asking for more money for your department just like all your colleagues." Denis sounded weary. He had heard similar pleas from many other members of the cabinet in recent months.

"Yes," Barbara replied, "I believe passionately in the National Health Service; it's the finest example we have of socialism in action. I want to see the underfunding of recent years corrected. The principle of 'care according to need' should be the foundation of Labour policy. The existence of the pay beds in our hospitals allows 'care according to the ability to pay' and surely that's unacceptable to us. Damn it, it's the sort of policy the Conservatives promote."

"And what sort of increase in your budget are you looking for?" Denis asked.

Barbara thought quickly. The officials in her department had shown her various projections suggesting what might be achieved with different sums of money but she hadn't really wanted to put a figure on it, but if she had to she would aim high.

"Something in the order of 9 - 10%," she commented, ignoring the look of astonishment on the face of her secretary, who was in the process of passing her the figures he had so assiduously prepared. For him, retirement beckoned and there were times when he wished that he served a more docile, less energetic Minister than the dynamic Mrs Castle. Yet he admired her vitality and 'never say die' attitude. It seemed to him that the more difficult the task that she set herself, the more determined she was to succeed. And there was no doubt in his mind that she was driven by a passionate sense of social justice.

Denis smiled sadly, "Come on Barbara, be reasonable. You've heard me say it often enough in Cabinet. There simply isn't the money available for anything remotely like that. All departments should be looking to hold their budgets flat, or at the most, looking for a 0.5% rise this year. Your Department is going to have to show restraint just like everybody else's. It seems to me that the NHS is a bottomless pit. There appears to be no limit to the amount of money that can be poured into it, without any very obvious benefit being apparent."

"But you cannot deny that health is a special case," Barbara argued passionately. "We're a Labour government. What can be more important than the health and well being of the people we represent?"

Denis sighed. "Barbara, everyone believes that they are a special case. The miners do, the farmers do and the armed forces do; even the staff here at the Treasury want more money. You would think that they of all people would understand that it just isn't possible. Let me explain to you what I've explained to your Cabinet colleagues. We've been in office now for about 12 months. In that time public expenditure has gone up by a massive 9%. You know as well as I do that inflation is over 20%. Over one and a quarter million people are unemployed, all of them being paid benefit. It simply cannot go on. We need to be looking for cuts, not for an expansion in service. We're building up a mountain of debt that is crippling us. It's not widely known yet, but shortly we shall be going, cap in hand, to the International Monitory Fund. We'll be looking to borrow at least three billion pounds this year to bail us out - and it won't be a free loan you know. There will be interest to pay in years to come. Even a 5% increase in your budget would be more than all the other departments would get put together. I can't understand why you always regard yourself as a special case. You've already had extra money for the disabled, for the deaf, for your child tax allowance."

"But you can't deny that the demands on the health service are increasing all the time," Barbara said, her voice now raised.

"No, and you can't deny that you've already won a formula for your department which guarantees to protect the NHS from increased demand and from the expense of new technologies." Denis retorted.

Barbara relished a good scrap, confident in her ability to put her case powerfully and succinctly. She replied heatedly, her arguments well rehearsed.

"Denis, the claims of some of the health workers are indisputable. Take the nurses for example. They must be regarded as a special case. They are held in high regard by the public; everyone loves nurses. The press will undoubtedly support their claim. Then there's the problem with the junior hospital doctors. When the public learn about the ridiculously long hours they work, the press and public will support them too."

"That's as may be," Denis Healey replied flatly, "but if there isn't any money, there isn't any money. Where do you think it comes from? It doesn't grow on trees. You know full well that we've put up income tax. The top rate is now 83%; we can't go higher than that. We've taxed business; we've put VAT on petrol. The public simply won't stand anymore, be it for the nurses or for anyone else."

Barbara thought quickly then decided to try a different tack. She turned to her old friend Michael Foot. She needed to see where his loyalties lay, hoping for his support.

"Michael, before the last election, as a political party, we made various promises to the public. We made a specific pledge to phase out private beds from NHS hospitals. Equality of access to Health Service facilities for all who are sick, irrespective of their wealth, is a just cause, a socialist cause, certainly one worth fighting for. To do that I need to change the contracts of the hospital consultants; I need to move them to a contract that commits them to work exclusively for the NHS. That's going to need a little bit of financial lubrication. Creating the NHS was Nye Bevan's crowning glory. It's the best thing that the Labour party has done since the war but to get the doctors to agree to it, he made one giant concession. He allowed them to treat private patients in NHS facilities. That was a grave mistake. My dream is to achieve what Nye failed to do. I want to purify the NHS by eliminating private practice. All I'm asking for is a little cash to oil the wheels."

There was a pause before Michael Foot replied quietly and sincerely. "Barbara, I know that you've made it your sacred mission to redress Nye Bevan's historical error. But you need to be careful. The consultants are a powerful group. Furthermore, their patients are influential people; business men, professionals and dare I say it politicians; people who need the convenience of selecting the date of their investigations and treatment. They won't be knocked over easily. And the public won't stand for further disruption in the hospitals. Remember what it was like three years ago when the ancillary staff went on strike. Your socialist idealism is your greatest strength Barbara, but be careful that it doesn't become your downfall."

"Phasing out the private beds was in our election manifesto. You and Denis both signed up to it," Barbara retorted stubbornly.

"Look, I'm truly sorry Barbara," Michael said, "but Denis is right. There can be no special cases; no exceptions to the rule. For my sins, I'm the guardian of the 'Social Contract' on pay restraint that was agreed between the Unions and the Labour party. Heaven knows, it was difficult enough to get the Unions to sign up to it and it's almost impossible to get them to stick to it."

"But Michael," Barbara replied, "surely we can show a bit of flexibility. We can give the consultants just enough to get them to sign up to the new contract and then, as their employers, we can claw it back over the next few years. It's a tactic that we've used before. Taken over the next four or five years, there won't actually be any extra cost at all."

"I'm sorry, Barbara but the answer still has to be 'No'. As a Government, we've agreed a pay policy. There can be no exceptions. If the policy were to be breached by any one group, especially people like the consultants whom the Unions regard as well off Tory toffs, the breach would turn into a flood."

Appreciating that pleading for understanding was not going to succeed, Barbara turned furiously back to Denis, trying a fresh line of attack. "Failure to implement a manifesto promise is going to infuriate those who fund the Labour party, the very people who put us into office. Don't forget that abolishing the pay beds has the unqualified support of Labour's National Executive and the TUC."

"But not of the Cabinet or the Parliamentary Labour party," Denis replied quietly, "and they are the ones who run the show."

There was firmness and finality in the Chancellor's voice and Barbara realised that she was not going to get the extra money she needed. Giving the nurses the pay rise she felt they deserved and eliminating pay beds from the NHS had suddenly become very much more difficult.

Chapter Five

It was ten o'clock on a Saturday evening. Paul was in the casualty department taking a short break and enjoying a mug of tea and some hot buttered toast. It had been a quiet shift with no major injuries to treat and fewer patients than usual. He heard the sound of a siren and the squeal of brakes as an ambulance pulled up outside.

"Sounds like more work for us," Paul commented to the nursing sister. There was no anxiety in his voice but his heart skipped a beat. Despite being quite experienced, he was aware that there were still certain medical emergencies that were beyond his competence. Staff working in casualty, be they doctors, nurses or paramedics, had to manage every situation that was thrown at them, whatever it might be. They could be dealing with a succession of minor sprains, cuts and bruises, none of them urgent or life-threatening, when the victims of a nasty road accident arrived critically injured or when an explosion occurred at the local chemical factory causing severe burns.

Paul suspected he was not alone in having such concerns. It was not a matter he had ever discussed openly, but he believed that many members of staff, if they were to be completely honest, would admit that occasionally they entertained doubts about their ability to cope. It was particularly injuries to the chest that concerned Paul. Specialist chest surgeons were available but they were 'on call' at home and took 30 minutes to arrive. If there were to be a stab wound to the heart or a severe crush injury to the chest, perhaps sustained at the local coal mine, Paul would be the one required to commence emergency resuscitation.

Sister left the office to help the ambulance crew to trolley the patient into the department. Two minutes later, she popped her head round the door.

"I think you ought to see this patient right away, Paul," she said. "She's got a nasty laceration on her hand."

Paul didn't need to ask into which cubicle the patient had been placed, he merely had to follow the trail of fresh red blood on the polished linoleum floor.

The woman looked to be about 35 years old. A quick glance at her casualty card told him that she was called Annie Nolan. She had a bloodied head scarf wrapped tightly around her right hand, which she clutched to her chest in pain. Paul thought the woman's face was vaguely familiar, although he couldn't place her.

"Hi, I'm Mr Lambert," he said. "Haven't I seen you somewhere before?"

Sister shot him an amused look but made no comment.

"You may have, Doctor. I live just around the corner." She looked frightened and unkempt, but it was the clothes she was wearing that reminded Paul why her face was familiar. She was wearing a cheap leather mini skirt, fish net stockings and a low cut blouse that revealed a vast cleavage. The blouse had once been white but was now grey and covered with blood. The hospital stood on one of the main thoroughfares that led to the city centre but on the opposite side of the road, a number of narrow side streets ran into a rundown residential area. Occasionally Paul had passed Annie on one of these street corners when returning to the hospital after a night out. She had once approached him and asked *'would you be looking for a little warmth and comfort this evening, Sir?'* No wonder Sister had been amused, when he had suggested that he recognised her.

Slowly and painfully Sister removed the scarf from Annie's hand and gently wiped away the blood and clots so that they were able to inspect the damage. Paul had never seen such an injury before. There was a deep cut across the base of all her fingers. The lacerations must have been inflicted by an incredibly sharp blade for the wound edges were clean and sharply defined. He asked Annie to make a fist, showing her with his own hand what he wanted her to do. She attempted this, grimacing at the pain that resulted. Her thumb flexed, but her fingers remained straight. He asked a second time. Again she tried but her fingers would not move. The cut had gone right down to the bone, dividing all the tendons that enabled her fingers to move. Unless these guy ropes could be reconnected, her right hand would be useless.

"How on earth did this happen?" he asked.

There was silence. "Come on Annie, we need to know." But Annie had clammed up.

"Are you right-handed?" Paul asked. She nodded weakly. That made the injury significantly more serious.

Paul turned to Sister. "Can you get a pressure bandage on these wounds for me, please? I'll ask the 'Orthopods' if they will come and see her. They're the specialists. They get more practice repairing tendons than we do."

"Annie," Paul said, "you're going to need this hand patching up under an anaesthetic but we'll get the experts to sort it out for you. Are you injured anywhere else?"

She pointed to a cut two inches long on the back of her left forearm and then took off her blouse. There was also a shorter laceration on her left shoulder. Again both injuries appeared to have been inflicted by an extremely sharp blade. Fortunately, however, neither was deep and Paul detected no damage to underlying tendons or nerves. He was certain that the orthopaedic surgeons would suture these two cuts whilst they were repairing her hand, so he simply asked Sister to apply a temporary dressing.

He had just returned to the office to write up an account of Annie's injuries when one of the staff nurses dashed in. "Paul, there's a major stabbing in the 'resus' cubicle; we need you right now." Again Paul experienced that twinge of doubt and muttered a quiet prayer that it would not involve the chest.

He followed staff nurse into the resuscitation area, a cubicle larger than the rest. It was equipped with a heart monitor and a suction machine. This was where the cardiac arrest equipment was kept and where patients with life-threatening conditions received emergency treatment.

Assessing blood loss in an Afro-Caribbean is not as easy as might be imagined. In a Caucasian, the profound pallor and cold moist skin is recognisable from the foot of the bed; not so for black skin. There was however, no difficulty in recognising that this particular West Indian gentleman, whom Paul later learned was called Cedric King, was 'in extremis'. He was barely conscious and had a large and expanding blood stain on his shirt.

"He's been stabbed," staff nurse said, rather stating the obvious. She was already at work setting up a drip and taking blood for cross match. "Pulse is 115 per min and his blood pressure barely 90/60."

"Get Sister to join us," Paul instructed.

Paul's quick examination revealed a single stab wound in the left upper abdomen, about an inch long. Inspection of the external wound offered no clue as to the extent of the injuries, but the whole of the abdomen was rigid, a sure sign of serious internal damage. Paul's attempt to examine it produced groans of protest. The knife, or whatever it was that had inflicted this injury, had clearly caused either massive internal bleeding or a perforation of his gut; possibly both.

"Blood pressure's falling," Sister shouted. "It's now 75 over 50."

"Right – we'll take him straight to theatre. Sister, get your girls to inform the staff there. Tell them to expect a patient for emergency exploration of the abdomen within five minutes. Get them to 'crash call' the anaesthetist and tell him to meet us in theatre. Call the laboratory urgently as well. We'll need four pints of blood, maybe more. If possible we'll have the same blood group, but there won't be time for a full cross match. Get one of your nurses to run the sample to the laboratory. We haven't time to wait for a porter. In the meantime, keep the plasma running."

There was no need to check that Sister understood these instructions; with years of experience working in casualty she would have organised things in exactly the same way, even if Paul had not been there. "And when you have a minute you'd better inform the police," Paul added.

Paul and Jimmy, the casualty orderly, rushed down the hospital corridor, pushing the trolley as fast as they could; a nurse running alongside holding the drip. They scattered visitors and staff as they went. Paul cursed the speed of the lift as they went up to the Surgical Five theatre on the first floor. Two minutes later they reached the theatre to find the staff hard at work, preparing for the emergency.

The duty anaesthetist, Bill Jones, a contemporary of Paul's and a steady head in an emergency, was already present. "What do you expect to find here?"

"Truly, I don't know." Paul replied. "He's clearly lost a lot of blood, so presumably some major blood vessel must be severed but the bowel may be damaged as well. We won't know until we get inside."

The truth was that the wound could be two inches deep, or twelve inches deep. It might be something Paul was able to deal with, but equally if it was damage to the aorta or inferior vena cava, the huge pipes that carry blood to and from the lower trunk and legs, the injuries would be beyond his capabilities. He had no experience of operating on these vessels. He rang Sir William, who was the consultant on call. It was his resident housekeeper who answered.

"I need an urgent word with Sir William."

"He's reading in his study, I'll ask him to come to the phone."

"No, wait," Paul said, "give him a message. Ask him...." but it was too late, she had put the receiver down and was already on her way to fetch the senior consultant.

Paul grabbed one of the junior nurses. "Hang onto this phone for me. When Sir William comes on the line, tell him we have an emergency stabbing in theatre. Ask him to come as quickly as possible."

In the anaesthetic room, one of the nurses was pumping fluid into Cedric's arm with a mechanical roller; Bill was passing the tube into the patient's throat through which the anaesthetic would be given. As soon as it was in place, he called to Paul.

"Paul, I'm going to bring him straight into theatre, we're in danger of losing him."

Paul glanced at the monitor. The blood pressure was almost unrecordable and the beep from the cardiac machine raced along. They dragged the patient from the trolley onto the operating table. Then abruptly the rapid beeping of the monitor became a continuous loud alarm and the weak flickering trace on the display screen became a flat line. The heart had stopped. Bill commenced cardiac massage, whilst a nurse squeezed the bag to blow oxygen and anaesthetic gases into the patient's lungs. Paul threw off his white coat, rolled up his shirt sleeves and pulled on a pair of surgical gloves, whilst one of the nurses dragged a plastic apron over his head. Sister passed him a scalpel. There was no time to cleanse the skin or to put drapes over the abdomen. Paul plunged the blade into the skin. There was no response from the patient; whether he was unconscious, anaesthetised or even dead, he had no idea. Making no attempt to identify the separate layers of the abdominal wall, he made a huge incision. The belly was full of blood, some of it liquid, some of it clotted. Sister produced a suction tube and the liquid blood rapidly disappeared into the litre bottle at the side of the table. Within a minute, the bottle was full and needed replacing. Paul scooped out the clots, two handed and placed them into a kidney dish. To his enormous relief, when the blood and clots were removed, the source of the bleeding was apparent. The large artery and two even larger veins feeding blood to the spleen had been divided. The application of several large pairs of forceps arrested the bleeding.

When a breathless Sir William entered the theatre a few moments later, he might have imagined that he was in a military hospital in a war zone. The patient, his underpants about his ankles and his shirt around his neck, had a huge wound in his belly, without a surgical drape in sight. Blood was dripping down the side of the operating table and forming a dark pool on the theatre floor. Paul was ungowned, still wearing his shirt and tie, with just a pair of gloves on his hands as a gesture of sterility; a nurse was wiping the sweat from his brow with a towel. The plastic apron which had initially been green was now heavily blood stained. Bill, the anaesthetist, was pumping on the patient's chest leaving Sir William in no doubt of the drama and urgency of the situation.

"Have I time to scrub, Lambert?" Sir William asked, his voice calm and quiet.

"Yes, I've managed to stop the bleeding," Paul replied.

"Good. In that case I'll join you at the table in a couple of minutes. If you have a cardiac arrest situation on your hands, I suggest that you pack the area with some large swabs. That will apply a bit of pressure and allow Jones some time get on with the resuscitation."

"That would be good," Bill gasped, now red faced and somewhat out of breathe from his physical exertion. "It will give us a chance to try to catch up with the blood loss."

The next five minutes was spent in furious non-stop activity. Blood and plasma were forcibly pumped into Cedric's veins. Then Bill injected adrenaline directly into his heart, the long intra cardiac needle being passed between the patient's ribs - but the heart failed to respond.

"Everyone stand away from the patient," Bill instructed as he placed the resuscitation pads onto the patient's chest. He applied a massive electric shock to the heart. It resulted in a violent muscular spasm which, for an instant, lifted the patient bodily off the table, but the cardiac trace remained flat and the alarm tone from the monitor continued unabated.

"Everyone back again," Bill shouted. He shocked the patient a second time. Miraculously, the heart started to pump again. Initially, the beat was hesitant and weak but very gradually its strength and rhythm improved until it was able to restore the circulation. To everyone's huge relief, the cardiac monitor once more gave out its reassuring regular, if rapid, beep. Then Sir William arrived at the table. Appropriately scrubbed, gowned and gloved he looked across the table at Paul's blood stained clothes.

"Lambert," he said, "I'll take over here for a minute. You'd better go and change and gown properly." Then he addressed the anaesthetist.

"Will it be alright if I tidy up in here?"

"I rather you didn't, Sir," Bill replied. "I'd prefer you surgeons to take a breather while I get some more fluid inside him."

In the changing room, Paul took off the bloodied plastic apron and placed it into the skip for disposal. He found that blood had dripped from it onto his trouser legs, shoes and socks, so he shed them and put them to one side. He would deal with them later. He put on a theatre top and pants then, with bare feet inside surgical wellington boots, he scrubbed properly and rejoined Sir William.

"We need to have a look round the rest of the belly," Sir William said. "Is it alright if we do that now?"

"Yes, that's fine," Bill replied. "He's been to the Pearly Gates and back but he seems to be perking up a bit now. I've got his BP up to 100. It's quite amazing!"

Sir William undertook a thorough examination of the abdomen. Fortunately, apart from the damage to the blood vessels to the spleen, he found no other injury.

"The next job is to remove the spleen," he commented. "It's lost its blood supply so it will die and get infected if we leave it in place. This really is your operation Lambert, but if you don't mind, I think I'd better do it to save time. The sooner we get this patient of the table the better, don't you agree, Jones?"

It was impossible not to respect Sir William; he was always such a gentleman. He didn't need to ask Paul's permission to remove the spleen. Cedric was his patient. At the end of the day, he was the consultant responsible for his care but even in this fraught situation, he had been at pains not to be perceived to be pulling rank on Paul.

Expertly, Sir William swept his hand round the back of the spleen and freed it from its bed. Then he applied ligatures to the blood vessels that had been damaged using the clamps that Paul had applied twenty minutes or so earlier.

"Right," he said, "before we close up, we need to investigate this stab wound. In due course the police will ask for a full report and this is an ideal opportunity to do a bit of detective work."

Together they looked at the entrance wound in the skin. It was about an inch in length. The edges could not have been more sharply defined had they been incised with a surgical blade. The knife that inflicted the injury must have been razor sharp.

"Look," Sir William commented, "it must have been made by a double bladed knife; the skin has been sharply cut at both ends of the wound. Can you let me have something to use as a probe, Sister? We need to know how long the blade was."

Sister passed him a pair of forceps, seven inches long which Sir William carefully inserted into the stab wound. From the entrance of the wound below the ribs on the left side of the abdomen, the instrument passed inwards and very slightly upwards for a full five inches.

"So," Sir William concluded, " the blade that inflicted this wound was incredibly sharp, was double edged, not less than five inches long, at least an inch wide and the direction of the blow was almost horizontal. You will need to include all that in your police report, Lambert. Right, it's time to close up. You do it. I'll assist."

"I'm afraid it's not a very tidy incision Sir," Paul confessed, "it was done in a bit of a hurry."

"As was entirely appropriate, I should imagine," Sir William replied, glancing at the blood in the suction bottles. "It looks as if you applied that clamp just in the nick of time."

Slowly and carefully, under Sir William's eagle eye, Paul closed the wound as best he could. It was an extensive incision and it was impossible to make a neat job of it. Looking at it when he had finished, reminded him of the bossed edges of a Cornish pasty! He hoped that it would heal satisfactorily, but given the patient's perilous condition, that was something they could worry about later.

Sir William and Paul went together to the surgeon's room to change. Paul was surprised to see what Sir William had been wearing before being called into the hospital. In the past, Paul had only seen him as the 'Senior Surgeon,' looking immaculate in his city suit. He had never seen his boss casually dressed. It was quite incongruous to observe him dressing into dirty brown corduroy trousers and an old woollen jumper which sported several holes! Sir William noticed Paul washing out his blood stained socks in the sink and placing them on the radiator to dry.

"I'll leave you now," he said, "but if you wait here for five minutes, I'll ask my house keeper to come across with a pair of my trousers and socks." He laughed. "I'll see if I can find a belt as well; my waist is rather larger than yours."

"That's very kind, Sir," Paul said. "I was wondering what I should be able to wear for the rest of the day."

Sir William started towards the door, then stopped and placed a hand on Paul's shoulder.

"You did a good job there, Lambert. Well done. It's important to know how to do things by the book but equally important to know when to break the rules. The patient should be very grateful to you."

Cedric King certainly ought to have been grateful to Paul for saving his life but subsequent events were to prove that he wasn't!

Chapter Six

Although Jimmy Ackroyd had suggested that the nurses' demonstration should take place at the Middleton Hospital, he changed the venue at the last minute. He had decided that a protest at the city's largest and most prestigious hospital would be more effective. Initially, Claire had been afraid that the event would be a flop, since she had only managed to persuade twenty or so nurses to attend. None had been willing to take time off work, partly because they were adamant that their action should not affect patient care, but also for fear of some reprisal by Matron. However, Claire need not have worried; when the day of the demonstration arrived, at least thirty City General Hospital nurses turned up, including Kate and a number of her friends.

Jimmy too was as good as his word. Nurses from other hospitals came and together with a handful of hospital cleaners, porters and laboratory staff, all members of the CoHSE union who had decided to add their support; the crowd looked impressive. Jimmy had suggested that the nurses should parade in their uniforms despite all of them being 'off duty'. He had also produced some banners and placards proclaiming '*FAIR PAY FOR NURSES*' and had arranged for both local and regional pressmen and photographers to attend.

Although the demonstration lasted for little more than thirty minutes, all the nurses were in high spirits and a party atmosphere quickly developed. They sang songs, shouted slogans, gave interviews and posed for photographs. The girls were delighted with the reaction from passersby, many of whom offered an encouraging word. Several motorists peeped their horns as they drove past and a couple of lorry drivers gave wolf whistles which the nurses chose to interpret as support for their cause. Jimmy judged the event to be a great success, particularly as it featured prominently in the newspapers the next morning.

When Claire saw that she could clearly be identified leading the rally in the press photographs she became concerned that she might be hauled before Matron but no such summons was issued. "She's probably quietly supportive," Kate suggested. "If we win better pay, her rise will probably be the biggest!"

The next day Jimmy rang Claire to congratulate her. "How do you feel it went?" he asked. "Did you enjoy it?"

"Yes, it was great fun, "she replied.

"And would you be happy to do it again?"

"Yes, of course."

"That's great," Jimmy said. "Similar action is being organised all over the country. We've already held a number of regional demonstrations. The next step is a mass rally. It will start at the Royal College of Nursing and from there we will march to Downing Street to hand in a petition to the Prime Minister. I'm sure that you will want to bring some of your friends along!"

Claire gulped, "Oh," she said. Things were moving rather faster than she had imagined.

*****

Whilst Claire and Kate were demonstrating outside the hospital gates, Cedric King was being monitored in a side ward on the Surgical Five Unit. He was as well as could reasonably be expected after the drama of the night before. Inevitably the local press got hold of the story. They described his condition as *'comfortable'* which was certainly a misnomer. Cedric was in a considerable amount of pain from his huge abdominal incision. Fortunately, though, his observations remained stable, there being no suggestion of further blood loss. For the first time since his arrival in casualty, he was conscious and the staff were able to communicate with him. Far from being grateful that he had been brought back from the dead, (not that he knew that at the time), they found him to be foul mouthed, rude and aggressive. Paul wondered whether this might be the result of his brain having been starved of oxygen at the time of his cardiac arrest but subsequently learnt that this was Cedric's normal personality. He wasn't asked about the events that had led up to the stabbing, nor did he volunteer any information. Paul chatted to the various police constables who sat in the corridor outside Cedric's side room, looking thoroughly bored, as they waited to interview him. Sir William though would not permit them to speak to him, saying that it would be unreasonable to do so before the patient had fully recovered from his anaesthetic and was able to give a coherent account of events.

"I don't think you need to sit here all day and wait," Paul suggested to one of the policemen. "We'll let you know when he is fit to be interviewed."

"My sergeant says I've got to wait, we don't want him to do a runner."

"That's not very likely," Paul replied. "He's not going to be fit enough to go anywhere for the next few days."

"We'll be asking you for a full written report of his injuries in due course Doctor, but it would be helpful if you could give me an outline now."

He listened with interest and made some notes as Paul described Cedric's life-threatening injuries and his cardiac arrest. "I suppose the woman with the cuts on her hand must have been involved in the same incident," Paul suggested.

"We weren't aware that there had been a second victim," the constable said, sitting up and taking notice. "Was she admitted as well?"

"Yes, she's downstairs on the orthopaedic ward."

"Do you think she's fit enough to be interviewed?"

"She's not my patient. I don't know how she is this morning, but her injuries were less severe than Mr King's."

"Well, well, that does make it interesting. It makes it even more important that we find the assailant."

"Perhaps the two victims knifed each other," suggested Paul.

"Look," the constable said, "I need to speak with my sergeant. We'll need to interview this second victim as well." To Paul's surprise, he then commented, "You might have done us all a favour, Doctor and not tried quite so hard to save him! There are far too many villains in this city."

"So he's known to the police is he?"

"He is indeed. He leads one of the most vicious gangs in the city. He's in the protection business; '*pay us a weekly sum, and we'll make sure that your shop doesn't catch fire*', that sort of thing. We've been after him for years, but never managed to pin anything definite on him."

Until he chatted with the policeman, Annie had slipped from Paul's mind; he had been totally engrossed with Cedric King and his injuries. Since Annie was being treated by the orthopaedic team, he was no longer involved in her care, but out of interest he rang the ward to enquire after her progress. It transpired that she was, at that very moment, undergoing surgery in the orthopaedic theatre. Since her injuries were not life-threatening, her operation had been deferred overnight. It was an ideal opportunity for him to watch a specialist hand surgeon at work; inevitably Paul would be called upon to perform this type of surgery at some stage in the future.

In the theatre, he found the orthopaedic team had already been operating for an hour and expected to be at least another two hours before they finished. They had confirmed that the cut on each of Annie's fingers had gone straight down to the bone, the tendons to all four fingers having been completely divided. Thankfully, all had been cleanly cut, making the task of rejoining them a little easier.

When Paul arrived, the orthopaedic consultant was busy suturing the ends of the tendons of the index finger together. It was a time consuming and meticulous procedure. The surgeon made the same observation that Sir William had made the night before. "I couldn't have cut these tendons more cleanly myself with a surgical blade. The knife that did this must have been incredibly sharp."

"Will she regain full function of her hand?" Paul asked. "She's right-handed. It will be a serious handicap to her if she can't."

"Hopefully she will, provided we can get these tendons to heal. But there's another problem. When we tested her sense of touch, we discovered that some of the nerves to her fingers have been cut. She's likely to have numb areas, particularly on her finger tips. That would be a real handicap. She would be at risk of injuring her fingers because she wouldn't be able to tell if she was handling something that was sharp or hot."

"Have you had a chance to ask her how she came by her injuries?" Paul asked.

"We did ask, but for some reason she refused to tell us. She wouldn't say a word."

Paul was puzzled. Both Cedric and Annie had severe injuries caused by a very sharp blade. Since they had presented to casualty within a few minutes of each other, it seemed likely that they had both been involved in the same incident but had there been one knife or two? Probably one, he thought, given that all the injuries had been caused by a razor sharp blade. Who had started the fight and why? Had they attacked each other or had a third party been involved? There were many questions for the police to answer but doubtless it would all become clear in the fullness of time.

*****

Two days later, the police interviewed Cedric King in his side ward. They spoke with him for over an hour. Paul, curious to know what had happened, hoped that they would share some information with him but they politely declined to do so, the sergeant explaining gruffly that to do so would be a breach of police protocol. He then asked Paul to prepare a formal written statement detailing his involvement with Mr King, including an accurate account of the injuries he had sustained. Having no previous experience of writing a police report, he went in search of Sir William to seek advice. He found him in his office adjacent to the surgical ward.

Sir William Warrender was tall and distinguished with a straight back, silver hair and a genial face. He wore immaculate dark grey three-piece suits and in the summer months sported a red rose in the buttonhole of his jacket, grown in his garden of which he was justly proud. Now within a few months of retiring, he was invariably courteous; always quick to praise and slow to chide. The hospital's benevolent senior surgeon, he was highly respected by his junior staff, being an excellent clinician and enthusiastic teacher. He was loved by his patients for his gentlemanly manner, his excellent communication skills and for the detailed explanations that he offered about their medical conditions, although these were a test of patience for the members of his surgical team who had heard them many times before. He was generous with his time and Paul had no hesitation in seeking his advice about the legal statement.

"In due course," Sir William explained, "someone is going to be charged with assault. The charge may be grievous bodily harm, but given the severity of Mr King's injuries, it's more likely to be one of attempted murder. The defendant may be the lady with the hand injuries but for all we know, a third party may have been involved. When it comes to the trial, your statement will be read in court and almost certainly you will be invited to answer questions on it. It's important that what you write is strictly accurate. Just stick to the facts and whatever you do, do not express any opinions. Later in your career you may be asked to be an 'expert witness' and be invited to give your medical opinion but in this case you are simply a witness as to the facts."

"Perhaps you would be kind enough to read it through when it's drafted, Sir?"

"Certainly; we'll look at it together before it's released."

The police also pressed Annie for a statement but she refused to speak with them, declining to give any account of how her injuries had been sustained. Nor would she answer any questions about her relationship with Cedric King. Later a more senior officer tried to extract some information from her but again she refused to cooperate. She wouldn't even defend herself when told that Mr King alleged that he had been stabbed in an unprovoked attack and that she faced a charge of attempted murder.

Inevitably there was much comment and discussion on the case in the hospital and later Paul and Sam Leonard, the orthopaedic registrar, discussed the King/Nolan affair and tried to imagine what might have happened.

"It seems to me," Sam began, "that we can assume they were both involved in the same incident. After all, they arrived in casualty within a couple of minutes of each other."

"That's right. The police have now confirmed that both Annie and Cedric were brought to the hospital from the same address; Annie's flat. Annie is a local prostitute. Presumably Cedric was one of her clients which means it's unlikely there will be any witnesses," Paul observed.

Paul thought back to the events of the night of the attack. He remembered Annie taking off her blouse. He had noticed that the blouse had cuts in it corresponding with the knife wounds on her arm and shoulder.

"Annie was dressed when I first saw her," he commented "but the nurses in casualty say that Cedric was only wearing a shirt and underpants when he came in. Apparently, he was wrapped in a blanket that had been provided by the ambulance crew."

"So did this all happen before or after the sex took place?"

Paul laughed. "I can hardly imagine that intercourse took place after the assault. Cedric would hardly have been in any fit state to perform! And I've really no idea what happens when a prostitute entertains a client. I rather imagine that both parties take their clothes off more or less at the same time."

"So if Cedric was half-naked perhaps the sex took place first and the fight afterwards."

"Or Cedric anticipated he would get his wicked way but Annie, for some reason, declined her services."

"So who started the fight and why? And how is it that they both suffered such severe injuries? Cedric is twice the size and weight of Annie. If there had been some dispute between them, he wouldn't have needed to use a knife. He could simply have knocked her over with his fist."

"I agree. I think it must have been Annie that started the trouble. Remember they were in her flat. She would have access to kitchen knives. After the sex, she could have got dressed then gone to the kitchen to get a knife. And I think she stabbed him when he was lying down. She's right-handed. Cedric was stabbed on his left side and if he was still lying on the bed that would explain why the knife went in more or less horizontally. Had they been standing facing each other, the blade would surely have had a downward trajectory."

"Then how do you explain Annie's injuries?" Sam queried. "She had wounds on the back of her left arm and shoulder. Those are surely wounds suffered in self-defence." He raised his left forearm and half-turned his back to illustrate the natural response to an impending attack. Surely they must have occurred when someone else, presumably Cedric, was holding the knife.

And there's something else we haven't considered. At some stage the tendons to her fingers were severed. After that it would be impossible for her to grip a knife firmly enough to plunge it into Cedric's belly. So unless she used her left hand to do the stabbing, Cedric was stabbed before Annie's tendons were cut."

"But if Cedric was stabbed first, how did he have the strength to seek revenge when he was bleeding profusely and in shock?"

"He would lose blood progressively; it would take time for the weakness and shock to develop. At first he would be in pain but still strong enough and probably angry enough to grab the knife and attack Annie in revenge," Paul explained.

"So the most likely scenario is that they had sex and then a dispute arose for some reason causing Annie to get so mad that she grabbed a knife and attacked Cedric. Then he counter attacked before collapsing from blood loss."

"If that supposition is true, it doesn't really explain why Annie won't cooperate with the police? She refuses to say a word to them, even though she may be charged with attempted murder. Surely she would say something in her own defence."

"Don't forget that Cedric runs a protection racket. It's possible that Annie is more afraid of Cedric and his gang than she is of the police and prison."

"I wonder if Sir William has any thoughts on the matter," Paul said, "after all he's worked in the hospital for 30 years or more; he must have been involved in similar events in the past. I'll ask him for his views when an opportunity arises."

But later when he spoke with the senior consultant, Sir William declined to speculate. "Lambert, as I said to you before, your role is simply to present the facts when asked to do so, not to pass an opinion or to hypothesize. You saved the man's life. That was your job and you did it well. Leave others to work out what happened and why. It's the police's job to investigate the crime, not yours. Then in due course, it's up to the legal profession to decide whether the evidence stands up in court, the jury's responsibility to come to a verdict and the judge's job to determine the sentence. By the way," he added "I've read the statement you drafted for the police; it's fine. Just sign it and leave things be."

"But aren't you curious to know what happened?" Paul queried.

"Of course I am. But I'm patient enough to wait until the judge delivers the jury's verdict," Sir William replied, with a twinkle in his eye.

Chapter Seven

Barbara Castle was deep in thought. She was sitting in her cabinet office polishing the speech that her officials had prepared for her presentation to the Royal College of Nursing.

Desperately she was trying to find the right balance between encouraging a sense of optimism, without at the same time raising the nurses' hopes too high and was struggling to come up with appropriate words and phrases.

"The nurses deserve a decent wage," she said to her permanent secretary. "Inflation has averaged 10% for each of the last three years. The nurses are essential to the success of the NHS; we can't run the service without them. We have to give them an award that recognises that."

"I don't doubt it for a minute," the civil servant replied, "but as the Chancellor said, '*if there isn't any money, there isn't any money*'. We might be able to squeeze enough out of our budget to give them a one or two percent pay rise by making cuts elsewhere. If you like, we can do some work on it in the next couple of weeks, though I doubt we'll be able to offer them more than that."

"Thanks a million; that's a fat lot of use," Barbara replied, throwing down her pen in exasperation.

"Well, you can praise them; tell them you hold them in high regard."

"Yes, I can do all that. I can make them feel warm and appreciated, tell them what wonderful people they are, tell them that we truly value their dedication and the exceptional care they offer to the patients *but* ... you always come to that little word '*but*'.... don't you? What is it that the Americans love to say; '*Everything before the 'but' is bullshit!*' I can blame Ted Heath for letting the national coffers run dry *'but'* the nurses want more money and I for one don't blame them."

*****

Although married to a nurse, Betty Newstead was not a nurse herself. Hers had been a legal training. As head of the RCN's labour relations department she was acutely aware that nurses' salaries had fallen woefully behind inflation. A veteran of many previous pay battles with the Department of Health, she knew that only dramatic action would shift the government's rigid adherence to its pay policy and Barbara Castle's forthcoming visit to the College of Nursing presented her with an ideal opportunity to force the issue. She planned to allow the Minister to feel the full force of the nurses' pent up frustration and anger but if a cast iron commitment to providing more cash was not forthcoming, she would issue her ultimatum.

Mrs Newstead was delighted to see that when the Minister arrived, the conference room was bursting at the seams. Many nurses were standing at the back and in the aisles. One or two of the more reserved members of the audience had come prepared to listen to what Mrs Castle had to say but the overwhelming majority were planning to tell her exactly what they thought of her; and they didn't pull any punches! For over an hour, Barbara was harangued as she sat on the platform, stony faced facing her critics. Speaker after speaker spoke vehemently on the appalling state of the nursing profession. They were underfunded, disillusioned, their morale was low, senior members of the profession were emigrating, recruitment had stalled, but their overriding concern was pay. Their salaries had been severely eroded by inflation. If the speakers were to be believed, some nurses were actually starving and having to prostitute themselves to fund their next meal!

It was obvious that when Barbara rose to speak she would have a rough ride, and so it proved. She followed the only course available to her; she praised the nurses, acknowledged the public's gratitude for the work they did, recognised their grievances, blamed the previous Tory government, explained the importance of the government's pay policy and hinted at a decent pay award in the future. She invited them to be patient until the country's finances were in a better shape but regretted that at present there was no money available to offer them the pay rise that they clearly deserved. Her audience were not impressed; she was heckled noisily, indeed at times her voice was drowned by catcalling from the floor. Thoroughly dejected, Barbara resumed her seat to prolonged booing and jeering.

Betty Newstead allowed the Minister to face the full fury of her audience for some considerable time before standing, walking to the rostrum and holding up her hands in an appeal for calm. Then she issued the ultimatum that she had prepared.

"Mrs Castle," she said her voice clear and authoritative, "you must set up a totally independent inquiry of our pay and conditions. If you do not, we will tell our members to resign 'en masse' and we will set up a private nursing agency and engage our nurses as temporary staff. The NHS will be forced to re-employ them on a wage determined by us. You have three weeks in which to comply."

With this statement, she resumed her seat to a standing ovation.

Barbara came away shocked at the ferocity of the attack she had faced but impressed by the strength of their sense of injustice. Later, though, as she licked her wounds, she wondered if the nurses had stumbled on a possible solution to the problem. If a truly independent inquiry were to support the nurses' claim, maybe a breach of the pay code could be blamed on the inquiry and not on her department.

The next day she told her staff of the mauling she had suffered at the hands of the nurses only to be greeted by more problems.

"I'm afraid that the National Union of Public Employees (NUPE) and CoHSE want to meet you," she was informed. "They're miffed that you've seen the RCN but not them."

"Why is it that as soon as we get a Labour government, the unions let their pent up frustrations explode?" Barbara raged. "I've only been in this post for a few months. They must think I've got a magic wand if they believe that I can solve all the problems left by the Tories at a stroke. I will see the unions but please stress to them that I'm busy and I won't be able to stay chatting all day. More importantly, make some preliminary arrangements for an independent inquiry on nurses' pay. I sounded out Lord Halsbury last night and he would be delighted to act as chairman. In the meantime I'll see if I can persuade the Prime Minister to see a small deputation of nurses. If the nurses give him as much ear ache as they gave me, maybe he'll realise just how aggrieved they are. We will need his agreement as well as that of the cabinet if we're going to organise an independent inquiry and we've only got three weeks!"

*****

To encourage a good turnout, Jimmy Ackroyd told Claire that the march from the Royal College of Nursing to Downing Street would not only ratchet up the pressure on the government but would also be a lot of fun. He was right on both counts. It was warm, dry and sunny day when Claire, Kate and ten other nurses from the City General caught the train into London. The girls had been given detailed instructions telling them how to cross the city to get from Euston Station to the College in Cavendish Square. Unfortunately, having successfully used the Victoria underground line to reach Oxford Circus, they walked the wrong way down Regent Street. They feared they would miss the start of the rally but when they eventually reached the College, found it had been delayed due to the vast number of nurses who had congregated and needed to be organised and marshalled. Claire and Kate were amazed to see just how many had made the effort to attend. There must have been a thousand or more, almost all in uniform.

"We ought to try and find Jimmy," Kate said anxiously, "to let him know we're here."

"I don't think there's much chance in this crowd," Claire replied, "and since we've brought our own banners with us, we really don't need him. We'll just tag along with the rest."

A loud booming voice interrupted them. "Please listen carefully everybody, I have an important announcement to make and I need you all to pay attention." It was a good-looking, young police sergeant speaking through a loudhailer. "This is an official demonstration which means that you have been granted permission to march to Downing Street but there are certain rules that must be obeyed. You will walk in a column, no more than four abreast. You will keep to the left hand side of the road and at all times you will obey the instructions of the official marshals. This is to be a peaceful rally; there will be no rowdy behaviour. The police have the authority to arrest anyone who causes trouble."

"You can arrest me anytime, darling!" a wag in the crowd shouted to laughter and applause. This set the mood for a joyful walk through Oxford Square, down Regent Street, taking a turn round Piccadilly Circus, before continuing south across the Mall with a glimpse of Buckingham Palace at the far end. Finally, they reached Whitehall and walked along Horseguards Parade before arriving at Downing Street. Little did they realise that on their journey they had passed the Treasury and been observed by the Chancellor of the Exchequer, who was to have a major role in deciding the success or failure of their protest!

As they marched, they sang songs, chanted their slogans and waved their flags and placards. All along the route they received messages of encouragement and support; commuters and shoppers clapping and cheering them on their way. Kate chatted and laughed as she walked, happy simply to enjoy the sunshine and the carnival atmosphere. Claire, more conscious of the purpose of the march, took every opportunity to share the nurses' grievances with anyone who was prepared to listen. When they reached the famous black door of Number Ten, the one that they had seen so many times on their television screens, their leader, a middle aged woman wearing a Sister's cape that neither Kate nor Claire recognised, waited until the press photographers had taken all the pictures that they wanted, then knocked on the door. Immediately it opened. No-one really expected Harold Wilson to appear casually smoking his pipe, but they had hoped that a few nurses might be allowed inside. Unfortunately, this was not the case, but the officer on the door promised that their petition would be seen by the Prime Minister.

When the door to Number Ten closed, it had been open for less than a minute, the police loudhailer addressed them once more. They were thanked for their good behaviour, asked to disperse quietly and wished a safe journey home. Kate and Claire decided to walk back to Euston to avoid the crowds on the buses and underground. Both were keen to pass on their reflections of the demonstration. Claire wished to tell her friends that she was certain they had put extra pressure on the government. She also wanted to see how the day had been reported by the press and television. She was not disappointed; it was the headline story on the BBC's nine o'clock news and the analysts were wholly sympathetic to their cause. Kate just longed to see Paul to tell him how enjoyable and exciting the day had been.

Chapter Eight

With mounting dismay, Barbara read the morning newspapers in her office and then asked her press secretary to join her.

"I take it you've seen this morning's headlines?"

"You're referring to the nurses' petition to Downing Street I presume. Yes, I did see it; and I saw last night's main news story on the television as well."

"I suppose it was inevitable that the story would be biased in favour of the nurses and that I would be portrayed as the nigger in the wood pile. Is there anything we can do to redress the balance, to get our message across? We don't have a majority in the House as you know, so there's bound to be another general election soon; we simply can't afford to have negative stories like this in the press."

"I'm afraid it's going to be difficult. Our message is that pay restraint is an essential part of economic policy. It's not a very sexy message and the nurses do have a special place in the affection of the public. If it comes to a battle between the government and the nurses, the press and the public are going to be on the side of the nurses every time! Nurses represent the acceptable face of militant trade unionism. They wear cute little caps, have shapely ankles and during their demonstrations, they break off from jostling with the police to smile prettily for the camera and chat up the press reporters."

"The truth is that I'm on their side as well," Barbara commented. "They deserve a decent wage and at the moment, they're simply not receiving one. Somehow or other I've got to persuade the Treasury to soften their line."

The next day, she invited Denis Healey and Michael Foot to join her for lunch in the Members' drawing room in the House of Commons. Denis was guardian of the nation's finances, Michael the defender of the pay policy. They found a quiet corner and over smoked salmon sandwiches and a bottle of Beaujolais, she raised the issue of nurses' pay.

"I take it you saw the press coverage of the nurses' demonstration," she began.

"Actually I saw the demo myself. I watched from the window as they marched past," Denis replied.

"Did you note the reaction they were getting from the public?" Barbara asked.

"Yes, I did and I can also see the way in which this conversation is going. The trouble is Barbara, that this country of ours hasn't the money to give them a decent rise, though perhaps we could manage two or three percent."

"But you do accept that the nurses should have more than that, that they deserve a significant rise?"

"Yes, I do," Denis replied honestly.

"And you know how much they are appreciated by the public and how events like yesterday's protest increase public sympathy? I had a meeting with the RCN recently; they are planning to increase the pressure in coming weeks. More rallies and more demonstrations, all of which means more bad publicity for us. There's a real threat of mass resignations from the NHS."

"But we cannot simply ignore the pay policy," Michael interjected. "You know how difficult it was to get the unions to sign up to it. They are constantly looking for an excuse to abandon it. If they see the slightest crack, it will turn into a flood."

As a waiter passed by, Barbara caught his eye. She tapped the now empty wine bottle. "Another of the same, please," she said.

"When do you think the next general election will be?" she asked innocently.

"Since the opposition can outvote us whenever they want, it's bound to be within the next three or four months," Denis admitted.

"So during the election campaign, the nurses are seen as wonderful, caring, blue-eyed angels and the press portray us as wicked devils determined to deny them what is rightfully theirs. That's going to cost us a whole lot of votes and quite a number of seats isn't it?"

"I do realise that there's a political element to this," Michael said," but can you suggest a way of satisfying the nurses without breaching pay policy?"

Barbara refilled their wine glasses. "Suppose we were to stand back, pass the problem to an independent panel and ask them to sort it out. In that way it wouldn't appear that we were the bad guys."

"That certainly might work. The risk would be that the independent body might make a recommendation that breached pay policy."

"That's a risk we would have to take, but if the body was chaired by someone who understood government policy, the risk would be reduced."

"Do you have anyone in mind?"

"Yes; Lord Halsbury. He used to chair the panel that advised on doctor's pay. I think he might be suitable."

Much to Barbara's relief, possibly mellowed by the wine, Denis and Michael agreed. She was even more delighted a few days later when both the Prime Minister and the cabinet, no doubt aware that the issue was a huge potential vote loser, decided not only that the recommendations made by the inquiry should be implemented without question but also that any award suggested should be back dated.

Chapter Nine

Sir William was in his office. He had ten minutes to fill before he was due to undertake his twice weekly review of the patients under his care. He made a point of being punctual. His recognised that his team of doctors were busy, hardworking people; he didn't wish to waste their time. He glanced at the group photos that covered the walls; one for each year that he had been a consultant, a catalogue of all the young doctors who had ever worked for him. He looked at the pictures fondly. He could remember them all by name, well maybe not all of them, but certainly the vast majority. Perhaps his memory was not quite as good as it had been when he was a younger man.

He had enjoyed his career and now, close to retirement, he allowed himself a warm glow of satisfaction. Throughout he had tried, not only to give his juniors a sound training in surgery, but to impart to them some of his own philosophies. He wanted them to remain humble no matter how senior they became, always to be caring and never to forget what a great privilege it was to be a doctor and allowed to share a patient's troubles.

He liked to teach 'surgical common sense'. He taught that gallant attempts at heroic surgery were rarely in a patient's best interest and that the quality of life was usually more important than its quantity. He realised of course, that some of the staff thought him old-fashioned and that they became impatient when his ward rounds took longer than those of his colleagues. He knew that some thought of him as an 'old woman' but he didn't care. He was happy to stick with his principles. Over the years, he had trained many surgeons and it pleased him to know he had influenced their practice. That would be his legacy.

Glancing again at the photos, he spotted Paul Lambert who had recently returned to his unit. Lambert had worked for him as a house man. Now he was back, this time as a registrar. Sir William felt a particular attachment to the young man. He had first noticed Paul when he had been a medical student. Initially, he had seemed somewhat shy and self-conscious, particularly when working alongside the nurses. But he had an easy way with patients, as shown by the case notes he wrote. Whereas most students' records were brief and factual, Lambert's included details of the patient's job and family, their hopes and fears.

Sir William recalled with a smile the day that he had appointed Lambert to be a house man. He would have liked the young man to work for him but had felt obliged to give his job to his nephew who qualified at the same time. Fortunately, his consultant colleague, Leslie Potts had been unable to attend the interviews and had given him the name of the candidate he wished to appoint. Sir William had taken one look at the dizzy young blond Leslie had selected, noted her short skirt, high heels and low neckline and had appointed Lambert instead! He thought it would do his colleague no harm to manage without a glamorous houseman for once! Leslie had been furious, which inevitably made things difficult for Paul when he took up his post but the deed was done and could not be reversed. It meant that Paul had started work under a cloud. For Paul though, this particular cloud proved to have a silver lining, for it was whilst working on Surgical Five that he met Kate Meredith, one of the student nurses. Paul had fallen head over heels in love with her and subsequently she had become his wife.

Looking again at the photographs reminded him that it was time to arrange a photograph of his present team. For the first time there would be a woman sitting next to him as his second in command. Long overdue, he thought. Victoria Kent had made a favourable impression during the short time that she had been working alongside him. She was quiet, thoughtful and compassionate. When she first arrived, he had wondered whether she would cope with the heavy work load and the stress involved with caring for critically ill people. How wrong he had been. When the going got tough, her Glaswegian grit appeared and she had proved herself to be the match of any man. She had overcome a lot of prejudice as she had climbed the surgical career ladder and Sir William knew it would not be too long before she became the first female consultant surgeon in the city.

Waking from his reverie, Sir William realised that the photographs on the wall and the memories they evoked had distracted him. He looked at his watch. Oh dear, it was five past ten. Fearful that he would lose his reputation for punctuality, he set off at a pace that belied his years, to join the team who were waiting to escort him round the ward.

"Sister, I do apologise for being a little late this morning," Sir William said as he entered the ward. "No excuses. I'm afraid that I was daydreaming rather than watching the clock."

"That's quite all right, Sir William," Sister replied. "May we offer you a drink or a biscuit before you embark on your round."

"That's kind of you Sister, but it's important that we attend to our patients first."

Victoria winked at Paul. They both knew that this exchange took place almost word for word, every time the consultant came to the ward.

"After you, Sister," Sir William said, as he held open the door for Sister and Victoria. He had the old-fashioned manners of an English gentleman; always holding the door for members of the opposite sex, no matter whether it was Matron, a visitor or the most junior of the student nurses. He valued every member of the team from the laundry maid to his consultant colleagues, treating them all with equal respect and he never failed to thank his staff for their support at the end of every ward round.

An expectant hush descended as Sir William strolled through the double doors of the main ward. To the fore were Sister, Victoria and Paul, closely followed by the staff nurse. Behind them a straggle of medical students tagged along and bringing up the rear was the houseman, pushing the trolley containing the patients' notes in time honoured fashion. As they reached the first bed, the houseman eased his way to the front of the crowd to present the patient's story to his boss.

"This is Mr Andrew Wood, Sir" Malcolm said. "He's 34 years of age and had surgery for his duodenal ulcer three days ago. His progress so far has been satisfactory, though he now has a slight chest infection. A sample of phlegm has been taken for culture and we have....."

Already Paul felt his attention wandering. He had the most enormous respect for Sir William, who was by far the most senior of the hospital surgeons. Perhaps he was no longer the most skilful operator, or the most knowledgeable, but he had achieved many great things in his professional life and was a wonderful role model for his trainees. He was widely respected, both inside the hospital and far afield. When away at other hospitals on training courses, Paul would often hear the comment *"You work for Sir William Warrender, don't you? You're truly very fortunate"* and there would be genuine envy in their voices.

But much as Paul liked and admired Sir William, there was a downside! Whereas Mr Potts would complete his round in an hour or less, Sir William took four hours or more. He believed passionately in giving adequate information to his patients. His explanations, perhaps concerning a forthcoming operation were lengthy and whilst much appreciated by patients, were a trial for the medical staff. Standing at a patient's bedside for long periods whilst the consultant repeated the same message over and over again was frustrating; legs became tired and the mind wandered, often thinking of all the other tasks that needed to be done when the round was over. It was unwise however to lose concentration because occasionally Sir William revealed pearls of common sense that were not to be found in surgical textbooks.

"I'm glad your chest is improving, Mr Wood," Paul heard Sir William say though his thoughts were still elsewhere. "Now how are your bowels? Have you managed a movement since your operation?"

This was another of the consultant's idiosyncrasies! Sir William never failed to ask his patients if their bodily functions had returned to normal after their operations. Furthermore, he would personally insert suppositories should these be required, a task that all other senior clinicians of Paul's acquaintance delegated to their juniors, or to the nursing staff. *'No one should be too proud to do a rectal examination,'* Sir William would say time and time again, whilst inserting suppositories into some poor constipated patient. *'If you don't put your finger in, one day you will put your foot in it.'*

"I've struggled to have a movement, but nothing has come through so far, Doctor," Mr Wood replied.

In a flash, Sir William's raised his right index finger like an umpire confirming a batsman's fate. It was a signal that Sister knew well; and it confirmed the patient's fate! Within the next minute, Sir William's chunky finger would be thrust up the poor man's anus, closely followed by a couple of suppositories!

"The rectal tray, nurse please," Sister said cheerfully.

As this ritual was taking place, the calm of the ward was suddenly shattered by a terrible scream of pain, then loud cries. They came from the corridor where the side rooms were situated. It was a deep male voice.

*"HELP ME. SOMEBODY F****** HELP ME. OH MY GOD, IM GOING TO DIE."*

A moment later, a junior nurse dashed towards the group of doctors and nurses, eyes wide in alarm, blood stains down the front of her apron.

By the time she reached Sister, she was sobbing. Her words came out in a torrent. "It's Mr King, Sister. I was just dressing his wound, then something awful happened. One minute he was fine, the next his wound exploded. Oh Sister, he had a coughing fit and then....." Her sobbing got worse such that she was unable to continue.

Sister turned to Sir William, "Please excuse me; I think I'd better go and see what's going on."

"Of course, Sister," the consultant replied. "I'm sure Staff Nurse will prove to be an able deputy. I suggest that Lambert and Miss Kent go with you as well," he added. With years of experience, he had already made the correct diagnosis. "It sounds as if Mr King will need to go back to theatre."

The scene that met their eyes when they entered the side ward was indeed dramatic, though not one that particularly alarmed Victoria, Paul or indeed Sister. It was a situation that they had all met before. Cedric was lying on his back, pale and shocked, not merely due to the problem with his wound but in fear that his days were at an end. The bedclothes were thrown back revealing that his long abdominal wound had parted from top to bottom. The entire length of his intestines had mushroomed out. His guts were lying in a pool of watery infected pink fluid in the bed beside him.

"My God, I'm f****** dying. Help. Help me please!" Cedric screamed.

"Don't be silly, Cedric, you're not dying," Victoria said calmly. "Mind you, we might just have to leave you to die if you don't stop all that terrible cussing. You've just got a little problem with your wound, that's all; it hasn't healed."

"But look at it, Doctor. It's awful. What the bloody hell is that?" Cedric moaned, pointing at the wet pink wriggling glistening mass.

"It's your guts, Cedric. But don't you fuss. We'll take you back to theatre, give you a puff of gas and stitch you up again. You'll be as right as rain."

Slowly, Cedric gained a degree of self-control, reassured by Victoria's words and calm demeanour. "But why the hell has it happened?"

"I think we'd best sort you out first Cedric, don't you, before we go into that?" Victoria replied, unwilling to enter a detailed debate at that moment.

Sister, who had slipped out of the room, now returned with some moist sterile towels. Gently she placed these over the exposed bowel. "Just leave those in place until you go to theatre," she said.

"I'll slip to theatre and get things organised," Paul said. "I take it you'll join me."

"Of course," Victoria replied. They both knew that one of Sir William's rules was that should a patient need a second operation; it should always be performed by a more senior surgeon.

Within the hour Paul was assisting Victoria as she washed away as much of the infected material as she could with warm saline. Then she returned the bowel to the abdomen and closed the wound, using especially strong thick sutures reserved for this purpose. The belly was then encased in a strong corset to offer the wound support as it healed, since wounds that had been infected often failed to heal strongly.

"Do you fancy a cup of tea?" Paul asked as they pulled off their gloves and masks and threw them in the bin.

"I do that," Victoria replied, "We've certainly earned one but perhaps we ought to go and see if the boss has finished on the ward."

"Must we? Sir William will have finished his round by now; he'll be entertaining the housemen with tales of his misspent student days."

Victoria smiled. "Oh, all right then. Stick the kettle on."

"There are some biscuits in the cupboard," the theatre sister said. "If you make a cup of tea for us as well, you can help yourselves."

Ten minutes later, the theatre staff and the two junior doctors were relaxing around a table covered in mugs of tea and packets of biscuits when the door opened and Sir William strolled in.

"I've just called in to see how it went," he said, his eyes scanning the scene.

They all jumped to their feet. "Well enough, thank you Sir," Victoria replied. "Let's hope it heals properly this time."

"Then I'll leave you to enjoy a drink," Sir William said with a grin, "I'm sure you've all deserved it!"

Following his second operation, Cedric's recovery was once again complicated, this time with a severe chest infection, blood clots in his legs and a mild heart attack. It was to be seven weeks before he was considered sufficiently fit to be allowed home. The staff on the ward, from senior surgeon to junior nurse, were happy to see him go. He had been an unpleasant, demanding, abusive patient. Just as bad were his visitors; a string of undesirable looking men of various nationalities, though mainly Afro-Caribbean. They tried to gain entrance to his side ward at various times of the day, but frequently late into the evening, which was a concern to the night staff. Accordingly a notice was placed on his door advising that visiting was restricted to official visiting hours - but this was largely ignored. All were tough looking, unshaven and, judging from their scars and broken noses, mainly gained a living with their fists. At times it seemed as if Cedric was running a business from his room, but whether this related to drug distribution or to a protection racket, no-one ever discovered. Unfortunately, the police, who had dutifully sat outside his room whilst they waited for his statement, had by this time disappeared and were not a witness to these comings and goings.

Chapter Ten

"Have you heard the news?" cried Claire in great excitement, as she burst through the front door of Kate and Paul's flat. The ringing of the door bell had been so loud and persistent that they had half-expected the neighbour's flat to be on fire.

"And what great news would that be?" Kate answered, relieved to find that it was only her great friend Claire and giving her a hug.

"Barbara Castle is visiting the hospital tomorrow!"

"Never," replied Kate. "At the moment, she's keeping a low profile. She's afraid of aggravating the situation by antagonising us and giving herself a bad press. She's hardly likely to walk straight into the lion's den and face more protests and demonstrations."

"No, it really is true. Apparently it's intended as a goodwill visit. She wants to show that she genuinely wants to help the nurses; she wants to prove that she's on our side."

"But it's perfectly obvious that she's not on our side. If she were, she would grant us the pay increase that we deserve."

"But it really is true Kate. I heard it from Jimmy Ackroyd, the union man. He rang me. I didn't believe it either at first so I quizzed one of the senior sisters. She got all hot and bothered when I questioned her but she didn't deny it. Barbara Castle is actually coming. It'll be a great opportunity to get our message across. Jimmy says the press are bound be there; probably television cameras as well. He says he will come too and bring some placards with him.

He wants me to arrange for as many nurses as possible to show up and have a demonstration. He suggests we give her a reception that she'll never forget!"

"I'm not sure that's a good idea," Kate commented. "Holding a demonstration on the street is all well and good but Matron will be furious if there's a rowdy protest here in the hospital. And Matron and the hospital big wigs are sure to be escorting Barbara Castle round. I would have thought a low profile protest would be more appropriate."

"Don't be such a coward. This is a wonderful chance to show the old cow just how strongly we object to her freezing our pay. We must seize the moment. There is a problem though; we don't know exactly at what time she's coming. Jimmy says we have to be prepared so that we can make our protest at short notice whatever time she turns up and whichever part of the hospital she visits."

"It's easy for him to say that but if we're on duty we can't just down tools, can we?" Kate observed.

"No, we can't, but we can make sure that some of us are available to make a protest whatever time she appears. The night nurses may be prepared to get out of bed and join the fun; so could those that are on shift duty. Come on Kate; be more enthusiastic. We mustn't let a golden opportunity like this pass us by."

"Agreed but we need to be careful. Matron's very proud of the reputation of the City General; she's not going to be happy seeing it shown in a bad light on the television, is she? Don't forget that she holds a lot of power, she writes our references and decides who gets promotion."

The next day, Mrs Castle did visit the hospital. She was accompanied by a posse of press men and a television crew who hoped to get some good pictures of her getting a rough reception from angry nurses. However Barbara was on a charm initiative. She was intent on gaining some good publicity and hopefully some votes from the visit. She steeled herself knowing that she would meet some disgruntled health workers but she vowed to woo them with patience, a disarming smile and some appreciative words; a skill at which she was an acknowledged expert. When she arrived, she was ushered into the hospital boardroom where she had her ear bent by the hospital's senior manager as she partook of some light refreshment. Then fifteen minutes later, she emerged to embark on her tour of the hospital, escorted by Matron, Sir William and the Regional Chairman.

It rapidly became apparent that it was not only the nurses who saw the visit as an opportunity to lobby the Health Minister. At every turn she was met by different groups of staff, all eager to impress upon her the depth of their feelings about their various grievances; ancillary workers disgruntled by their poor pay, junior doctors angry at their 80 plus hour working week, nurses frustrated that their pay claim had been refused and consultants furious about the threat to private practice. She listened patiently to their various complaints, never once giving the impression of being rushed. She spoke cheerfully with them all.

Claire, heeding Kate's warning, did not wave a placard or chant a slogan. Instead, she headed a small group of nurses and as Mrs Castle walked by, she asked politely if she could hand her a letter.

"Of course you can," Mrs Castle replied smiling, "I will read it on my journey back to Westminster but perhaps you would give me the gist of it now."

Claire had not reckoned on being able to speak personally to Mrs Castle and, aware that the press were taking photographs, answered hesitantly. "The letter says that our pay has fallen significantly behind that of other workers. It also says that all our patients agree that we deserve more money for the long hours that we work and for the responsibility that we carry."

Barbara Castle's response was to gather the group of nurses around her.

"In that case I agree 100% with your patients," she said to their great surprise. "You do a wonderful job. Everyone in Government is immensely proud of you and truly grateful for the work you do. And thanks to the terrible inflation created by Mr Heath when he and the Tories were in office, you have definitely fallen behind pay wise. But of course, you do know that you've already got your pay rise, don't you?"

"No, we have not," replied Claire, almost shouting with indignation.

"But you have," Mrs Castle said patiently. "The government has already agreed to accept the report of the independent inquiry, no matter how much it costs. Furthermore your increase will be backdated to May. You are actually entitled to it now. The work you are doing this month is being paid at the new higher rate. We're just waiting for Lord Halsbury to put a figure on it. Didn't you know that?"

Although a couple of the nurses in the group did already know, Claire didn't.

"No, I didn't know that," she stammered, then answered defensively. "But we don't know how big the increase will be, do we?"

Barbara smiled reassuringly. "No, at the moment, you don't, but the people who are deciding on the amount are completely independent and the Government has promised to implement it in full. However large the rise may be, be assured it will be paid."

"And when will that be?"

"Even I don't know that yet," she said still smiling, "but I don't think you will be disappointed when the figure is announced. Now I'm afraid that I must move on; there are other people I must speak to before I leave - but it has been nice chatting with you."

Later, Kate quizzed Claire on the meeting.

"Did you believe what Mrs Castle said," she wanted to know.

"Funnily enough, I did," Claire admitted. "She was very easy to talk to. It was a bit like having a chat with my own granny. On the telly she seems shrill and strident but she wasn't like that at all. She seemed sincere and appeared genuinely to want to help us."

"That's encouraging. I suppose that we shall have to wait until this Hayleybury man makes his report. Did you ask Mrs Castle when the report would come out?"

"He's called Halsbury actually. She said she doesn't know the date herself but if the increase is to be backdated we might get a tidy little lump sum. That would be very useful."

"Yes, it would be very welcome but we mustn't count our chickens too soon. Paul says politicians speak with forked tongues. You can't always believe what they say."

Chapter Eleven

"Thank you Sister but I won't stop for a cup of coffee today," Mr Potts said.
"I've been asked to see a patient on one of the medical wards."

The ward round had just finished but the consultant didn't have time for a drink
and a chat.

"There's a woman there," Mr Potts continued, waving a referral letter in the air,
"whom the physicians are worried about. She's losing weight and they don't
understand why. Apparently they've run every test in the book and they still
can't work out what's the matter with her. That's typical of physicians, always
so indecisive! I suppose we'll have to go and sort things out for them."

Mr Potts sounded pleased to have the chance to play 'one-upmanship' with his
medical colleagues. Paul was well aware of the rivalry which existed between
physicians and surgeons, a rivalry which dated back hundreds of years to the
days of the *barber surgeons*. In those times, surgeons were not qualified as
doctors and therefore not entitled to be addressed as such. They were usually
barbers who offered 'extras'. They pulled teeth, straightened broken bones,
lanced boils and stitched wounds. They were classed as mere 'tradesmen' and
considered a 'rough lot' by the physicians of the day. They were pointedly
referred to as *mister* in a derogatory fashion.

Meanwhile the physicians, by virtue of their medical training and qualifications,
considered themselves to be vastly superior. They believed that they were
engaging in a scientific profession as they cheerfully applied bloodsucking
leeches to patients with anaemia and treated syphilis with purgatives! Later, as
the benefits of surgery became appreciated, formal qualifications were
introduced. Surgeons are now required to complete a medical degree to become

a *'doctor'* before they become doubly qualified as surgeons, entitling them to adopt the title *'mister'*. Over time, the enmity between physicians and surgeons has become little more than friendly rivalry, but nothing pleases surgeons more than being able to cure a patient by performing an operation when medical treatment has failed.

When Mr Potts had said *'we'll have to go'*, it wasn't quite clear to whom he was referring. No-one was bold enough to ask for clarification, so the whole team felt obliged to follow him as he stalked off down the corridor. Although these consultations on other wards took Paul and Victoria away from their regular duties, they found them interesting and educational. Whatever the nature of the patient's problem, it was rarely straightforward. It broadened their experience and was a good opportunity for learning.

Mr Potts strode purposefully along the main hospital corridor, relating a story about an incompetent manager with whom he had recently crossed swords. He led the way into the medical corridor which was just as drab as the surgical corridor that they had left. Paint was peeling off the ceiling, there was city grime on the windows and tired dog-eared posters on the walls. Reaching the female medical ward, he burst into Sister's office without knocking, the surgical team hot on his heels, like the cavalry in full charge in days of old. Sister, who had been working quietly at her desk alongside her staff nurse, looked up sharply, a frown on her face and a reprimand on her lips but, recognising the consultant surgeon, held her tongue.

"Ahh, Mr Potts, you took me by surprise," she said, her voice failing to disguise the irritation she felt at the manner of Mr Potts' entrance. "You will have come to see Mrs Twigg, I suppose."

"I'm not sure of the lady's name, Sister dear," Mr Potts replied, oblivious to Sister's displeasure. "It's the woman who is losing weight; the one who's got Dr

Longfleet baffled. I gather he's finally decided that he hasn't a clue what's the matter with her and needs the wisdom and experience of a surgeon to make the diagnosis for him."

Pleased with his quick response, he looked to his surgical entourage for approval. His manner was jovial, but there was arrogance in the words. There was a view that hospital consultants could be categorised according to their personality; surgeons haughty and self-confident, physicians indecisive and insecure, psychiatrists distant and preoccupied, their heads in the clouds and pathologists, only confident of a diagnosis when the patient was dead. This was exemplified by a medical joke which was popular at the time.

It concerned doctors from different specialities who were on a duck shooting expedition. As the first two ducks flew over, the physician, with his reputation for procrastination, raised his gun but then hesitated, unable to decide which duck to shoot first, thereby allowing both ducks to fly to safety. When it was the psychiatrists turn, the same thing happened, the psychiatrist later explaining; *'I didn't shoot because I couldn't decide whether the ducks were real or a figment of my imagination.'* Finally, it was the turn of the surgeon. As the birds flew over, two shots rang out in quick succession and both ducks fell to the ground. The surgeon promptly turned to the pathologist saying; *"Well, tell me what they died of then."*

The beauty of the story was that it could be varied according to the audience. The one favoured by junior doctors being the one in which the surgeon, having shot the ducks, turns to his lowly house officer and shouts; *'Well don't just stand there dithering, boy. Go and fetch them.'*

Sister reached for the phone. "If you'll excuse me for a minute Mr Potts, I'll call the house officer. Mrs Twigg has been with us for many weeks now. She's had a great many investigations. He will be able to tell you about them."

"That's fine, Sister dear," replied the consultant. "You call him by all means, but I'm a busy man. I haven't got the time to wait for the houseman. I'll make a start without him."

With that, he exited the office, turned left and marched onto the main ward, his army of junior doctors and medical students following obediently in his wake. Victoria turned to Mr Potts' houseman and whispered urgently; "Get the notes Janet; we're going to need them."

Sister promptly replaced the telephone, quietly indicating to her staff nurse that she should call the medical house officer. She followed a few steps behind the visiting team, but stopped outside the office door. She watched a smile on her face, as the surgical cavalry hesitated then came to a halt halfway down the ward, uncertain of the location of its target.

Coughing politely, she said primly; "Perhaps you would allow me to show you the way, Mr Potts?" before turning to the right, away from the main ward. She knocked on the door of one of the side rooms.

She just had time to say, "Mrs Twigg, I have a visitor for you. You remember that....." before Mr Potts entered, his surgical retinue hot on his heels. Three strides took him to the patient's bedside. His team crowded in after him, completely filling the small room. Mrs Twigg had been sitting in her bed, quietly reading; a tartan woollen blanket around her shoulders but was visibly frightened by this sudden invasion. She slid further down the bed in an unmistakable act of self-protection.

If ever a person had an appropriate name, it was Mrs Twigg. She was a tiny bird like figure, barely five feet tall, who could not have weighed an ounce more than six stones. Her face was pale and pinched; cheek bones prominent against dark sunken eyes. Her arms, partly hidden by the blanket were like matchsticks, every anatomical feature sharply defined. Her hands, no more than skin and bone, looked skeletal; her nails claw-like, white and shiny as if made of enamel.

"Good morning, Mrs......," boomed Mr Potts as he towered over her.

"Mrs Twigg," Victoria added helpfully.

"That's right, Mrs Twigg. Don't look so frightened woman; no one's going to bite you."

If these words were intended to reassure, they missed their mark. Mrs Twigg cowered from him, fear written large on her face. Instinctively she pulled the bedclothes protectively to her chin as if to shield herself from attack.

Sister was now at her patient's side, across the bed from the consultant, a protective arm around Mrs Twigg's shoulders. "This is Mr Potts," she said quietly, "one of the consultant surgeons. You will remember that Dr Longfleet said that he would be coming to see you."

"That's right," reiterated Mr Potts, his voice echoing around the room. "Dr Longfleet has asked me to sort you out. Now, what seems to be the problem?"

"I'm not really sure," Mrs Twgg replied hesitantly after a long pause. "I just don't feel very well."

"Not very well in what way?"

"I think it's my tummy," Mrs Twigg responded in a voice that was barely audible.

"But what symptoms are you getting in your abdomen, woman?" Mr Potts demanded, clearly irritated at these vague replies.

"I'm really not sure." Mrs Twigg's voice quavered, her eyes turning towards Sister in a mute appeal.

"Well are you getting pains anywhere? Have you been vomiting? Have you been unable to eat? I've come here to help you so tell me what's been troubling you."

Quite overcome by the manner of the interrogation and the crowd of people in the room, poor Mrs Twigg started to cry softly.

"I need to know what symptoms you're getting. How on earth can I help you if you won't help yourself?"

But there was no response; Mrs Twigg had retreated into silence

"God give me strength," the consultant muttered, before turning to the medical students. *"Volo me aegrum virum saltem dimidio cerebro convenire posse,"* he said quietly, shaking his head sadly.

Those students who had studied Latin at school tried to hide their sniggers. Non Latin scholars looked puzzled. Mrs Twigg, realising that a personal comment about her had been made, looked hurt; her eyes again turning to Sister seeking help. Sister, also conscious that an inappropriate remark had been made, though not understanding what had been said, looked daggers at Mr Potts but said nothing.

Paul and Victoria glanced at each other, the same thought passing through each of their minds. Sir William would never have behaved like this. He would have put Mrs Twigg at ease, restricted the number of people round the bed and then questioned her quietly and gently. How could Mr Potts be so insensitive? Surely if his own wife had been subject to such lack of feeling he would have been absolutely furious, the first to complain. Paul's eye caught Janet's, the feminist house officer whom Mr Potts loved to provoke. Her face was a picture of furious indignation. It appeared that her feelings were about to find forceful expression. Hurriedly he frowned and put a finger to his lips as a warning. Mr Potts was in no mood to have his conduct questioned.

Fortunately, at that moment the medical registrar appeared and was able to defuse the situation by giving Mr Potts a summary of Mrs Twigg's history and investigations.

He said that Mrs Twigg was 45 years old, a mother and part time secretary who had enjoyed good health until two years previously. She had then been troubled by vague abdominal pains and had started to lose weight. Her GP had given her some simple medication but when this had no effect, he referred her to the hospital. At first, it was thought that she had a stomach ulcer. However she didn't respond to therapy. Then she developed bowel symptoms which also failed to improve with treatment. All the while she had been losing weight; in total, she had lost over four stones.

In the course of her illness, a wide variety of blood tests had been performed, an array of x-rays had been taken and numerous medications tried but all to no avail. Despite Dr Longfleet's best endeavours, no firm diagnosis had been reached and her weight had continued to fall. Further, she was now severely anaemic and undernourished despite having received blood transfusions and a highly nutritious diet. She was in danger of a sad demise if the cause of her troubles could not quickly be discovered and treated.

"We'd better have a look at your abdomen," Mr Potts said, pulling down the bed clothes and lifting the patient's nightdress without asking or waiting for her permission.

Paul was startled by what he saw. Mrs Twigg's ribs stood out dramatically, like the timbers of an old wooden sailing boat. The bones of her pelvis, lacking any fatty layer, were prominent ridges in contrast to the hollow of her abdomen. The flesh on her buttocks and thighs had been lost, her skin hanging loosely in folds from her body. The victims of Belsen could not have looked more emaciated.

Mrs Twigg winced as Mr Potts gave her abdomen a cursory examination. He then stood back.

"Right," he said, addressing the patient. "There's absolutely nothing at all for you to worry about. We'll get you across to my ward and we'll soon have you sorted out." He looked across the bed. "You can arrange that for me, can't you Sister?"

Without further explanation and denying Mrs Twigg the opportunity to ask questions, he turned abruptly and left the room. It had been a typical Leslie Potts performance; the sort of thing Paul remembered from his days as a house officer three years before. Mr Potts had a self-confidence which at times bordered on arrogance. He clearly had little doubt that he would rapidly succeed where his medical colleagues had failed. He had shown little thought or consideration for the patient or her feelings and simply didn't recognise that his engagement with Mrs Twigg was so unequal. He was standing, confident and healthy, fully dressed, supported by his team, armed with his medical knowledge and the authority to decide on his patient's treatment. She was lying, in a strange, frightening environment, ill and anxious, half naked, her nightdress barely covering her modesty as he laid his hands on her, fearful of what the future might hold.

Paul wondered how someone who behaved in such a manner could have risen to become a consultant. Had he perhaps hidden his true feelings when he was being supervised as a trainee? Or had he become insensitive by virtue of having seen so many patients, that he had simply forgotten that they were human beings and had come to regard them merely as academic problems? He wondered if there was any higher authority to which he could express his concerns about his boss's behaviour but of course there wasn't. The consultants were the highest authority; that was what enabled some of them to act as Gods!

Yet, Paul was also aware that his boss was capable of performing surgery that was technically brilliant, that he was able to perform life saving operations that were beyond his fellow consultants and that his knowledge of surgical matters was second to none. What a shame that these attributes were not matched by an equally good bedside manner.

Paul's every instinct was to stay behind to console Mrs Twigg, but he knew he was expected to follow Mr Potts as he led the way back to the ward office. No doubt Sister would remain at the bedside, comforting her patient and apologising for Mr Potts' abrupt manner, whilst privately cursing him for causing Mrs Twigg unnecessary distress. She would probably explain that the consultant was an extremely busy man but reassure her that he was also very clever and would do his best to make her better, whilst inwardly wishing she could give him a few lessons on how to improve his intolerable behaviour.

As they left and walked back along the corridor towards the surgical wards, they chanced to meet Dr Longfleet coming in the opposite direction. With his entire surgical team and half a dozen students as an audience, Mr Potts was in his element. He addressed his colleague in a jocular tone, a beaming smile on his face.

"Ah, Bill. I'm so glad to see you. We've just been to see that emaciated lady of yours, Mrs......"

"Mrs Twigg, Sir," Victoria prompted once again.

"Yes, that's right, Mrs Twigg. She looks half dead to me. You must have been starving her! She certainly seems to have got you foxed. Perhaps you should have admitted defeat earlier and called for our assistance months ago when she had a little more flesh on her bones. I guess we shall have to take a quick look inside that abdomen of hers and solve the mystery for you."

Dr Longfleet was a quiet, intelligent and experienced physician who said nothing, nor did anything, without a great deal of thought. Although an inch or two taller than Mr Potts and probably a dozen years older, he was slim and had a slight stoop, suggesting that his responsibilities lay heavily on his shoulders. His small pinched face with its beak-like nose wore a permanent worried frown and he peered at the world like a timid owl through small, metal round-rimmed NHS glasses. In the exchange that was to follow, he was no match for the ebullient surgeon. He spoke hesitantly in a voice that was scarcely more than a whisper.

"Oh, er, hello Leslie. Thank you for coming to see Mrs Twigg. I'm very grateful to you. I cannot deny that she has been causing us a lot of concern and we have performed many investigations without getting to the root of her problem. But when we asked you to see her, we weren't actually thinking about surgery. We thought you might care to go over the various investigations we have performed and give us the benefit of your opinion. I really don't feel that an exploratory operation is the answer."

"Nonsense, dear fellow," Mr Potts said in a voice loud enough to startle two student nurses who happened to be passing, "You've obviously done every test under the sun. I'm sure a quick look inside her belly will solve the problem. Obviously we'll let you know what we find. Then we'll feed her well, fatten her up and you can have her back to recuperate."

"But that's the point, Leslie. She is eating well, but the food she takes doesn't do her any good. She doesn't seem to absorb it. There's clearly something amiss with her intestines, but I doubt that it's anything that can be removed surgically. We really wanted you to consider the entire file and advise us if we are missing something."

Mr Potts laid a condescending hand on his colleague's shoulder. "You worry too much, Bill. Just leave the matter with us, dear chap. We'll have her fit and well before you can say Jack Robinson."

Dr Longfleet looked unconvinced. "But Leslie, I, ...er, think that perhaps...." but his colleague had already turned to leave and the physician lacked the confidence to press the matter. However, the expression on his face suggested that he was far from happy at the prospect of his patient having an exploratory operation.

Back on the surgical ward, after Mr Potts had departed, Janet turned angrily on Paul. "It's no good you '*shushing*' me like that. Only a man could behave in such a deplorable fashion," she said scornfully. "Someone needs to tell him that his conduct is simply not acceptable."

"That may be so," Paul replied crossly, "but don't let that someone be you, unless you want your medical career to end before it's begun. I was only trying to help you."

Paul turned to Victoria. "Did you study Latin at school?"

"Yes, I did."

"So what did the boss say after he'd frightened that poor lady into submission?"

"It came out of the blue and took me by surprise but part of it was '*dimidio cerebro*' 'which means *'half a brain'* so I guess it was probably something about Mrs Twigg only having half a brain!"

Paul shook his head sadly. "It's amazing what you can get away with when you're the boss."

Chapter Twelve

Malcolm collared Paul one day after lunch in the doctor's residency. "Paul," he said, "do you have a minute? There's something that I'd like to show to you. I thought I'd better let you see it before I unveil it on the ward."

Malcolm led the way to his room and when the door was securely closed showed off his latest creation. Paul looked and silently groaned. Malcolm had designed and constructed a wooden box some two feet long and nine inches wide. The top was hinged and when the lid was opened, a number of compartments of different shapes and sizes were revealed. A handle was attached, also made of wood. The design was good, the handiwork beautiful. The box had dove-tailed joints, brass hinges and a lock inset into the front.

"It's a beautiful piece of work," Paul said, knowing how hard house officers worked and how little spare time they had for rest and relaxation. "Did you make it yourself?"

"Yes, I did," Malcolm said. "I was off duty last weekend and spent all my time on it."

"It's for carrying cards and equipment on the ward isn't it?"

"Yes, and I want to know if you think Mr Potts will take exception to it. He doesn't seem to approve of my various ideas. I really don't wish to be embarrassed on the ward again."

Paul knew exactly what Mr Potts was likely to say if he saw it. With sarcasm flowing from his lips, it would be something along the lines of '*I'm not having anyone looking like a joiner traipsing after me while I do a ward round. Get rid of it at once!*'

"Look, I'm sorry Malcolm but I honestly don't think that the boss will approve. In fact, I doubt it would be wise to let him see it. I do understand that it saves time to have everything you need to hand when examining a patient, but I'm afraid the boss won't see it that way."

Malcolm looked crestfallen. "But why should he object?"

It was a perfectly reasonable question for Malcolm to ask but Paul knew that they were not dealing with a reasonable man. "Take my advice. Use it when you're working on your own, but for Heaven's sake don't take it on any of his consultant ward rounds. He's God around here and if he's decided he doesn't like your bright ideas, then he's not going to change his mind."

Advising Malcolm in this way, brought to Paul's mind similar advice that he had received as a houseman from his registrar; a man called Mohammed Khan whom Paul held in high regard. '*Don't try to buck the system,*' he had said. '*You won't change it. It was here long before you arrived on the scene and it will still be there long after you are gone.*'

Following Paul's advice, Malcolm used his latest innovation when working on the wards but was always careful to leave it on the floor in a quiet corner of the office whenever Mr Potts was around! It wasn't long though before Malcolm became quite a celebrity in the hospital, as he carried his carpenter's box around with him wherever he went. Someone referred to him as 'Chippy' and the name stuck. He became known as 'Chippy Chapman' for the rest of his time on the unit.

*****

It had taken over three hours but Sir William had finally completed his review of the patients under his care and had accepted Sister's offer of a drink and a biscuit. It was a good opportunity to sit in the office and discuss some of the cases they had seen, out of earshot of the patients. Too often though, the discussion drifted away from patients and Sir William would engage in his favourite hobby; reminiscing about his own life as a junior doctor in the days when he was a trainee surgeon. It was clear that he had thoroughly enjoyed those early days, particularly the practical jokes that they played on each other. He invariably emphasised how hard he had worked, what unrelenting taskmasters his consultants had been, and how the job was unpaid. *'In the good old days, we were apprentices'*, he would say. *'Our reward was to be taught good clinical practice – not like the trainees of today who expect to be paid as well as taught.'*

When Sir William mentioned the subject of pay, it offered Paul an opportunity to discuss with the consultant a subject which had started to worry him; the vexed question of the doctors' dispute with the government. Not only were the consultants at loggerheads with Mrs Castle but the junior doctors were getting restless as well, with their insistence that their excessively long hours be appropriately remunerated.

A couple of weeks previously, Sir William had asked Paul if he knew whether there had been any meetings of the junior doctors at which the possibility of industrial action had been debated. It was something that he had subsequently discussed with Victoria and had discovered that she held very definite views on the matter.

"Sir William's absolutely right," she had commented. "There hasn't been a meeting so we haven't a clue what the doctors here think. There's been some wild talk in the medical press of working to rule, even of going on strike but surely no doctor would be prepared to do that; I would certainly hope not anyway! So yes, I'm certain there ought to be a meeting to see how people feel."

"Sir William feels that the consultants pay too little regard to our problems," Paul said, "particularly to the number of hours we are required to work. He's persuaded them to invite a member of the junior staff to sit with them at their meetings. He wants someone to represent the junior doctors' views. He suggested that I might be prepared to do it."

"Did he now?" Victoria replied, sounding impressed. "That would be a real feather in your cap and a very useful thing to have on your CV. I should jump at that if I were you, Paul."

"But I've never taken much interest in medical politics and we're all so busy with our noses hard against the grindstone that I'm not sure I have the time or energy to do it."

"I wouldn't turn it down in a hurry if I were you," Victoria advised. "Opportunities like that don't come along too often."

Paul knew that he couldn't accept Sir William's offer without the approval of the other junior doctors. Conventionally their spokesman was the 'Mess President' but Paul's inquiries revealed that the post was vacant. He therefore called a meeting so that the matter could be discussed. Perhaps unsurprisingly, when it became known that he had been asked to sit at the consultants' table, they promptly elected him as their President! The meeting also made Paul realise, somewhat to his surprise, just how many of his colleagues felt a deep sense of injustice at their long hours, and how extremely angry they were that the hours they worked beyond 40 was so poorly remunerated. Some had already decided they would 'work to rule' if asked to do so by their national representatives. They were emboldened by the fact that the consultants were also threatening industrial action in their fight to preserve the pay beds.

Now, as their representative, Paul needed to know what the reaction of the consultants would be, should the juniors decide to take industrial action. Specifically could Sir William give an assurance that junior doctors would not be victimised.

"Sir," he began, somewhat hesitantly, "I need some advice on the industrial action that is threatening the Health Service at the moment. May I have a few moments of your time?"

"Yes, of course Lambert, and since there's no time like the present, let's go to my office where we won't be interfering with Sister or the housemen. I'm sure they have plenty of work to do. Miss Kent, if you're free, perhaps you would like to come along as well."

Safely in his office, where they couldn't be overheard, Sir William offered the two registrars a seat. "Now Lambert," Sir William said, "what is it that's on your mind?"

"Sir, it's about the industrial action that's being discussed both in the national press and by the British Medical Association (BMA). It raises some awkward questions that are causing the junior doctors some concern."

"Yes, these are unhappy times. I'm saddened that some consultants have already started to reduce their workload. It's something that I never imagined I would see. It portrays our profession in a very bad light."

"It seems that some of the junior doctors are considering going down the same road, Sir."

"Do you have any idea how many?"

"I'm afraid I have no idea at all. If there's an official call for action, I guess some will participate and others won't."

"A mixed bag, just like the consultants then."

"Yes, but the juniors are worried. You see Sir, if a consultant and his junior both restricted their work in some way, or indeed if they both worked normally, there wouldn't be a problem. The concern would be if a junior decided to take action against the wishes of his consultant."

"Yes, I can see that might lead to difficulties," Sir William conceded.

"As the senior consultant in the hospital Sir," Victoria asked, "could you instruct your colleagues not to disadvantage a junior doctor who took industrial action?"

Sir William laughed. "My God I wish I could. At times I would love to be able to keep them in order but I'm afraid I can't. Managing consultants is a bit like herding cats. They're a very independent minded lot! You see, the system doesn't work like that. All consultants have equal status. It's one of the great weaknesses of the organisation."

"What about Dr Digby. He's chairman of the consultants' committee," Paul asked, "surely he has some authority?"

"Sadly not, Lambert. In theory the hospital managers are in charge but in practice they have little control. Dr Digby and I can try to lead by example but we have no authority over our colleagues. But I will raise your concerns at the next meeting. I'll propose that the juniors should be allowed to act without fear of any retribution."

"Thank you, Sir that should help a little."

"If I may though, I would offer a word of advice. None of us should forget that the victims in all of this are the patients. As far as is possible we must safeguard their interests. I suggest that should juniors ever take action, they should guarantee that there will be no disruption to the care of casualties or emergency patients. Let any disruption be limited to non urgent cases. Also I feel that it would be appropriate to give the hospital management at least a weeks' notice of any impending action, so that appropriate arrangements can be made."

"Thank you for that, Sir. Another meeting of the juniors is scheduled in the next couple of days. I am sure that will be agreed."

With that, Sir William looked at his watch, excused himself and left to have his lunch. Paul slipped away to casualty to treat a patient with belly ache who had been waiting to be seen. No sooner had he arrived than his pager sounded.

Surprisingly it was Kate. She knew not to disturb him at work unless it was urgent. She was in a state of high excitement, bursting to tell him her news. "Paul, we've got a 30% rise."

"How much did you say?"

"Thirty percent!"

"That can't be right. It must be a mistake."

"No, Paul, it's not a mistake. I didn't believe it when I was told. I thought someone was pulling my leg. So I listened to the BBC news. And just as Mrs Castle promised when she came to the hospital, it's going to be backdated to May when the inquiry was set up. It means that we'll get a lump sum."

"Well then, the BBC must have got it wrong. No-one ever gets a thirty percent pay increase."

"Well, we just have. Check for yourself if you don't believe it." And when Paul checked, he was delighted to find that Kate was correct. The Halsbury report had indeed recommended an average salary increase of just over 30%, loaded in favour of senior nurses; student nurses getting proportionally less. Even more surprising, the government had accepted the recommendations, implemented them in full and back-dated the award!

Chapter Thirteen

The day after Mr Potts' visit to the medical ward and his subsequent encounter in the corridor with Dr Longfleet, Mrs Twigg was transferred to Surgical Five. Patients such as this were medical detective mysteries. Paul knew that occasionally the answer could be found by a careful review of the patient's story, a thorough clinical examination followed by some detective work in the medical library. It would be wonderful if the surgeons could resolve the problem that had baffled the physicians; better still if he could be the one to do it, particularly if this could be achieved without resorting to the knife. In Mrs Twigg's emaciated state, an operation would be a risky undertaking.

It was clear that Dr Longfleet had invited his surgical colleague to see Mrs Twigg with a view to applying some thought to the case, not simply to look inside her abdomen hoping that, by chance, this would reveal a condition that required surgical correction. His particular expertise was in endocrinology, the study of glands and hormones, not in diseases of the gut. Paul recalled how the house officers had enjoyed a laugh at his expense at the last hospital Christmas revue. To the tune of *'June is bursting out all over'* they had sung a witty lyric about him:

June is bursting out all over, where once she was skinny and so thin,

'til she went to see Bill Longfleet, at his rooms down in St John Street

and he fed her on synthetic oestro Gin.

Endocrinology is charming, testosterone for men is quite the thing,

so if you're short of male emotion, just take Billy's little potion , and your love affairs will really start to swing.

So, if your libido is low, take Bill Longfleet's pills and go!!

Paul was concerned that so little consideration had gone into Mr Potts' decision to operate and resolved to take a particular interest in Mrs Twigg himself. His conscience would simply not allow him to stand by until the surgery was undertaken.

He started that evening by taking time to go through her extensive medical records. There was no doubt she had been exhaustively investigated. When her troubles had started she had weighed ten and a half stones. There was a suggestion that she might have had a stomach ulcer and also evidence of some mild inflammation of the bowel. Unfortunately, when treatment for these conditions had been applied, there had been no improvement whatsoever. And all the while, her weight loss had continued. Whilst she had been in hospital, she had been weighed twice a week; the chart showing a continuing downward trend. She now weighed precisely six stones and seven pounds.

At one stage a psychiatrist had been asked to see her. He had noted that Mrs Twigg seemed a little depressed, but had concluded that this was the result of her illness, rather than the cause of it. Specifically, he did not think that she had anorexia nervosa, not least because the nursing staff confirmed that she had not lost her appetite, ate her meals and seemed to enjoy them. Paul noted however, that the central part of the bowel, the small intestine, had not been investigated. Since this was the part where many of the nutrients in food are absorbed, it struck him that this was a notable omission. He felt excited. If this discovery led to the correct diagnosis, Mrs Twigg might be spared an unpleasant operation. It would also be good for his reputation! It would certainly be a feather in his cap if he could solve the mystery that had defied a consultant physician. All trainees needed some 'Brownie points' if they were to progress up the career ladder in the highly competitive specialty of surgery.

Laying aside her notes, Paul then went to the ward and asked Mrs Twigg to be patient while he listened carefully to the story of her illness; a story she had repeated innumerable times to the many doctors she had already met. Concentrating on conditions that arose in the small bowel, he searched for any clues that might suggest some rare cause of disease; strange habits, unusual pets, exposure to noxious substances or travel to exotic locations. And he struck gold! Two years previously, Mrs Twigg had travelled to Nigeria. Her sister worked for Oxfam and she had gone to Africa to visit her. She had stayed for a month.

"Were you ill when you were there?" Paul asked.

"Well I had a little diarrhoea," she replied, "but no more than anyone else."

"Did you tell the doctors on the medical ward about it?

"No, I don't think so. They didn't ask and it didn't seem important. Anyway, it was a long time ago."

Paul reviewed the notes again. The trip to Nigeria had not been picked up by Dr Longfleet, nor had any tests for tropical diseases been performed. He realised that this was almost certainly the breakthrough for which they had been searching. His knowledge of diseases that could befall travellers to exotic countries was limited but he did recall from his student days that there were many infections that could affect the small bowel. One of them must surely be the cause of Mrs Twigg's profound weight loss. A diagnosis would be reached without an operation after all.

Excited, he went to the hospital library. On a top shelf, he found three books on tropical diseases. They were covered in dust; there was rarely need to refer to them in an inner city hospital in the UK. He picked up the slimmest volume but even this ran to 800 pages. He flicked through its pages with dismay. Despite being medically qualified, he recognised only a tiny fraction of the diseases that were listed. Most had long unpronounceable Latin or Greek names and were caused by all manner of noxious organisms. There were diseases caused by fleas and lice most of which he had never heard. Then there were a variety of different worms such as the dreaded tapeworm, as well as round worms, thread worms, whip worms, hook worms and Guinea worms that could be over a metre long. Paul shuddered at the thought of that! Most of them were endemic in Africa. Many were associated with a fever but importantly, most caused vague abdominal pain and weight loss, the very symptoms that Mrs Twigg had!

He discussed the situation with Victoria.

"Did Mrs Twigg have a fever when she was on the medical ward?" she asked.

"Occasionally her temperature was raised, but it was never very marked," Paul replied.

"And I take it that there haven't been any tests to look for weird and wonderful bugs in the stool?"

"No."

"Then we need to monitor her temperature and to ask the laboratory to examine the stools," Victoria commented. "An x-ray of the small bowel is the next logical step; but we'll need to get Mr Potts' permission first. It involves quite a lot of irradiation and takes the radiologist the best part of an hour to perform."

"Then let's request it now," Paul suggested. "It always takes a day or two to arrange and we can always cancel it if the boss doesn't agree."

"Well, let's hope he does agree. We certainly need to persuade Mr Potts not to charge in with an operation!"

Chapter Fourteen

In due course Paul learned that he was to be called as a witness for the prosecution in the case of The Crown versus Miss Annie Nolan. The charge was one of 'attempted murder'.

Paul was required to present himself at the criminal court in the city centre at nine am on the first Tuesday of the following month. With no previous experience of appearing as a witness and ignorant of court procedures, he again sought the advice of Sir William.

"Lambert, you are quite right to be concerned. Appearing in court can be quite an ordeal and it's sensible to prepare yourself in advance. Here in the hospital, you are in an environment with which you are familiar, in which you feel relaxed, but for our patients things are quite different. For them the hospital is a strange, unfamiliar, frightening place. The same is true in court except now it is you who are out of your comfort zone and the lawyers who are at home. But there are some things you can do to prepare yourself.

You will be interrogated on your statement, so go over it carefully before the trial. Always take time to stop and think before answering a question; don't be rushed into saying something that you can't substantiate. Always confine yourself to facts. In the event that you are asked for your opinion, don't be too definite with your replies. Phrases like... *"in my opinion it is possible that"*.... are useful. Remember that barristers are slippery customers; they like to lead you on. They will often present a scenario to you and ask you to agree with it. If they do, it is tempting simply to say '*Yes*' but much safer to say '*I agree that what you are suggesting is possible.*' Remember, you are only there as a witness to the things you saw and the actions you took. As I say, just stick to the facts."

Paul had been anxious before he went to see Sir William but came away feeling even more apprehensive about the forthcoming trial. Nonetheless, he went over his witness statement several times and determined that when he was in court, he would try to stay cool and follow his consultant's advice.

The summons that Paul received had been accompanied by a letter from the prosecuting barrister, requesting a meeting an hour before proceedings were due to commence. The court clerk showed him to an office where the barrister was waiting.

"This is Dr Lambert, one of the witnesses," the clerk said by way of introduction.

The barrister, Vincent Egerton QC, was far younger than Paul had expected, perhaps no more than 35 or 40 years of age. Tall and slim, he had a stern bony angular face, notable for a sharply pointed nose and grey eyes that complimented his jet black hair. He spoke with a clipped, high pitched, slightly nasal voice, with an accent that suggested a 'privileged' home and an expensive education. Mr Egerton was sitting behind a mahogany desk, the inlaid top covered with legal papers, some loose, others rolled and neatly tied with red ribbon. To one side, Paul saw his barrister's wig on top of a pile of leather bound books. He did not rise when Paul entered; instead he waved loftily at a chair across the desk. For three or four seconds, he simply looked at Paul, his eyes focussed on Paul's face. His gaze had a staring, penetrating quality, suggesting he could infiltrate your skull and discern your innermost thoughts. Paul reminded himself that Sir William had said that he had nothing to fear in this, his first court appearance. He was there simply to testify to the facts, but this man's gaze made him feel distinctly uneasy. Already he felt that he was on trial - not Annie Nolan.

"Right, Lambert," he said sharply, his inspection of Paul complete. "Have you appeared in court before?"

At the City General, Paul was accustomed to being referred to simply as 'Lambert'. Just like his teachers when he had been at school, the consultants rarely used a prefix. It was hospital custom and practice and Paul took no offence at it. Outside of the hospital however, to address somebody simply by their surname, would be regarded as being impolite, bordering on rude. Paul presumed that the barrister was establishing the relationship that he felt would be appropriate between them. When Paul confirmed that this was indeed his first court appearance, Mr Egerton proceeded to instruct on how Paul should present his evidence.

"I shall lead you step by step through the statement that you have provided. I take it that you have familiarised yourself with it?" Paul nodded. "It will all be entirely straight forward. I want you simply to answer my questions. Do not be tempted to add any additional thoughts that you may have, no matter how relevant you think they may be. Is that absolutely clear?"

Again, Paul nodded. "You will be the second witness that I shall call. The first will be Mr King, the victim of this appalling attack. I want you to listen carefully to his evidence. It is possible that when I have led you through your own statement, I shall ask you a question or two that may arise from what he says. Are you happy with that?"

For a third time, Paul nodded. "Then that will be all, thank you."

The entire meeting had lasted precisely three minutes and Paul had spoken not half a dozen words. He was shown to a waiting room. The proceedings were not due to commence for a further hour. Then information was fed through that there had been a delay, expected to be perhaps thirty minutes. No explanation of the delay was offered. For two hours, Paul sat twiddling his thumbs thinking that he could have been doing something useful at the hospital if the court officials were more efficient and considerate of the time of others. He vowed that if ever he was called to court again, he would bring a book or a newspaper with him.

Finally, a clerk came to collect him and he was led into the court. There he saw Cedric King for the first time in six months. He had been accustomed to seeing Cedric as a patient, lying in a bed and he had not appreciated just how huge he was. Broad across the shoulders, he was not less than 6 ft 2 inches tall. At first, Paul scarcely recognised him. The Rastafarian dreadlocks had been shed in favour of a neatly parted 'short back and sides' and the pyjamas that he had worn in hospital (occasionally accompanied by a multicoloured woollen hat) had been replaced by a smart grey suit, whose buttons struggled to contain his enormous belly.

Then, Annie was lead into the dock. By comparison, she was a tiny mouse-like figure, dwarfed by the stout prison guard at her side to whom she was hand-cuffed. She looked petrified and seemed to shrivel in size as she cowered from the curious gaze of the jury, other members of the court and the visitors in the public gallery. It was as if she was trying to make herself invisible. Everyone was instructed to stand as the judge made his appearance. Judge Phillips waddled slowly up the steps to his throne. He was almost as wide as he was tall. Before taking his seat, he stopped and looked around his courtroom as if to assure himself that everything and everybody was in its proper place. He looked to be at least seventy years of age. Wisps of white hair protruded from beneath his grey wig. His face was lined and lacked expression. As Paul was to discover as the trial progressed, having taken his place in his high chair, he scarcely moved. With eyes half-closed and head bent forward as if he were hard of hearing, there were times when it seemed that he might have nodded off; though equally it was possible that he was simply concentrating hard on the proceedings.

As Paul surveyed the court, the polished oak benches, the dark panelling on the walls, the jury segregated to one side watching intently from their box, the public gazing down from the gallery and particularly the barristers and the judge with their robes and fancy wigs, he found it hard to decide whether the scene was one of dignity and great solemnity or of farce and pantomime. Paul recognised a number of faces in the public gallery. He had seen them visiting Cedric in his hospital side ward. Although Cedric's appearance had changed markedly, theirs had not. They still looked a rough tough group of men whom Paul would not have wished to meet on a dark night!

After some preliminary remarks by the judge addressed to the jury, reminding them of their grave responsibilities, Cedric was invited to take the stand. He was sworn in and proceeded to give his evidence. If Vincent Egerton had spent very little time with Paul, he had clearly rehearsed Cedric at great length. The answers that he gave to the prosecuting barrister's questions were delivered confidently in a slow deep monotone, as if they were being read or had been memorised. From time to time his counsel needed to prompt him. At one stage, he caused a laugh when he gave an inappropriate answer to one of the questions. He then apologised *'Oh sorry Sir, that's the answer to the next question isn't it?'*

As Cedric gave his evidence, Paul watched the judge and the defending counsel but they appeared to be taking little notice. Presumably they knew exactly what Cedric would say, having read his written statement in advance. His account of events on the night of the stabbing was that he had gone into one of the local pubs with a crowd of his friends to celebrate a significant win on a horse he had backed at the local betting shop. During the evening, he had drunk several beers, though not to the point of being drunk. He stated that he fell into conversation with a woman that he now knows to be Annie Nolan, the defendant. They struck up a friendship and in due course walked to Annie's flat, where sexual intercourse took place. Cedric insisted that this was consensual. He then alleged that before he was fully dressed, Annie had demanded money from him. He was adamant that he did not know that she was a prostitute. He stated that he had never found it necessary to pay for sex. He thought he had been '*doing her a favour*' and he was dammed if he was going to give her any money. He said that Annie then flew into a rage and attacked him with her fists. He simply laughed at her and pushed her aside, but she found the knife that he carried in his belt and attacked him with it, inflicting the wound that had so nearly killed him.

He was asked if he had done anything to provoke the attack but he denied this strenuously. When asked again if he had been inebriated at the time, he acknowledged that he was 'merry', but insisted that he had not been drunk. He was questioned as to why he found it necessary to carry a weapon, a six inch double bladed knife. Did he not know that if was illegal to carry an offensive weapon? He acknowledged that he did know that it was illegal, but said that in the environment in which he lived, he felt more secure carrying it, although he would never have dreamed of using it. He carried it as a deterrent.

Vincent Egerton then led him through the period that he had spent in hospital. Cedric stated that he had actually died whilst on the operating table, his heart had stopped and he had only survived thanks to the expertise of the medical staff. He made great play of the fact that his wound had burst open and that all his intestines had ruptured into the bed. This was stated to be a further life-threatening episode, as were the chest and cardiac problems that had occurred during his recovery. Clearly the barrister wished the jury to agree with him that the crime was indeed '*attempted murder*' not merely '*grievous bodily harm*'.

Cedric was not asked, nor did he offer any explanation of Annie's injuries. At the time it seemed bizarre that Cedric had not been invited by Mr Egerton to explain how these had occurred and it was only later that Paul was to understand the reason why. Otherwise the account that Cedric gave, sounded entirely credible. Paul's understanding from the nurses in casualty had been that Annie normally 'conducted her business' from a street corner adjacent to the hospital but there seemed to be no reason why she shouldn't pick up a client in a pub. It also seemed possible that confusion had arisen as to whether Cedric understood that he was expected to pay for services rendered. The account of events also supported Paul's theory that Cedric had been stabbed after sexual intercourse had taken place whilst he was lying on the bed, though Mr Egerton had not actually ascertained whether Cedric had been standing, sitting or lying when the assault took place.

Cedric was dismissed and a few moments later Paul was called to give evidence. Now it was his turn to be interrogated. As he took the stand, he told himself not to be nervous. There seemed to be no need. Mr Egerton had been extremely gentle with Cedric. Questions had been posed quietly and politely. Nothing unexpected had been asked. The barrister had simply led Cedric through his prepared statement. Paul reminded himself that he was only going to testify to the facts and not offer any opinions. But he couldn't help feeling anxious in this strange environment. His mouth suddenly felt dry and he was conscious of his heart beating in his chest. He clearly understood Sir William's remark about the apprehension felt by patients when they were in an alien hospital setting.

With his right hand on the bible, he was sworn in. '*I swear by Almighty God, that the evidence that I shall give shall be the truth, the whole truth and nothing but the truth.*' He was about to add, *'so help me God'*, and was surprised to discover that those words were not actually written on the card! He stopped himself just in time.

Mr Egerton asked Paul's name, his job and established that he was on duty at the City General Hospital on the night in question.

"Tell me, Dr Lambert, did you see my client Mr Cedric King in the casualty department of the hospital and did you treat him for wounds that he had received?"

Paul noticed that in the arena of the courtroom he was addressed with a title, albeit an incorrect one. For a moment he thought of pointing out that, as a surgeon, he was Mr Lambert, not Dr Lambert, but then thought better of it.

"Yes, I did," he confirmed.

"Please will you describe for the benefit of the jury, Mr King's physical state when you first saw him?"

"He was bleeding profusely and was in a state of shock."

Paul was then asked to describe Mr King's injuries and invited to refresh his memory from his statement if he so wished. But there was no need; it was simply a matter of relating the facts.

"Would you say that his injuries were serious?"

"Yes, I would."

"Would you say they were life-threatening?"

"Yes, they were."

And so it went on, Mr Egerton leading Paul through a series of questions, establishing that Cedric had a major operation under a general anaesthetic, that he required an eight pint blood transfusion and that he was in hospital for seven weeks. The questions were all entirely straightforward and gradually Paul began to feel more relaxed and confident.

"Did you make an examination of the wound and if you did, would you please describe it to the jury? Also tell them of any conclusions you may have reached about the knife that inflicted the injury."

Paul explained that the wound was cleanly cut at both ends, suggesting that a double bladed weapon had been used. Since the wound was five inches deep, he suggested that the blade must have been at least five inches long, and not less than an inch wide at a point at this distance from its tip.

"Dr Lambert, I am now going to show you a knife. I would like you to look at it carefully."

He passed Paul a horrendous looking dagger, at least six inches in length. It was heavy with a dark wooden handle; and it was double-bladed.

"Dr Lambert, would you agree that the injury you treated was entirely consistent with an assault with such a knife?"

"Yes," Paul said cautiously, "the injury may well have been caused by such a blade."

"And would you agree," Dr Lambert, "that in all probability, it was this particular blade that caused Mr King's life-threatening injury?" the barrister asked quickly and confidently.

It suddenly struck Paul that in the last few minutes, there had been a subtle change in the interrogation. Mr Egerton had assured him that he would only be asked questions of fact, but he now realised that he was being asked for his opinion. He recalled Sir William's cautionary words and vowed to be careful. He suspected that he had very nearly fallen into a carefully contrived trap.

"Not necessarily," Paul responded cautiously, "but it's possible that a blade such as this could have caused the injury that I treated."

For a second, Paul wondered whether he saw the slightest look of irritation on the barrister's face but if he did it was gone in a flash.

"You said in your evidence Dr Lambert that the horrendous bleeding suffered by my client was caused by an injury to the blood vessels leading to the spleen. Will you please tell the jury the tissues through which the blade must have passed to reach this point?"

"The blade would have passed through the skin, the fat beneath the skin, then the abdominal muscles and then a layer of fat inside the abdomen, before it hit these vessels."

"And can you confirm that it passed through three distinct layers of muscle?"

"Yes, I can."

"Do you agree that the tissues you have described are generally known as 'soft tissues'?"

"Yes, that is correct."

"And as such they would not offer a great deal of resistance to a blade as sharp as this one?"

"No."

"So a stab wound five inches deep, caused by a very sharp blade such as the one I have just shown you, would not require a great deal of force to inflict it."

Paul thought carefully. Strictly speaking, the words, as spoken, were a statement and as such they didn't require an answer. The inflection of the voice though posed them as a question. Paul realised he was being asked for an opinion.

He paused before answering. "No, in my opinion it would not have required a great deal of force."

"And therefore, it could well have been inflicted by someone of a very slight build; a slim woman, such as Miss Nolan, for example."

Another statement, despite the inquiry in the voice. Paul decided not to reply.

"Well, Dr Lambert?"

"It *could* have been inflicted by such a person," Paul said, emphasising the word '*could*'. But it could also have been inflicted by someone of average or heavy build."

"Dr Lambert, I would now like you to consider how such a wound might be caused. Since the wound was to the victim's left side, presumably the attack was from an assailant who is right-handed."

"I am not sure that I understand," Paul responded.

Mr Egerton came and stood in front of Paul. He raised his right arm holding a pen in his fist to mimic a knife. "To stab you in your left side, I would have to be using my right hand, wouldn't I?"

"Not necessarily. You are assuming that both parties were standing face to face. I understood from Mr King's evidence that this confrontation took place in a bedroom. Mr King might have been lying on a bed at the time. You are also assuming that the assailant had the use of their right hand at the time of the attack."

Mr Edgerton looked puzzled. "What do you mean by that?"

Sir William later explained to Paul that a good barrister would never ask a question to which he didn't already know the answer.

"Well, if the question refers to Miss Nolan, at some stage, she sustained a nasty injury to her right hand." Again Paul was sure that he detected a flicker on Mr Egerton's face, this time of surprise, before the mask clamped down again.

"How do you know that?" he asked. Another mistake; again this was a question to which he clearly did not know the answer.

"I know because I treated her in the Accident and Emergency department less than five minutes before I treated Mr King. In my opinion, after she sustained her injury it would have been very difficult, if not impossible, for her to grip a knife in her right hand."

There was a prolonged pause. Paul glanced at the judge. He had been listening to Paul's evidence with much the same bored expression that he had listened to Cedric's, but now he looked alert and interested.

"Mr Egerton," he said his voice a deep growl. "It is now nearly 12.30 and in view of this development, I expect that Dr Lambert is going to be on the stand for some time. Would this be a good opportunity for us to break for lunch?"

"Yes, my lord, I think it would," the barrister said.

"Right," said the judge, "the court will reconvene at 2.30."

"All stand," shouted the court clerk, and everyone rose while Judge Phillips wobbled down the steps and left the court. Still standing in the witness box,

Paul was stunned. Mr Egerton's response to his last two answers suggested he had been completely unaware that Annie had also been injured in the fracas that had taken place. It seemed inconceivable, yet he had looked genuinely surprised at the news.

In an instant Mr Egerton was at Paul's side. "Lambert, come with me," he ordered. He marched Paul back to his office, tight lipped and angry. As soon as they were on their own, he slammed the door.

"When did you treat Annie Nolan?" he demanded to know, his voice was sharp and cold, his eyes piercing.

"It was the same night that Cedric King was admitted. She arrived a few minutes before he did. I had already examined her when I was called away because Cedric was so seriously injured."

"Did they come from the same location?"

"I don't know for certain but I have been told that they did."

"What were her injuries?"

Paul described the lacerations on Annie's right hand and went on to explain that the division of the tendons leading to her fingers meant that it would be impossible for her to grip a knife. He also mentioned the minor injuries to her shoulder and arm. There was a long pause.

"I see," he said. His face had lost the superior confident expression to which Paul had become accustomed. He looked distinctly worried. "Okay, Lambert, that will be all. I shall have no further questions for you this afternoon."

Paul was being dismissed but the events in court puzzled him. "Didn't you know that Annie was injured?" he asked the QC.

"No, I didn't."

"Surely, you get copies of the defence statements?"

"Yes, normally we do. But Miss Nolan decided not to make a statement."

"Not even to her defence team?"

"No, not even to them. I understand that she simply clammed up. She hasn't given an account of events to anyone; not to the police and not to her defence counsel."

"Why on earth would she do that?" Paul asked.

"I really couldn't say," Mr Egerton replied flatly. But Paul knew the answer and he suspected that the barrister did as well. He remembered what the police had said about Cedric's 'occupation'. He was in the protection racket. His weapon was fear. Annie was afraid to describe the events that had occurred in her flat, so afraid in fact, that she was prepared to be found guilty of attempted murder, rather than to defend herself in court.

"Does that mean that I'm now free to go?"

"No, it doesn't. Technically you are still on the witness stand. The judge will be the one who will tell you when you are allowed to go."

Chapter Fifteen

Paul had expected to be called back at two thirty but it was after three thirty when the trial recommenced. Once more, he found himself in the waiting room and irritatingly, there was again no explanation of the cause of the delay or information as to when the trial might be resumed.

When Paul was eventually called, he was directed once more to the witness box. The judge turned to Mr Egerton.

"Dr Lambert was your witness when we took a recess," he said. "Do you have any more questions for him?"

Having been assured that the barrister had no further questions, Paul was surprised to hear him say, "yes, just one or two, my lord." Had he been deliberately misleading Paul, or had he had second thoughts?

The prosecuting counsel began by reminding Paul that he was still under oath.

"I would like to ask you a few questions Dr Lambert about Mr King's convalescence after his operation. I understand he was in hospital for seven weeks altogether. I presume therefore that there must have been one or two complications."

"Yes," Paul said, "he developed an infection in his wound."

"Would you describe this as a minor infection, or a major one?"

"Oh certainly a major one," Paul responded confidently, "one of the worst that I've seen. It must have been very unpleasant for him."

"Unpleasant in what way?" he was asked.

"Well, after an operation the wound is always painful, but if it becomes infected, the pain is increased."

"And what causes the infection?" he was asked. Paul didn't realise it at the time but he was being lead into a trap, this time a trap that would ensnare him.

"It's due to organisms, bugs, which get into the wound. We know that because we were able to identify them in laboratory tests."

"And does this infection by bacteria or bugs as you call them, interfere with the healing process?"

"Yes, most definitively. Healing is always impaired when infection is present. Mr King's wound failed to heal."

"What do you mean by that?"

"Well on the tenth day after his operation, he suffered what we call a 'burst abdomen'. All the stitches parted and his entire gut mushroomed out through the wound, like a volcano exploding." Mr Egerton was now rattling off his questions in staccato fashion, scarcely allowing Paul time for thought before being bombarded with the next.

"You describe events in a very dramatic way, Dr Lambert."

"Well, it's a very dramatic event."

"And how does it affect the patient?"

"Well, it's shocking for the patient, both mentally and physically. It's extremely frightening to witness your guts as they suddenly burst from your abdomen and then see them alongside you in the bed. And it can lead to a patient's death."

"I understand that as a result of this volcanic explosion, Mr King had to go back to theatre to have his wound re-sutured, and it then took a further five weeks before he was sufficiently fit to be allowed home." He paused and looked at his notes. "And did you re-suture the wound yourself, Dr Lambert?"

"No, it was done by somebody more senior."

There was a long pause while Mr Egerton perused his notes allowing Paul a moment to reflect. The questions he had been asked had been straightforward; he was confident that his answers had been factually correct but he wondered in what way they were relevant to Annie Nolan's trial.

"I have been looking at the operation note that you wrote Dr Lambert, after you had performed surgery on my client. It states quite clearly that you did not wash your hands before this operation."

For the first time, it dawned on Paul where this line of questioning was going. This devil of a lawyer was trying to pin the blame for Cedric's torrid post-operative convalescence on him. He felt a surge of anger flow through him.

"Yes, that's right," he admitted.

"The operation note also states quite clearly that you did not put any antiseptic on the skin before you started to operate. Is that also correct?"

"Yes."

"Nor did you put any sterile drapes around the wound."

"No, I did not."

"Surely that's highly irregular and presumably that is why Mr King had such a difficult time, indeed as you said yourself 'a *life-threatening*' time after his operation."

Angry though Paul was, he now began to think a little more clearly.

"But you must remember," he said, "that Mr King had a stab wound; I don't suppose the knife was sterile when it went into his abdomen."

"I grant you that," said Mr Egerton coolly, "but it was your wound not the stab wound that became infected. And wasn't the wound that you created ten times as long as the stab wound? And wasn't your wound open for an hour or more?"

Paul was forced to admit that this was true. "So I think we must conclude," Mr Egerton said, a superior tone to his voice "that the infection was caused by your surgery."

This was a monstrous misrepresentation of events. Paul knew he had to defend himself.

Angrily, he replied. "I concede that the organisms probably got in, as you say through the surgical wound that I created. But there was an extremely good reason why I didn't wash my hands, or put an antiseptic on the skin, or placed drapes around the wound to sterilise the area in the usual way. Mr King was bleeding to death. It was infinitely more important to stop the bleeding than to worry about possible future infections."

"And that is your opinion, doctor?"

"Yes, that is my very definite opinion."

"But that is the opinion of a very junior surgeon, is it not?"

Paul riled at that, his anger welling up once again. "I am four years qualified and I'm a Fellow of the Royal College of Surgeons."

But Mr Egerton knew more about him than he imagined. He had obviously done some homework. Paul wondered whether this was the reason behind the delay before the afternoon session. "Tell me Mr Lambert, what training do you still have to undertake before you are able to apply to be a junior consultant?"

"Well, I have to complete my job as a registrar and then all being well, hold a senior registrar job."

"And would it be fair to say that you can expect to be a registrar for another two years?"

"Yes, that's reasonable," Paul replied.

"And then a senior registrar for a further four years?"

"Yes," admitted Paul through gritted teeth.

"And although you say you have been qualified for four years, as I understand it, the first of those four years was your probationary year, when you weren't a fully registered doctor and not permitted to treat patients unless under supervision. Of the remaining three, I believe one was spent in the university studying anatomy when you did not see any patients at all. Is that also correct?"

"Yes." Paul felt like a mouse. Whichever way he ran, the cat was covering his retreat, blocking him in.

"So in practical terms, you have two years experience of surgery and six years of training in front of you. You are therefore one quarter of the way through your surgical training. And I think you said yourself that you called for someone more senior to deal with Mr King's wound after it burst asunder; a wound that you created Dr Lambert."

He turned to the jury to deliver his final insult. "I think therefore members of the jury that it's fair to conclude that Dr Lambert is a junior and inexperienced surgeon."

Without allowing Paul a chance to comment, he addressed the judge. "Thank you, my lord; I have no further questions for this witness."

*****

The counsel for the defence was Lionel Baxter QC. Twenty or so years older than Mr Egerton, he was small in stature, very stooped and with his wig and black gown, resembled a grey haired crow. He spoke with a soft Scottish accent in a quiet voice, allowing long pauses between his questions.

"Now Dr Lambert, you treated Miss Nolan, I believe?" Again, this was a statement, dressed up as a question.

"Yes," Paul replied.

"And you say she arrived in casualty before Mr King?"

"Yes, but only by a few minutes."

"Now isn't that interesting," he commented, addressing the jury. "I wonder if that reflects the order in which the two parties were injured." He turned back to Paul. "Dr Lambert, will you please describe for the benefit of the jury, the injuries sustained by Miss Nolan, particularly the injuries to her right hand."

Paul explained that Annie had suffered a cut across the base of each of the fingers on her right hand.

"So that the jury can be absolutely clear where these injuries were, please will you demonstrate with this ruler the exact site of these cuts?"

Paul turned the palm of his right hand to face the jury and placed the ruler across the base of his four fingers.

"And how deep were these cuts?"

"In every case, they went down to bone. All the tendons were cut."

"I am sure that you understand that I am not a doctor, nor indeed are the members of the jury, so perhaps you would explain to us in lay terms what tendons are and how they enable the fingers to move?"

Paul explained that there are no muscles in the fingers. The muscles that move the fingers are situated in the forearm. From these muscles there are strong string-like cords, called tendons going to each of the finger joints; the ones on the front causing the fingers to bend and those on the back, causing the fingers to straighten.

"So if I have understood you correctly doctor, if all the tendons on the front of all the fingers were cut, Miss Nolan would not be able to bend her fingers. She would not be able to make a fist and she would certainly not be able to grip a knife."

"That is correct."

"And how do you think that she sustained these injuries?"

"I'm afraid that is something I don't know." Paul answered, aware that he was being led.

"But surely you can conclude that at some stage, a sharp blade must have been drawn across her hand."

Paul thought hard before answering. "Yes, I believe that to be a fair assumption."

Mr Baxter picked up the knife that had been exhibited before.

"Do you think that it is possible that this blade could have inflicted these injuries?"

"Yes, it *could,* but equally the injuries could have been caused by a different blade. "

"And at the time, presumably the knife must have been held by somebody else?"

"Yes, or I suppose held by Miss Nolan in her left hand."

"I suppose that is *theoretically* possible," Mr Baxter said thoughtfully, "though it must be extremely unlikely because we know that Miss Nolan is of course right-handed." Mr Baxter paused allowing the jury time to digest the implication of this statement before continuing. "Now, Mr Lambert, please will you tell the jury of Miss Nolan's other injuries."

Paul described the injury on the back of Annie's left shoulder and the one on the middle of her left forearm on its outer aspect. Mr Baxter picked up the knife and handed it to Paul.

"It is possible," he said addressing the jury, "that it may later be suggested by the prosecution that Miss Nolan's wounds may have been self-inflected; in other words, that Miss Nolan not only stabbed Mr King, but also injured herself."

He turned back to Paul. "May I ask you to take the knife and show me how someone might inflict this injury upon themselves?"

Paul took the blade and applied it easily to his left forearm but try as he might with both left hand and right, it was impossible to apply the tip of the knife to the point on the back of the shoulder where the injury had occurred. Then Mr Baxter walked towards Paul, took the knife from him and stood at Paul's side, the blade held in a firm grip in his right hand. It truly was a vicious weapon. He then turned away to replace the knife on the table but suddenly span round, screamed and lunged, his hand raised, as if to stab Paul's head. Alarmed, Paul shrank from him but trapped in the witness box, wasn't able to take a step back. Instinctively he raised his left arm to protect his face. Mr Baxter's hand came down and Paul was struck on his left forearm, on its outer aspect halfway from wrist to elbow. It wasn't the knife. During the moment, his back had been turned, the knife had been exchanged for the ruler. Now Mr Baxter froze; the ruler held firmly in his hand remained in contact with Paul's arm.

"Is this where Miss Nolan was cut?" he asked.

"Yes, it was."

"And was the line of the cut, in the line that this ruler is now positioned?"

"Yes, it was."

Quietly satisfied that he had demonstrated that this wound was almost certainly suffered in self-defence, he turned to the jury. "Now isn't that's interesting," he said quietly. "I have no more questions for this witness my lord," he said.

*****

Paul left the courtroom burning at the injustice of the mauling that he had received at the hands of Mr Egerton. He had belittled Paul, called him junior and inexperienced. He obviously held Paul responsible for Mr King's long and complicated convalescence; blaming him for the pain and suffering caused by the severe infection and burst abdomen that had occurred. It was grossly unfair. Damn it, he had saved the villain's life. There simply hadn't been time to take all the precautions that normally prevent such infections. Yet Paul felt that to some degree he had let himself down. Despite the pressure that he had been under in the witness box, he should have been more definite about the extreme urgency of the situation. He hadn't mentioned the cardiac arrest, the patient's non-existent blood pressure or the fact that the anaesthetist had needed to transfuse eight pints of blood. Yet if Paul had defended his actions more vigorously, no doubt the barrister would have suggested that his inexperience *'as a junior surgeon'* had led him to panic and make injudicious decisions.

Paul was also confused. He couldn't understand why Mr Egerton had turned on him. The trial was supposed to reveal who had inflicted Cedric's stab wounds, not to discuss his post operative problems. So the next day, when Sir William asked him how the case had gone, Paul explained what had happened and poured out his anger. Like Paul, Sir William was also amazed that the prosecution team had not known of the injuries that Annie had suffered, but suggested that it probably explained Mr Egerton's attack on Paul.

"When the QC realised that both parties had been injured," he said, "and that Annie's wounds had almost certainly been suffered in self-defence, he would recognise that the charge of attempted murder was less likely to succeed. With it the chances of obtaining damages from Annie would go, not that it was likely that she had much money anyway. However, he would realise that as a doctor, you have medical insurance. So if he could lay the blame for most of Cedric's problems on your shoulders, there could be a significant pay out for his client. It's not at all uncommon," Sir William continued, "that if there's an accident in which no one can be held responsible, there may still be some money to be made, if the legal team can find fault with the medical treatment."

Chapter Sixteen

There was a loud knock on the door and Mrs Castle's political advisor dashed in. He looked concerned.

"Can I interrupt you for a moment, Barbara? There's something here that we must talk about." He threw a copy of '*Private Eye*' onto Barbara's desk as he spoke.

Barbara looked up, irritated. "Just give me the gist of it, I'm busy."

"There's a story here that says you had an operation in the private wing of the University College Hospital (UCH) recently. They allege that you went in as a private patient under an assumed name."

Barbara looked up bewildered, "Do they say what sort of operation?"

"Something gynaecological apparently."

"That's nonsense. I've never been in the UCH," she said. "It must be another of their lies."

"Are you absolutely sure? With all this kerfuffle about private beds, it's the sort of story that the press will latch onto. The Telegraph and the Mail would love to be able to prove that you had been a private patient, just when you're in the process of ridding the NHS of pay beds. I need to scotch the story before it gathers momentum. Can I tell the press that you've never been a patient in UCH, either publically or privately?"

"Yes, absolutely," Barbara replied. "I may have visited friends in the private wing in the past, but I've never been treated there."

"That must be the source of the story and it makes my job very easy. I'll kill it off immediately. I'll get them to issue a correction and also insist that they print an apology."

Later that evening, over supper at home, the phrase *University College Hospital* rankled in Mrs Castle's mind. Had she been a patient there or hadn't she? Could she be absolutely sure? She shared her worries with her husband.

"Yes," he said, "don't you remember. It's a number of years ago now, but it wasn't anything gynaecological. You came back from one of your overseas trips with sinus trouble. You had an operation and I'm sure that it was performed at UCH."

"Oh my God," exclaimed Barbara as the full horror of the situation struck her. She now remembered, with frightening clarity, that she had been treated in a private side ward. She had asked to be admitted as an NHS patient, but the Cabinet Office had insisted that she should have a private room, so that she could read her cabinet papers in peace and meet some of her staff if needed. Yet that very afternoon she had issued a statement to the newspapers categorically denying that she had received private treatment. The press would crucify her. Not only would they delight in telling their readers that she had indeed had private treatment, they would also accuse her of a cover up. Yet she had issued the statement in all innocence.

She begged her husband for advice. "What on earth shall I do?"

"I guess you need to speak to your press adviser," he said, "and the sooner the better."

In desperation, she tried to phone her press secretary but was unable to contact him.

The next day, after a sleepless night, her worse fears were confirmed. When the newspapers reached her desk, she found that the story of her treatment as a private patient was on the front pages. Not only that, but the surgeon who had operated on her, had confirmed his role in the episode. "What the hell has happened to patient confidentiality?" she raged.

Feeling physically sick, she called a crisis meeting in the office. She decided that the only policy was to be utterly open and frank with her staff.

Addressing her press secretary, she said firmly, "I owe you an apology. Yesterday I stated quite emphatically, that I had never had treatment at UCH, but my husband reminds me that I have. I didn't want private treatment. I certainly didn't ask for private treatment but it was organised for me to minimise the disruption to my work."

An arrangement that applies to the many business leaders who keep the country going, her secretary reflected, though he was wise enough to keep his thoughts to himself!

For a moment, the room was silent whilst the impact of the revelation sank in.

"Before we issue a further statement, Minister, I think we need to make absolutely sure of the exact status of your stay in UCH. You might have been in an 'amenity bed', paying for the use of the side ward but not having private treatment from the consultant. We also need to check whether you've had private treatment at any other time. It isn't just the press who will be digging at this story. The Tory party will have their private detectives on the job as well. They would love to be able to dish up a bit of dirt."

"And what's the best way of doing that?" Barbara asked.

"Well, if you don't mind, I think we ought to speak with your General Practitioner. He will have all your records and the Cabinet Office will probably be able to confirm whether you had a private room at the UCH."

"Please chase this up as quickly as possible," Barbara begged, still horrified at the situation that had arisen, "and in the meantime, perhaps we need to put out an interim press statement?"

"There's no need for that. In the statement we put out last night, we took the precaution of saying that you hadn't *recently* had any treatment at UCH. That at least is honest and it will buy us some time whilst we get a fuller picture."

"That at least is some relief. Thank you. Now, whilst you're here, you had better give me the background to this trouble that I've been hearing about at the Charing Cross Hospital. You've arranged for me to meet with the warring factions and I need to be prepared."

Barbara was dismayed when the nature of the problem was explained to her. Quite suddenly a local dispute had blown up at the Charing Cross Hospital in London. The new 16 million pound hospital had been completed only four years previously. It included a private wing on the 15th floor that was nicknamed '*the Fulham Hilton'*. Feelings against the services provided for the privileged few in this wing were running high, not least because it had been built with NHS funds. The hospital's ancillary workers were angry that they were required to provide 'silver service' for the patients in the private beds without receiving any extra pay. They knew that the consultants were being well remunerated for the service they provided, though the doctors had been quick to point out that they sacrificed nearly twenty percent of their NHS salaries for the right to treat private patients.

As a result, the local NUPE branch, led by a vociferous local representative called Mrs Esther Brookstone, was involved in a fight to close the private wing. She was a medical secretary at the hospital and had made a name for herself in the national press as the *'battling granny'* leading the protest against the private beds. Services to the patients in these beds was being curtailed which inevitably angered the consultant medical staff.

Management suggested that the private patients be transferred to other wards, thus releasing the beds on the 15th floor for NHS patients. Unsurprisingly, this idea was supported by the unions but rejected by the consultants. In a series of 'tit for tat' moves, NUPE then threatened to withdraw all domestic services from the private wing, effectively closing it. In retaliation, the consultants were threatened a work to rule in the rest of the hospital.

"I know that you will be reluctant to intervene in a local dispute, Minister, but it's threatening to disrupt the national negotiations on the elimination of the pay beds. I suspect it will prove to be a preliminary skirmish to the main battle with the British Medical Association that will inevitably follow. The story is receiving a lot of coverage in the national press, attitudes on both sides are hardening and I feel the time has come to bang a few heads together. If you like I can prepare a briefing paper for you. There are a number of levers that we can use to bring some common sense to the situation."

"Yes, please do that," Barbara replied. "I'm sick and tired of the consultant's *'holier than thou'* self-righteous attitude. See if you can provide me with a needle or two to puncture their over-inflated egos. They're far too full of their own importance."

"I'll have something on your desk later this afternoon. Then if you're agreeable I'll set up a meeting, probably on Wednesday. If we can get the Charing Cross issue resolved we shall have a much better chance of settling the national dispute with the BMA."

"Thank you," Barbara responded.

"And on Wednesday, you'll have something to look forward to whilst you're practising your powers of diplomacy. In the evening you are to be the guest of honour at the grand banquet of the Royal College of Obstetricians. You'll need to be nice to that particular group of consultants. I understand that the hospitality at their college is absolutely first class."

"I've no doubt that they do themselves proud," Barbara responded. "Let's just hope that the Charing Cross meeting doesn't give me indigestion and that I can get there in time to enjoy their hospitality. It's highly unusual for a Secretary of State for Health to get any largesse from the consultants!"

Chapter Seventeen

"What are the latest blood tests on this patient, my dear?"

Mr Potts had arrived at Mrs Twigg's bedside during his next ward round and had directed the question at Janet, his house officer.

"Please do not patronize me, Mr Potts. I am not *'your dear'*," Janet replied primly.

"Then please accept my apologies Miss....." he paused. "Look, you'd better tell me if it's Miss or Mrs or perhaps M/s so I don't get into any further trouble." Mr Potts smiled; he enjoyed these exchanges. To him, toying with this tall elegant blond young doctor was a game, a little light amusement that enlivened the round.

"I have already told you Mr Potts, that it's Miss Smith, but since my marital status is of no relevance on this ward round, I should appreciate it if you would call me Dr Smith."

"That's fine. That's what I shall do young lady but I've no doubt you will correct me should I forget!" Further teasing by Mr Potts was curtailed as the calm of the ward was shattered by a loud hammering noise. It seemed to be coming from the corridor leading to the ward.

"What the hell is that confounded racket! For Heaven's sake Sister, how are we supposed to concentrate on our patients? Send someone to sort it out."

"Yes, of course." She turned to the group of nurses, "Staff nurse, would you mind?"

Staff nurse went to investigate but before she reached the end of the ward, the banging had stopped. She looked down the corridor, checked the office and investigated each of the adjacent rooms in turn but could find nothing amiss; there was no obvious explanation for the noise that had so rudely interrupted the round. She returned a minute later. Mr Potts shot her an inquiring glance. Staff nurse shrugged her shoulders.

"I'm afraid that I've no idea what it was, Sir," she said. "The banging stopped before I reached the office and there were no workmen there at all."

"Well, at least it's quiet now," Mr Potts responded. The ward round continued and the incident was quickly forgotten.

"Now, let's get down to business." He turned to Mrs Twigg. "I'm pleased you've come over to the surgical side of the hospital. This is where we really get things done. As you know, Dr Longfleet has run dozens of tests but hasn't managed to sort you out. He and I have had a little chat about you. We both agree that we need to have a look inside that tummy of yours to find the cause of your troubles. I'm sure you feel that's the best way to put you on the road to recovery." Dr Longfleet hadn't agreed with him, in fact he held the opposite view, but Mrs Twigg wasn't to know that!

Mrs Twigg, overawed by the consultant's domineering tone was too frightened to speak, let alone to contradict him. He towered over the timid little woman, who cowered before him like a field mouse faced by a hungry tom cat.

Mr Potts took her silence as consent.

"Right, that's good. I'll do the operation for you just as soon as there is a vacant slot on my theatre list." He turned to Janet. "Perhaps you could see to that, my dear.... I do apologize, I mean Dr Smith," Mr Potts added, with a grin on his face and a sideways glance and a wink to the rest of the team.

He had spent less than a minute at her bedside and was ready to move on.

"Sir," Paul said somewhat timidly, aware of the consultant's unpredictable mood swings, "Victoria and I have been reviewing the history. We have learned that Mrs Twigg spent some time in Africa a couple of years ago. It raises the possibility of tropical diseases that haven't been investigated. Also no tests of the small bowel have been undertaken, so it might be useful to get that part of the gut x-rayed. We might get some further information without resorting to surgery." As he spoke, he glanced at Mrs Twigg, who nodded weakly.

"I'm sure that Mrs Twigg feels that she's had sufficient tests already and just wants to get on with an operation to sort things out," replied Mr Potts, speaking for the patient without consulting her.

It was difficult to pursue the conversation in front of the patient, so Paul did not persist. He decided to wait until the ward round was over and then argue his case in the privacy of the office.

The next patient's problem was apparent to anyone with a sensitive nose, long before they actually arrived at his bedside. The offensive aroma from his infected in-growing toe nail wafted freely down the ward.

The screens were pulled round the bed.

"Sister, can you remove that dirty dressing and let us see the nature of this disagreeable problem," Mr Potts said, his nose wrinkled in disgust.

Paul had seen some unpleasant infections in his time but few worse than this. The toe nail was lost in a sea of pus and the whole foot was swollen and covered in livid red streaks. As the bandages were removed the smell became almost overpowering.

"Possem secare eius pedes oderem removere," commented Mr Potts grimacing and smiling at the medical students. *'I could cut off his foot to get rid of the smell'.*

The patient looked surprised then angry. "Aut linguam exideam ut humanitates emendet," he replied coldly. *'Or cut off his tongue to improve his manners'.*

"Look," Mr Potts stammered, red faced, "I'm most awfully sorry, I never ...."

But the patient interrupted him and gave him a lesson both in good manners and in Latin grammar. "Actually, Mr Potts, you were in error when you used a 'purpose clause' – the purpose of the amputation would be to get rid of the smell. In such a clause, the verb should be in the subjunctive mood. Therefore to be absolutely correct, you should have used 'ut' instead of the infinitive. You should have said *'Possem secare eius pedes ut odorem removerem'.*"

"Sir, I apologise most sincerely," Mr Potts began again, "I wouldn't have used Latin had I any idea ....."

Again he was interrupted. "You wouldn't have used Latin had you known that I was the Professor of Classical Studies at the University but it wouldn't have mattered had I been unable to understand. Is that what you were trying to say?"

Everyone on the ward round, Victoria, Paul, Janet, Sister and her nursing staff, as well as all the medical students knew that was exactly what the consultant was intending to say. Yet none of them was particularly upset that Mr Potts was getting his 'come-uppance'! Ever since becoming a consultant, Mr Potts had criticised and demeaned his students and junior staff. He delighted in embarrassing them in front of their peers or in front of the nurses. Now he was on the receiving end and was clearly not enjoying it. There was a long uneasy silence.

Finally, Mr Potts spoke. "Sir, I apologise. I should have known better. May I be allowed to start again?"

"You may," the Professor replied. "I have come to seek your advice about this exceedingly painful toe. I know that the smell is offensive. I had presumed that as a doctor, you would understand that the odour is a symptom of my condition, not a sign of poor personal hygiene. So, yes, it would be best if you started again and perhaps this time we can conduct the consultation in a more civilised fashion."

Paul had never seen his consultant so visibly shaken. The rest of the round was completed in record time. At each bed side, he listened as Janet presented the patient to him, agreed with the management that Victoria and Paul suggested and then moved on without comment.

The moment that the round was over, Mr Potts stated that he had urgent matters to attend to and was not able to linger for a drink. Paul realised that he wanted to lick his wounds in private but he needed to plead for a little time to investigate Mrs Twigg.

"Before you go Sir, may I have a word about Mrs Twigg?" Mr Potts looked daggers at him but said nothing. Paul ploughed on.

"Mrs Twigg has had no tests to look for tropical diseases. I know that it's some time since she was in Nigeria but an infection in the bowel could explain her symptoms. It could also cause her to be malnourished and lead to her weight loss."

But Mr Potts was unimpressed. "An African disease would be associated with an obvious fever and profuse diarrhoea," he stated. "I'm sure a cancer hidden in the pancreas or liver is the cause of her problems. The quickest way to get to the bottom of it is to explore her belly. I'm sure that's what Mrs Twigg wants."

Paul knew that he ought to 'stick to his guns' but lacked the confidence to do so. He also wanted to say, *'perhaps we should ask the patient that'*, but hadn't the courage to say so.

Victoria though was not so timid. "Some stool cultures and an x-ray of the small bowel shouldn't prove to be too much for Mrs Twigg, Sir. It wouldn't take more than a couple of days and it might avoid surgery."

"Alright," conceded Mr Potts. "As it happens, my next theatre list is already fully booked, so you have until Friday to run your tests. But we can't wait any longer than that. If we do, poor Mrs Twigg will fade away altogether. And I bet you a pound to a penny, we will end up exploring the abdomen."

Paul heaved a sigh of relief. He was certain it was the right thing to do and was grateful to Victoria for her support. He was also thankful that he would not have to admit that the bowel x-ray had already been arranged and was in fact scheduled for the next day.

Whilst Victoria and Paul had been chatting with Mr Potts, 'Chippy' Chapman had returned to the office to retrieve his 'carpenter's box', which he had hidden behind Sister's desk to avoid it being seen by Mr Potts. To his surprise he found he couldn't lift it. He tried again but to no avail. The box was firmly stuck to the floor, though Malcolm couldn't imagine why. He put both hands round the handle and tugged with all his might, he tried rocking it from side to side, but still it wouldn't budge. Mystified, he opened the lid but the contents were as he had left them. He emptied the box and solved the mystery. A huge nail had been hammered through the base securely fixing it to the floorboards.

"What the hell....." he began, then he remembered the hammering that had disrupted Mr Potts' ward round.

Grimly, he turned to Staff Nurse. "Did you see who was responsible for this?" he asked.

"No, I didn't," she replied, "but Bill Taylor was in the office when I looked in and, now I think about it, he did have a guilty look on his face."

"Was there any one else in the office with him?"

"No. I'm sure he must be responsible."

Bill was the house officer from Surgical Three, the rival surgical unit situated on the ground floor, immediately below Surgical Five. Furious at what had been done to his precious box, Malcolm vowed that he would find an opportunity to have his revenge. But that would have to wait; the immediate problem was releasing it from the floor. He considered using brute force but quickly decided that to do so would irreparably damage the box which he had spent so much time crafting.

It was Sister who came to his rescue. "Chippy, you get on with your jobs; I'll get the hospital maintenance team to free it."

That evening, Malcolm discussed with Paul how he might settle his score with Bill. Various schemes were proposed, cotton wool in the ball of his stethoscope, itching powder on the collar of his white coat, glue in his theatre boots and so on, but all these ideas seemed a little childish and rather unsuitable. The matter was left unresolved, but later Malcolm said that he had the germ of an idea. He suggested that there should be no further talk about the episode with the tool box, while he developed his thoughts. He didn't want Bill to have any suspicions that he was planning to have his revenge.

Chapter Eighteen

Barbara was angry that patients were being treated as pawns in the 'private beds' dispute between the consultants and the ancillary workers at the Charing Cross Hospital. She hoped that an agreement which allowed a normal service to be resumed would be reached quickly as she was looking forward to her evening meal with the obstetricians. But the tension was palpable in the air even before her meeting with the Unions and the BMA began.

She nodded to the national leaders of NUPE and CoHSE. She knew them both well of course, but didn't wish to be seen to be on familiar terms with them. She spoke briefly with the consultants from the Charing Cross Hospital and to Dr Derek Stevenson who led the BMA's negotiating team. She introduced herself simply as 'Barbara' to Mrs Brookstone, the medical secretary and local union representative. She proved to be a rather retiring grey haired granny, not the aggressive, militant, trade union representative portrayed by the press.

"I'm here," Barbara began in forthright fashion, "because I'm distressed that the work at the hospital is being disrupted. Your actions are harming patients and that is unacceptable."

She turned to address the union leaders. "You should leave the phasing out of 'private beds' to parliament. It's a Labour Party manifesto commitment and I expect to see it included in the Queen's Speech and then implemented. It is quite unnecessary for you to take pre-emptive action."

She then spoke angrily to the consultants. "Your threat of action against NHS patients in the hospital is irresponsible. You know that a working party is busy agreeing your new contract and looking at the 'pay beds' issue. Taking industrial action now, before its report is published, is likely to be counterproductive.

Dr Stevenson," Mrs Castle continued, now addressing the BMA's senior negotiator, "you have been asked to move some patients from the private wing to other parts of the hospital, yet you have refused. Are you refusing because their treatment might suffer as a result?"

"No, not at all," he replied.

"Then why are you objecting?"

"We're objecting because there's an important principle at stake; a principle of law and order. The law allows private practice within NHS hospitals and until the law is changed, the law should be enforced."

"Are you saying then, that if the law were to be changed," Mrs Castle challenged, "you would abide by it, even if you didn't agree with it?"

"Yes, of course, we wouldn't wish to break the law."

Barbara decided it was time to use one of the needles with which she had been armed. "Do you realise, Dr Stevenson, that the NHS act of 1946 does not require me to allow private beds? It empowers me, as Secretary of State, to authorize them if I think them reasonable. Had I wished, I could have withdrawn authorization when taking office. Had I done that, would you have been prepared to accept it?"

This news came as a shocking revelation to the BMA representatives. They had believed that this was the trump card that would safeguard the private beds, at least until the law could be changed. It was only after an urgent whispered conference with his colleagues that Dr Stevenson replied. "No, we would not, because it is our belief that private practice within the NHS benefits patients. We expect this to be recognised in the new consultant's contract."

"Then it is clear that your objection is not on the grounds of law and order at all," Mrs Castle retorted. "You are merely fighting the government's policy."

Having disillusioned the consultants on their right to have 'pay beds', Mrs Castle turned to Mrs Brookstone.

"Esther, do you realise that the government is already committed to phasing out private beds? Do you really think its right that your union should disrupt the whole hospital when your government is actively delivering your objectives?"

Although Mrs Brookstone answered in a quiet voice, there was determination in her words. "Mrs Castle, I am not a militant activist at all and speaking personally I don't want any of our patients to be harmed. But the truth is that the members of my union simply don't trust politicians anymore. They don't believe they will honour their promises. They don't believe they will get rid of the 'pay beds'. My members are fed up with the long waiting lists that NHS patients have to put up with. They don't see why people should be allowed to jump the queue."

Then she threw a copy of the Daily Mirror onto the table and pointed to the headline on the front page. "People like this pop star are admitted to the private wing, by-passing the waiting list. They make impossible demands of the ancillary staff. They want extra menus and special food. They want telephones and televisions. Their visitors come and go with no regard for the official visiting hours, disrupting the work of the staff. I repeat, we don't want to harm patients; we just want all patients to be able to share the facilities in the private wing. That will enable us to shorten the waiting list. And another thing," she added as an afterthought, "the consultants get well paid by the private patients but the rest of the staff have to look after them for nothing. That's neither right nor proper."

"It's perfectly proper," Dr Stevenson interjected. "Consultants forego twenty percent of their salary for the right to treat private patients, yet still have to work five full days for the NHS. I don't suppose you've told your union members that."

Barbara thought for a moment. There was clearly an impasse, the consultants demanding to use the pay beds and the local union refusing to service them. All the while patients were being disadvantaged and bad publicity for the Labour government was being generated. Somehow she needed to find a compromise. She decided to ask for an adjournment; she needed time to think and to speak to the two sides separately.

Whilst Barbara was having a private chat with Esther Brookstone, her secretary interrupted to tell her the results of their detective work into any private treatment she might have received in the past.

"Your GP was extremely helpful. He went through all your records. It seems that you had a chest infection in 1968 and saw a consultant at Guy's Hospital."

"Heavens, I do remember that now," groaned Barbara. "I got flu very badly in January and my doctor said I should have an x-ray. The office sent me to Guy's Hospital for one. Then I had to go back for a follow-up, because there was an abnormality on the chest x-ray."

"Was the follow up appointment at his private rooms or at the hospital? Apparently, the letter that your GP received came from Harley Street."

"I honestly can't remember," Barbara replied, "but if I did go to Harley Street, it would be because the consultant asked me to go there. I would never have gone there out of choice." She thought for a moment. "Did my GP turn up any other occasions when I've been treated in hospital? I certainly can't remember any."

"No, he didn't."

Barbara sighed. "At least that's a blessing."

"So how are we going to handle this latest development?" she was asked.

"We're going to have to issue a press statement and do the best we can. Have you got anything drafted?"

"Yes, I have. Essentially it says that you are a passionate believer in the NHS, you greatly value the work of NHS staff and that you normally have all your treatments through the NHS."

"Not as strong I would have wished, but I suppose that it's the best we can do in the circumstances," Barbara admitted, whist remaining extremely doubtful that it would throw the press hounds off the trail.

"I had another telephone call this morning," her secretary added, eager to end their meeting on a bright note, "from the College of Obstetricians. They wanted to know whether you had any special dietary requirements for the banquet tonight. They have a cracking menu lined up for you; salmon en croute, rack of Welsh lamb or fillet steak, and all manner of tasty starters and exotic desserts."

"Well, at least that's something to look forward to," Barbara replied as she nibbled on a dry biscuit.

When the meeting reconvened, she invited the consultants to consider a proposal that the unions had suggested; that the ancillary workers action would be called off if the working party on the new consultant contract and the right to do private practice could be speeded up?"

"I don't believe for one minute that would lead to a resolution," Dr Stevenson retorted. "We feel sure that that the findings of the working party have already been prejudged. You told us yourself only a few minutes ago that the elimination of the pay beds will be passed into law. For all we know, the report could ban private practice outside the NHS as well as removing the NHS pay beds. And we are particularly shocked that you haven't denounced NUPE's harmful action against patients in unequivocal terms."

Mrs Castle's response was curt and angry. "But haven't you given me an ultimatum. You've threatened industrial action if you don't get what you want? It seems to me that everyone is prepared to damage the health service to secure their own ends. No-one gives a damn about the patients. There's no difference whatsoever between the consultants and the unions. Regarding the working party, I can assure you that nothing has been prejudged, but there isn't any secret about the government's policy to phase pay beds out of NHS hospitals."

Barbara looked at her watch. It was already ten past seven. She felt tired, she was hungry and was irritated by the consultants. It seemed to her that their sole objective was to obstruct government policy. She was damned if she was going to back down.

"Look," she said to the consultants, "this meeting has already dragged on for five hours. I suggest we have a further break in which you consider two things. Firstly, that you have agreed that there is no aspect of clinical freedom involved at Charing Cross and secondly that there is an offer on the table to speed up the working party report. Consider your position carefully, remembering that the press will expect a statement at the end of our discussions. You can let me know when you wish the meeting to resume."

Back in the privacy of her office, Barbara turned to her secretary. "These consultants are absolutely impossible; they're so obstinate. Thanks to them I've missed my lunch and if we can't get agreement soon, I shall miss my banquet with the obstetricians as well." She had a cup of lukewarm tea in one hand and a curled up sandwich in the other. "I've been told repeatedly what a wonderful spread they lay on. Incidentally, has anybody rung them to say that I'm battling with their colleagues and may be a little late?"

For three hours, the consultants discussed the situation in private, whilst Barbara fumed in an adjacent room. Her secretary slipped out to try to find some food but the sandwiches that he managed to buy were a poor substitute for the salmon en croute and fillet steak that she had been promised. It was ten pm before the consultants declared that they were ready to resume the meeting. Mrs Brookstone retired to a side room whilst the consultants and national union leaders continued their battle.

"Well, Dr Stevenson, can you tell me what you've decided?" Barbara asked.

"Yes, I am happy to say that we will assist in the speeding up of the working party. We believe that it should be possible for it to reach some positive conclusions within the next six weeks. However, if in our opinion the conclusions are not positive, we reserve the right to reconsider our position. But there are conditions. Firstly, that you should state categorically that you deplore the industrial action of the union. Remember it is the union, not the doctors, who have disrupted the care of patients. Secondly, that in the meantime there should be no reduction whatsoever in the number of private beds nationwide."

Mrs Castle exploded. "What the hell can I say Dr Stevenson that I haven't already said? I've said a dozen times that I deplore industrial action, be it practised by the unions or threatened by the consultants. But I am pleased to hear you say that speeding up the working party meets with your approval. However I can't possible commit myself to retain the present number of private beds. In the Commons next week, I'm going to come under pressure to plan the removal of at least half of the pay beds as a part of government policy. But I might have a chance of defending some of those beds if the problems at Charing Cross are resolved."

It took until two the next morning before it was agreed that Mrs Castle would reiterate her condemnation of industrial action, that there would be no reduction in the number of pay beds pending the working party report, that the unions would call off their industrial action and the consultants would remove their threat of retaliatory action. In the meantime, a proportion of private beds at Charing Cross would be redistributed to other wards, thus allowing some NHS patients to enjoy the private beds on the 15th floor.

Finally, Dr Stevenson rose from the table. He was shaking hands with the national union representatives when Mrs Castle interrupted, "Hey, Mrs Brookstone hasn't agreed to this yet, she may have some comments and we certainly need her agreement."

"That's an intolerable suggestion, Mrs Castle," a member of the BMA team exclaimed. "We have agreed, the national union representatives have agreed, what on earth has it got to do with Mrs Brookstone?"

"I think that since Mrs Brookstone is the local NUPE representative, the one who actually called this industrial action, she has a great deal to do with it," Mrs Castle explained. "I will go and speak with her. Perhaps one of you would come with me?"

Mrs Castle met a tired and irritated Esther Brookstone who had been waiting in an anteroom for many hours to hear the result of the meeting. Barbara laid great stress on the government's intention to phase the private beds out of every NHS hospital in the land. Further it had been decided that some of the patients from the private wing at Charing Cross would be moved to general wards, which would release beds in the private wing for NHS patients.

But Mrs Brookstone was not happy. "Our objective," she said, "was to get rid of all the beds on the private wing. Our members do not see why they should give special treatment to rich people who are able to buy their way to the front of the queue. I'm not sure that I shall be able to sell this package to my members."

Mrs Castle turned to the hospital consultant. "How quickly can you move NHS patients onto the private ward," she asked.

"By tomorrow morning, we could have at least six NHS patients in there."

Mrs Brookstone remained unhappy. "We really haven't got what we came for."

"I think you have got a great deal," Barbara retorted. "You know that the government is going to phase out all pay beds, you know that the process is to be speeded up and you now have a mixed wing instead of a private wing."

In the end, Mrs Brookstone conceded that this was the best deal she was going to get and the meeting finally broke up at three in the morning after a further argument over the wording of the press statement! Although she was pleased that this local dispute had been settled, Barbara was painfully aware that national negotiations with the doctors would be resumed when the working party report was published. Since that would decide the issue of the pay beds throughout the country, not just in a single hospital, the stakes would be far higher and the battle would inevitably be even more bitterly fought. She remained determined however that this was a battle that she would win. She vowed not to rest until all the pay beds had been eliminated; she would not allow the rich and privileged to undermine the socialist principles on which the NHS had been founded.

Chapter Nineteen

One afternoon, a few days later, Malcolm was furious to discover that for a second time his precious 'work box' had been nailed to the floor. No one actually heard or saw the deed being done, nor was any suspicious activity noticed; nonetheless Malcolm was in no doubt of the identity of the culprit. He became more determined than ever that he would be avenged. On this occasion, he was able to free the box himself, for having anticipated that Bill Taylor might be tempted to repeat his childish activity, he had borrowed a claw hammer and kept it available in his room. There were however to be unforeseen and unfortunate consequences.

That evening, Sister Morrison was sitting at her desk in the Surgical Three office supervising the 'nurse's handover', the routine that took place each evening when responsibility for the patients was passed to the night staff. Around her, in a wide semicircle, her nurses sat listening intently. Sister was detailing the progress that each of the patients had made during the day and giving the staff their instructions for the care to be given through the night. She had worked a long and tiring shift and was looking forward to putting her feet up when she got home. She was just speaking of the final patient when a drop of water fell onto the nursing record that she was holding in her hand. Surprised, she looked round to see where it had come from. Then a second drop arrived, larger than the first. Alarmed, she looked up at the ceiling. Immediately above her head, the white plaster had turned a dirty grey colour and was bulging ominously over an area three feet across.

"Oh, my God," she exclaimed. More drops fell, now onto her hands and the adjacent desk, their size and frequency increasing. And as she watched a crack appeared at the apex of the swelling. The drops became a steady trickle.

"The whole ceiling's going to come down," she screamed as she jumped to her feet, taking evasive action. "Quick, help me to move this desk and these patient records."

Even as she spoke, a huge area of plaster crashed down directly onto the desk at which she had been sitting just a few moments before. It was followed by a cascade of several gallons of dirty brown water. All the patient records that had been on the desk were soaked. The watery debris splashed onto the nurses' shoes and stockings, covering the floor and splattering the surrounding walls. There was bedlam as the nurses scattered in all directions, some in a state or shock. Fortunately, none of them were injured. In a matter of seconds the office was transformed. A few moments earlier it had been neat, tidy and orderly; now it looked as if a tornado had ripped through. It was Sister Morrison who recovered first.

"Nurse Webster," she said, "Surgical Five is above us; run upstairs and see what the problem is. Some fool must have left a tap running."

Two minutes later, the student nurse was back. "There's no problem upstairs," she reported, "everything's fine."

Sister looked up at the ceiling from which a steady trickle of water still emerged, adding to the lake on the floor. "Then one of the pipes must have burst," she concluded.

Quickly, she organised her staff. She ordered the night staff to commence their usual nursing duties, and then asked for volunteers from the day staff to stay behind to help to clear up. She arranged for buckets to be placed under the continuing leak, told the switchboard to call the maintenance team and then got busy with mops and towels tidying up the mess.

Unfortunately, the hospital plumber had gone home for the night and it was thirty minutes before he could be called back. All the while water poured into the office. He studied the building from outside and agreed that the Surgical Five office lay immediately above the Surgical Three office. He went up to investigate. He inspected the floor for any signs of dampness but could find none. He failed to spot a tiny hole in the lino where Malcolm's box had been anchored earlier in the day. With water still streaming into the ward below, he shifted all the office furniture, rolled back the lino, then started to raise the floor boards. Twenty minutes later, he identified the problem; a neatly punched hole in a cold water pipe. He scratched his head wondering what had caused it. Had he been aware that only a few days earlier his colleague had come to Malcolm's assistance, he would probably have put two and two together. As it was, having identified the appropriate stop cock, he repaired the leak, before replacing the floor boards and lino.

It wasn't until the next morning that Bill Taylor realised what had happened. He arrived at the ward as usual then turned into the office only to find that the room was empty. All the furniture had been moved into a side ward which was now being used as temporary accommodation whilst the office waited to be cleaned and decorated.

Bill observed the floor, still wet from the drenching it had received the night before, noted the dirty stains on the walls and the buckets catching the last few drops of water that seeped through the ceiling where a large section of plaster was missing.

"What on earth has happened here?" he exclaimed before, with sudden horror, he realised the cause of the problem. He experienced a terrible spasm of guilt but decided in the same moment to play the role of innocent bystander. So long as no-one pointed a finger of blame at him, he would keep quiet and hope the 'burst pipe' would be assumed to be an *'act of God'*. As it happened, the only other person who knew otherwise was Malcolm but his sense of loyalty to his colleague meant that he wasn't prepared to report the matter to the management; he would settle the score in his own way and in his own time.

Chapter Twenty

As it happened, had Paul or Victoria taken the 'pound to a penny' bet they had been offered by Mr Potts on the chances of further investigations solving the mystery of Mrs Twigg's illness, they would have lost their money. None of the tests they requested added anything to their understanding of the problem. Her temperature chart remained as flat as a pancake, no African parasites were found in her stools and the x-ray of the bowel was normal. And so it was that on Friday morning, with an anticipation normally associated with reading the last chapter of a good detective novel when the identity of the murderer is about to be revealed, Paul joined Mr Potts and Victoria in theatre as they prepared to open Mrs Twigg's abdomen. The skin was painted with antiseptic iodine, sterile drapes were laid around the operation area and when the anaesthetist gave the nod, Mr Potts set to work.

As a surgical trainee, Paul found it educational to observe different surgeons at work. On the ward, Mr Potts was dour and taciturn, a man of few words. He conducted his rounds quickly, rarely spending more than a couple of minutes with any of his patients, making it necessary for his junior staff to return later to explain the decisions that had been made. But his personality changed when he walked through the doors of the operating theatre. In theatre he came to life and took centre stage. He was the director, the producer and the leading player all in one. He selected the work to be performed, he chose the cast, his was the name at the head of the bill; he was the star of the show. When operating he became expansive, verbose and indeed 'theatrical'. Not for him the thin baggy green cotton trousers, tied with a 'pyjama' cord round the waist, or the shapeless shirts worn by the rest of the staff. He wore a specially designed tailored blue cotton suit, with his name prominently embroidered on the pocket. He tied a white crepe bandage around his forehead to act as a sweatband and wore one of the newly designed surgeon's torches, a modification of the original miner's lamp, on his forehead.

Mr Potts had a supreme confidence in his own ability. He delighted in demonstrating his technical skills to his staff, particularly to the young nurses. He loved telling tales of disasters that had befallen other surgeons. Having watched him on numerous occasions though, Paul knew that occasionally this self-assurance was misplaced. Different surgeons operated at different speeds. Sir William was slow, methodical and excessively cautious because he checked and double-checked every stage of the procedure. His operations took a long time but despite his slight tremor, he was an extremely safe surgeon. By contrast, Mr Potts was far faster. He was technically superior to his senior colleague. At times his work was quite brilliant; he was capable of performing extremely intricate and delicate procedures with a skill that was the envy of others. However, once or twice Paul had seen him get into trouble causing unnecessary bleeding; overconfidence having caused him to be a little too casual when dealing with a large artery or vein. Thanks to his ability and experience, he had always been able to retrieve the situation, but for a moment the reason for his sweatband had become apparent.

"Now," Mr Potts declared as he took the scalpel that Sister offered him, "we shall soon find out what's confounded the physicians for the last two months. There comes a time when one little peek inside the belly is better than a hundred blood tests and x-rays. My guess is that she has a tumour tucked away somewhere, possibly hidden in the pancreas or the liver. Those are both areas which are difficult to demonstrate on x-ray. Then we shall be able to chide Dr Longfleet for taking so long to seek our advice," he added, winking at the nurses.

Paul had never seen such a thin abdominal wall, even in a child. Mrs Twigg's skin was as thin as gossamer and as fragile as tissue paper. There was no fatty layer beneath it at all. Her muscles were also incredibly wasted, as thin as a slice of bacon, instead of being as thick and healthy as a decent steak. Within a couple of minutes, Mr Potts had made an incision four inches long. He started by examining the stomach, duodenum and pancreas, inspecting and feeling each in turn but could find no abnormality. He then turned his attention to the intestine and examined its entire length. Again he drew a blank, so he extended the incision upwards to look at the liver, spleen and gall bladder. Everything was completely normal.

"This is very strange," he said "There must be a tumour in here somewhere."

He extended the incision downwards, such that it now stretched virtually from the ribs to the pelvis. This allowed an examination of the uterus, tubes and ovaries. Thanks to the lack of any fat inside the abdomen, all these organs were very easily seen and palpated but, once again, all were entirely normal.

For the first time, Mr Potts seemed to have doubts.

"Miss Kent," he said, "have a good look round. See if you can find anything, perhaps something I've missed."

Five minutes later however, when Victoria's search had also proved fruitless, Mr Potts was forced to the conclusion that there was no abnormality in the abdomen.

"Damn," exploded Mr Potts. "That fool of a psychiatrist was obviously wrong. She must be a bloody anorexic after all." He turned to Victoria. "Keep her in hospital for a couple of weeks. Put her in a side ward and get Sister to monitor every single scrap of food that goes in and comes out. We'll soon find out what she's up to."

With that, he looked at the clock on the theatre wall. "I must be off now. I've some more profitable work to do at my private rooms. Close the belly for me Miss Kent; and do it carefully. She's so wasted; it will be a miracle if it heals."

He stormed out of the theatre without a further word, throwing his cap and mask onto the floor as he left.

*****

For the next ten days, Mrs Twigg remained imprisoned in her side ward. At first, she was confined to her bed but even when she was able to sit out, she was not allowed through the door. Since the side room had a wash basin but no toilet facilities, a commode was provided for her. All the food and drink she was given was monitored, as were any remnants of food that she left on her plate; not that there were many, for she appeared to have a reasonable appetite. Her weight was recorded daily. She dropped a pound or two in the first few days after her operation, which was to be expected, but to everyone's dismay and consternation, her weight loss continued.

Two weeks later, Mrs Twigg was five pounds lighter than she had been when she left the medical ward! Dr Longfleet inquired after her progress and there was an awkward silence when he heard that an exploration of the abdomen had been performed but had not revealed any disease. He frowned but made no comment. As her weight fell, the anxiety of the surgical team increased. It was inevitable that within the next week or so, like frail grannies twice her age, she would develop a chest infection and, since she was far too weak to cough to clear her phlegm, she would die. Amazingly despite her emaciated condition, her abdominal wound healed. However, she remained as much a mystery to the surgeons, as she had to the physicians.

Paul and Victoria agonised over the situation. They spent hours in the medical library scouring high powered medical text books looking for rare and obscure causes of weight loss. They studied the latest research and academic journals. They reviewed reports of malabsorption, allergies, infections, hypersensitivities and neurologic abnormalities of the gut. They spoke with consultants at the London School of Tropical Medicine hoping for enlightenment but all to no avail. As the days passed, Mrs Twigg got weaker and weaker until she was barely able to get out of bed unaided. Eventually, even Paul and Victoria were forced to accept that it was only a matter of time before the pathologist undertook a post mortem examination to identify whatever it was that had defied diagnosis during life.

Chapter Twenty-One

A weekend when Kate and Paul were both 'off duty' from Friday teatime until Monday morning was a rare luxury, one that they cherished. It allowed them an opportunity to become 'normal people', doing the everyday things that 'normal people' do. Living in a flat within the grounds of the hospital and with both of them working long and irregular hours, gave them an odd sense that they were living in a parallel world, alongside mainstream society. They often ate in the hospital canteen and tended to socialise with their medical and nursing friends. It was refreshing to have a weekend when they could go to the shops for their weekly supplies or visit the bank or post office. If the weather was fine and they felt energetic, they might take a long country walk or go on a cycle ride to gain some much needed exercise. However if they were exhausted, maybe after some disturbed nights, they would be content to do jobs around the flat, invite friends round for a drink and have a couple of early nights to catch up on their sleep.

It was at 10.30 on such a Saturday morning that the postman delivered the letter that was to cause so much heartache.

"Who do we know in London," Paul asked, "who uses expensive envelopes and sends their mail first class?"

"You'd better open it and find out," Kate replied.

"It's from some solicitors," Paul said, "Quinell, Purvis and Weekes. What on earth do they want?"

The letter was quite short and very direct. Paul read it twice with a sinking feeling in his stomach.

"Are you OK, Paul?" Kate asked.

In silence, he passed the letter to her.

'*Dear Mr Lambert,*' it read,

Re. Cedric King, aged 42.

We act on behalf of the above named client who has suffered both physically and mentally as a direct result of your negligent medical attention. Please be informed that the extent of his injuries, which result from your negligence, have been assessed at £25,000.

Within the next two weeks, we will write to you again, detailing an inventory of the damages claimed.

Yours sincerely,

James Purvis (on behalf of Quinell, Purvis and Weekes)

It was the word 'negligence' that hurt Paul most. It hit him like a bucket of ice cold water. He didn't consider himself negligent at all; on the other hand, he believed himself to be a conscientious doctor and a hard working member of the team. It was his nature to complete a task on the ward, rather than hand it over to a colleague, even if that meant going off duty late. Kate frequently chided him for his inability to delegate tasks but he found it difficult to relax unless he had undertaken the job himself. He gained great satisfaction when the operations and treatments carried out on their surgical unit were successful. He worried excessively about his patients when they were not doing well, checking and rechecking their progress to ensure that everything possible was being done for them. He felt that he always put the patients first. How dare they suggest he had been negligent?

"Who is Cedric King? Was he the man who suffered that stab wound?" Kate asked, reaching across the table and taking his hand. Paul knew exactly who he was and the mere mention of his name brought every detail of his treatment flooding back into his mind. He recalled vividly the night when Cedric had come to the casualty department, the emergency operation, his cardiac arrest, even going home wearing Sir William's socks and trousers. Damn it, without that operation he would now be dead. How dare they?

"Yes. He's the man who was stabbed in the belly; the case in which I had to give evidence in the Crown Court when that wretched barrister blamed me for all his post operative complications."

"But you saved that man's life. He would be pushing up the daisies now if you hadn't operated on him. How ungrateful can you get?"

Paul thought for a minute, grim faced. "I'll need to tell the Medical Defence Union (MDU) about this. They're the experts in defending doctors when they get into trouble. Heaven knows, I pay them enough for my insurance cover."

"Will this mean another court appearance?" Kate asked.

"With me in the dock this time you mean? I doubt it, though I suppose it's possible. I gather these things are usually settled out of court."

"I'm sure Sir William will support you. I remember you telling me that he complimented you for your swift action on the night of the stabbing. Why don't you go and see him?"

It was Monday lunch time before Paul was able to have a private word with Sir William in his office. Sir William listened to Paul's concerns, read the solicitor's letter then laid a hand on Paul's shoulder.

"Lambert," he said quietly, "this claim has absolutely no chance of succeeding. I will see to it personally. They are just fishing and hoping the MDU will make a small payment to settle the case without them incurring too many legal costs. Acknowledge the solicitor's letter, inform them that you will be represented by the MDU and let me know how things develop. And don't worry," he added kindly.

But despite Sir William's reassurance, Paul did worry!

*****

Victoria was chatting to Sister in the office on the female ward when one of the hospital porters came in with the morning post, mainly laboratory reports and other interdepartmental mail.

"What's so attractive to the birds on the roof of the Surgical Three theatre?" he asked.

"What do you mean?" Sister Rutherford asked.

"Well, Surgical Three is on the ground floor. You can see its roof as you approach this ward along the top corridor. There are always a few birds flying about the hospital grounds, picking up scraps of kitchen waste but there must be a dozen or more pigeons on that roof at the moment. They've been there regularly for the last few weeks. There must be a reason for it."

"If you've got a moment, can you show me what you mean?"

"Of course, no trouble."

They walked down the corridor, looked through the window and sure enough, ten or more pigeons were busy pecking at the flat roof of the theatre.

Victoria looked at Sister and she looked at Victoria. Simultaneously the same thought had occurred to them both. Sister looked thoughtful. "Are you thinking what I'm thinking?" she asked.

"We need to be certain before we challenge her," Victoria said.

"Fair enough," Sister replied. "I suggest that we let her have her lunch, then watch from this window."

Their suspicions were quickly confirmed. Mrs Twigg was supervised while she ate most of the food that was on her plate. The remains of her meal were removed and she was then left to her own devices. Ten minutes later, from the vantage point on the corridor, they saw her throwing something out of the window.

"We know she ate the food," Victoria said, "so she must be making herself vomit by putting a finger down the back of her throat. Then, when nobody's looking, she's feeding her vomit to the birds. No wonder all the investigations we've performed have been normal! Would you believe that a chance remark by one of the porters has solved the problem that has confounded the best medical brains in the hospital? He's probably saved her life as well!"

Victoria rang Paul to tell him that all the questions surrounding Mrs Twigg's illness had finally been answered, or as she actually said, "Sister and I have finally 'twigged' the cause of the problem!"

Paul received the news with mixed emotions; surprise and delight that the mystery had been solved but also with a sense of anger that all along Mrs Twigg had put her life at risk and caused so much anxiety and distress. They considered whether Mr Potts should be informed immediately of Mrs Twigg's behaviour, or whether it would be better to tell him on his next ward round. They agreed that nothing would be lost by waiting until his next routine visit.

"She's made complete fools of all of us. The boss is going to be furious," Victoria commented.

Inevitably there was concern as to how Mr Potts would react when he was told the cause of Mrs Twigg's troubles. There was always a sense of unease when he was on the ward. Partly, this was because his natural manner was brusque but there was also a sharp edge to his tongue. If a member of his junior doctors made a mistake, they earned a brisk reprimand, unless of course they happened to be female with a pretty face and shapely ankle.

Victoria suggested it would be best to inform him of the latest developments in the office, realising that it would be difficult to tell the full story at the bed side, in Mrs Twigg's presence. Rather cautiously she raised the subject and told him what they had discovered. When she had finished there was a long pause, finally broken by a grim faced Mr Potts.

"Damn the woman. She's quite deliberately deceived the lot of us, me included; she's nothing but a bloody nut case risking her life like that!"

"But that doesn't mean she's not ill, Mr Potts," Sister said stiffly.

"Maybe she is, Sister, but she doesn't need a surgeon. She needs to go back to that wretched psychiatrist."

He stopped and paused. "Have you told her that we now know what she's been up to?"

"No," Victoria said, "but she must have guessed. Since we found out what she's been doing, one of the auxiliaries has been sitting with her for a couple of hours after each meal to give her food time to digest."

"I presume that she's still in the side room? It will probably be better to bring her out on to the main ward. We can keep an eye on her more easily there. And Lambert, get that psychiatrist to see her again."

So, the saga of Mrs Twigg came to an end and she actually started to gain some weight before she was transferred to the care of the psychiatrist. All in all, it had been a fascinating story with the moral that it was a mistake to believe that every patient always told you the truth!

Chapter Twenty-Two

One Saturday some weeks later, it was Surgical Three's turn to take responsibility for accident and emergency patients and Bill Taylor, as their houseman, had to take his fair share of work in the casualty department. Although the hospital employed casualty officers, they only worked on weekdays and then only from nine in the morning until nine in the evening. The housemen were responsible for manning the department through the nights and at weekends. This night shift was referred to as the '*graveyard slot*' because it threatened to be the death of the housemen who were required to work it; they had worked the day before and were required to work the day after.

Fortunately, the department was also staffed by some longstanding and extremely experienced nursing staff, including a couple of excellent senior sisters. Never-the-less, to be 'first on call' for a catchment population of half a million people was a daunting prospect for an inexperienced young doctor and it certainly wasn't in the best interests of the patients they served! The housemen lived in constant fear that some dire emergency would arrive and require immediate attention before a more senior doctor could be roused from their bed in the medical residency to offer advice and assistance.

During the early part of his shift, Bill had treated some minor sports injuries such as sprained ankles and twisted knees. Then there had been the usual run of medical ailments, such as cases of constipation, indigestion and sore throats, problems that ought to have been sorted out by their G Ps. These were local residents who came to casualty, either because their GP was not on duty, or because they thought, often mistakenly, that they would be seen faster at the hospital. Later he had seen an elderly couple who had been involved in a minor road traffic accident. None of these problems had been serious and Bill had managed them all without needing to seek more senior advice.

Midnight approached, the time when, having been encouraged by landlords to down a quick final drink at 'last orders', the pubs discharged their intoxicated customers onto the street. Some were disinhibited, others disorientated with a tendency to fall off curbs or walk into lampposts. A few, in belligerent mood, took offence at some minor comment or criticism, got involved in a fight and sustained an injury. Unfortunately, the local 'Bobbies' felt obliged to bring these disagreeable and disruptive miscreants to hospital to have them medically examined before locking them up in the cells for the night and then transporting them to the magistrate's court the following morning.

Bill, having put in a full day's work on the ward before commencing his shift, was weary, ready for bed and felt abused. These alcohol-related problems were self-inflicted and he had little sympathy for them. Moreover, some of the patients were aggressive, others were 'lippy', making comments to the nurses that they thought were clever and funny but were in fact, usually inappropriate and occasionally crude. However, he knew his job, he was conscientious and, tired though he was, he continued to work his way round the cubicles as he had done throughout the evening. When the cubicles and the waiting room were finally cleared, he went with a weary sigh to sit in the office to enjoy a well earned snack of tea and toast. He was just about to retire to the hot and noisy bedroom where the duty doctor could grab an hour or two of sleep if the flow of patients allowed, when one of the staff nurses came into office. "I'm afraid there's another case for you to see Bill," she said. "I've put her in cubicle two."

With a look of resignation on his face, Bill went to see the patient, hoping desperately it would be the last and that when he finally got to bed, he would not be disturbed too frequently before morning. The woman on the couch in the cubicle was young, blond and attractive. She wore a university college scarf around her neck and Bill was pleased to observe that she seemed to be sober. With her was a man in his mid-twenties, who appeared an unlikely companion. He was big, burly and looked unkempt. He had two days growth on his chin, a bruise on one cheek and a cut above his eye which Bill judged to have been recently inflicted. Unlike the girl, who was nicely dressed with a pencil skirt, black leather shoes and a tight fitting jumper that exaggerated a shapely figure, he wore dirty jeans, an old food stained sweater and steel capped boots. Bill picked up the casualty card and introduced himself. The girl was called Penny; she was a 21 year old student who lived in one of the University halls of residence.

"Tell me what happened and where you are hurt," Bill said, noting that the receptionist had written 'road traffic accident' on the casualty card.

"I fell off my bike earlier this evening," Penny explained. "I landed heavily on top of the bike and the end of the handlebars stuck in my chest. I didn't think too much of it at first, but it really hurts now."

"Have you hurt yourself anywhere else or is it just your chest?" Bill asked.

"I have a pain in my knee and my elbow aches a bit but nothing serious."

"Is the chest pain there all the time?"

"No, if I keep absolutely still it doesn't hurt at all; but as soon as I move it hurts a lot - and if I cough, it's absolute agony. It's like a dagger stabbing into me."

"It sounds as if you have injured a rib; you might even have cracked it. Have you noticed any change in your breathing?" Bill asked, knowing that a fractured rib might easily have punctured a lung.

"Yes, I do feel a bit tight chested; you know slightly short of breath."

"Okay, well I'd better have a look at it. Can you slip off your top please?"

Penny looked at her companion. "Would you mind Pete," she said.

"I don't mind staying to look after you," her companion replied in a gruff voice, looking at the pretty young woman who was about to disrobe.

I'm sure you wouldn't, thought Bill. "Quite sure, thank you," Penny replied in a firm voice.

"In that case, I'll just wait outside in case you need me," Pete said as he left, somewhat reluctantly.

After Pete had left the cubicle, Bill asked whether he was a friend of hers, curious to know the relationship between this rather rough looking character and the well spoken girl who clearly came from an upper class background.

"Good gracious me, no!" she exclaimed, as she slipped off her sweater. "He's the caretaker at the hall of residence. The college tutor asked if he would mind driving me here to be seen."

Bill was a rather shy bachelor who had only recently passed his final medical school examinations and qualified as a doctor. As he gazed at the slim figure lying on the couch before him, the skimpy red bra struggling to contain a full figure, he wondered how long it would be before medical professionalism completely obliterated his more natural male emotions. His face flushed slightly, aware of the conflict in his mind. "Would you like me to get a chaperone, he asked?"

"No. You're a doctor aren't you? You must have examined dozens of women of all shapes and sizes."

He had indeed examined many female patients in the short time he had been qualified but most had been elderly women with folds of loose flesh hanging from their rather dumpy bodies. None had been as gorgeous as the young woman lying in front of him at that moment.

'Inspection first, percussion second and auscultation third. Start with the back of the chest' he said to himself, repeating the instructions his tutors at medical school had given him as he attempted to distract himself from Penny's beautiful body.

"Inspection first," he said out loud. "Sit up straight and take a deep breath for me please." The chest moved symmetrically but Penny winced as she felt a stab of pain in her side. Then, in text book fashion, he diligently percussed the upper, middle and lower regions of her back, carefully comparing one side with the other. No abnormality there. Finally, auscultation. Bill took his stethoscope out of his pocket. "Breath in," he instructed as he listened for any abnormal sounds, "and out," he said. He decided there was an equal volume of air flowing into both sides, nothing to suggest a punctured lung.

Now he had to examine the front of her chest. He knew that to undertake a complete examination he should asked Penny to remove her bra; that is what he had been taught to do at medical school - but he found himself too embarrassed to ask. Once more, he inspected, then percussed and then listened to the upper and lower parts of her chest but this time omitting the middle region!

Then Bill placed his hands on either side of the chest to undertake the test for a fractured rib. He pressed firmly to apply compression to the entire rib cage. Penny squealed with pain. "My God that really hurt," she complained.

"I am afraid that means you've broken a rib," Bill said. "Pop your top on and I'll arrange an x-ray for you."

"But doctor, the pain that really hurts is in my left breast. That's where the handle bar really stuck in and I'm worried because I seem to have developed a lump there. You don't think it could have done any damage do you. My mum had breast cancer when she was only in her 40's and I am petrified that I might get that too. You will check it for me wont you, while I'm here, just to make sure?"

Uninvited, she slipped off her bra.

'Observation, then palpation,' Bill said to himself. Observation first. As he looked at the nubile figure before him, his emotions were once more in turmoil. A hint of perspiration appeared on his brow.

"Lie back on the couch and put you left arm behind your head," he said, knowing that this was the correct patient position for a breast examination.

'No asymmetry between the two breasts,' his medical training said. *'What a beautiful figure,'* his male brain responded.

"Where does it hurt?" he asked, attempting to control his emotions.

She pointed to an area behind her left nipple.

'No obvious bruising,' the doctor in him decided. *'How desirable,'* his baser emotions replied.

Tentatively he laid a hand on her breast. His fingers could detect no obvious swelling. He probed more firmly.

Suddenly, the girl recoiled and screamed at the top of her voice. "Get off. Get off you fiend." Immediately Bill recoiled, backing away, hands raised in a posture of innocence.

"But I....."

But his protestations of innocence were drowned out as Penny continued to shout. She sat up and started flailing at him with her fists, breasts bouncing up and down like balloons on a restless sea, all the while screaming at the top of her voice, "Rape, rape, help, someone please help me!"

Bill continued to protest, but Penny was now wide eyed and hysterical.

In a flash, Sister appeared through the door. "What on earth is going on?" she cried. Summing up the situation in an instant, she glared at Bill. "How dare you?" she said, as she gathered the sheet from the couch and threw it round Penny who was now cowering in a corner, crying uncontrollably, hands across her chest, trying to protect her modesty.

"But I.... I did nothing," Bill wailed. "I was simply examining her. She said she had a pain in the breast. I wouldn't dream of...."

Again, he was interrupted, this time by Pete who entered, his face enraged.

"It's him, it's him," Penny screamed pointing directly at Bill. "He's a sex maniac, a pervert, a rapist. He's been groping me."

Pete reached Bill in one stride across the small cubicle. He picked him up by the lapels of his white coat and lifted him bodily off the floor, his feet dangled in fresh air. He thrust his face within two inches of Bill's. "You filthy little swine, you'll pay for this you pervert."

At that moment, two more figures entered the crowded cubicle unannounced; one was Malcolm, the other Paul. Malcolm held an eight millimetre cine camera to his eye. It purred quietly as he focussed on Bill's petrified face and then panned the camera to Penny, now discreetly draped with the hospital sheet. She had a huge grin on her face. Malcolm continued filming for a couple of minutes taking time to photograph all the characters in the charade which he had so carefully planned. Initially, Bill had looked terrified, then when he saw Malcolm, he appeared bewildered. It took quite some time before it finally dawned on him that he had been duped. He growled at Malcolm.

"You bastard, you utter despicable bastard."

Satisfied that he had a complete photographic record of the scene, Malcolm stopped filming. The revenge that he had planned had gone with a precision of which the military would have been justly proud. It would give him great pleasure to arrange a film show for his fellow house officers when the film was developed.

"Let me introduce you to Penny," he said to Bill. "She's actually my sister. She's a drama student at the college of performing arts. She's a great actress isn't she?"

Then he turned to Penny's companion. "And this is Roger. He's not really the caretaker at the college; he's actually the captain of the London Irish rugby team. He's Penny's boyfriend. He played in a match this afternoon which explains why his face has been knocked about a bit."

Malcolm turned to the casualty nursing sister. "I'm sorry Sister that we didn't let you in on our little secret, but I must say you acted your part to perfection. We thought you might not be quite so convincing, if you knew in advance what was going to happen. Now Paul," he said, "would you be kind enough to fetch my little box of tricks so that I can put my camera back in a safe place?"

Paul slipped out of the cubicle and returned a few seconds later with Malcolm's 'tool box'. With a glance at Bill he opened the lid, put the camera safely inside.

"I trust that will teach you not to mess with my belongings in future."

Chapter Twenty-Three

Leslie Potts tapped his pen impatiently on his leather topped desk. It was an expensive pen, inscribed with his name, a gift from an Iraqi sheikh, given in gratitude *'for services to his wife'*. He ran his fingers along the smooth hand painted porcelain shaft then removed the diamond encrusted cap and admired the 18 carat gold nib. When he had been a student at medical school all those years ago, he would never have imagined that the humble haemorrhoid could be so profitable! He glanced at his watch, another gift from a grateful patient and his brow creased into a frown. He would wait a little longer but if his next client didn't arrive within the next five minutes (when working in his private rooms he thought of them as clients not patients), he would leave. He was too busy and his time too precious to be wasted. He needed to return to the hospital at the end of the session to rally his consultant colleagues into action to fight the threat to the NHS pay beds.

Glancing round the consulting room he reflected that he had done well for himself since those distant university days. It was a large well proportioned room, tastefully furnished. There was a rich fabric paper on the walls, a beautiful polished mahogany folding screen to allow clients privacy as they undressed and two inlaid glass fronted cabinets displaying antique surgical instruments; an amputation knife, forceps for extracting teeth, various metal probes and a speculum for internal examination. In the far corner stood a Victorian chaise longue upholstered in satin, where a relative or companion could sit whilst the patient was being examined.

Although he only worked in these private rooms for two half days a week, Leslie owned the house, indeed he owned its neighbour as well. The houses formed part of a Georgian terrace in one of the best streets in the city. Initially, built as private residences, town houses for rich industrialists, he had converted the rooms into medical consulting suites which he rented out to his colleagues. As a surgeon, private practice was far more lucrative than it was for his medical colleagues at the City General Hospital and infinitely more rewarding than for colleagues who worked in the more remote parts of the country. There was very little private practice available in the smaller towns and only a limited amount in the shires.

He stretched his legs underneath the desk and made himself comfortable, a self-satisfied smile on his face. He had spent a good deal of time, a fair amount of energy and quite a lot of money cultivating the GPs in the more well-to-do city suburbs, persuading them to refer their patients to him and his investment was paying dividends. If the number of private referrals continued to rise, he would soon be able to give up his NHS work altogether. Offering his services to the Royal College of Surgeons as an overseas tutor and examiner had been a master stroke. It involved some tedious journeys to distant parts, some interesting experiences in foreign hotels and the requirement to swallow indigestible food with a smile on his face, but it was proving to be well worthwhile. He now attracted a regular stream of exceptionally wealthy Middle Eastern patients who believed, with good cause, that standards of medical care were higher in England than they were in their own countries.

However, Leslie was painfully aware of the gathering storm. To enable him to keep abreast of political developments, he had recently become a council member of the British Medical Association. As a result of attending meetings at BMA house in Tavistock Square, he was well aware of the threat to private practice. Ever since the Labour Party manifesto had been published there had been no doubt of the government's intentions but hearing it confirmed in the Queen's Speech a week ago at the 'Opening of Parliament' had been a body blow.

'My government will introduce legislation in the course of this session to phase out all private practice from NHS hospitals,' the Queen had said.

Curse that blasted Barbara Castle and her socialist dogma. The Health Secretary would have written the words that Her Majesty had read to the nation and Mr Potts could imagine the pleasure it must have brought her. Although he had been a consultant for just ten years, Mr Potts could double his NHS salary by operating privately. But to earn at this level, he needed access to the pay beds in the City General Hospital. There were a limited number of beds in the small independent hospital in the city but they didn't have the x-ray and laboratory support that was available at the City General. He vowed to do whatever was necessary to safeguard his interests and those of his fellow consultants and if that involved industrial action, so be it. This was a battle that had to be won.

His reverie was interrupted by the ringing of the telephone on the desk. It was his receptionist, speaking from the room next door.

"Your last patient of the day has arrived Mr Potts, a Mrs Amira Kabbani. She's brought a letter from a surgeon in Damascus."

"OK, bring her through," Mr Potts replied in a resigned voice. This was irritating. Normally, the more private patients he saw, the happier he was but at this particular moment, his desire to get to the meeting at the hospital to put pressure on his fellow consultants was far more important.

*****

Paul entered the committee room with some trepidation but was pleased to find that Sir William was already present and grateful when the senior consultant beckoned Paul to sit next to him. When preparing for his first appearance at the hospital consultants' meeting, Paul didn't anticipate having to make an active contribution, other than to seek an assurance that junior doctors would not be disadvantaged if they participated in industrial action; indeed he was happy to sit and listen to his seniors' discussions. He had studied the agenda carefully, imagining that the meeting would focus on patient care, improving quality and reducing waiting times, but he was to discover that this assumption was incorrect.

After a list of '*apologies for absence*' had been noted and the minutes of the previous meeting read, agreed and signed, the chairman Dr Digby welcomed Paul to his first meeting. There then followed a long discussion under the heading '*requests for equipment*'. Paul learned from Sir William that a budget was available for the consultants to spend as they thought appropriate. A cardiologist wanted a new ECG machine costing £145 whereas a respiratory physician thought a spirometer priced at £130 would be a better investment. The argument swayed to and fro for a good fifteen minutes before the chair decided that in the absence of agreement and to save time, the matter should be put to the vote. The ECG machine won a narrow majority. The chest physician looked miffed but was mollified when the chair proposed that the spirometer could be purchased at the next meeting when more funds became available; a suggestion that was immediately and unanimously agreed.

The next item proved even more contentious. Mr Harrison, the hospital's senior manager, requested that the finance department be relocated to the room currently used as the consultants' dining room. He suggested that in future the consultants should dine in the hospital canteen. He explained that the finance department had recently taken on extra staff to deal with an ever increasing workload and that the present accommodation was proving to be inadequate. This proposal provoked outrage amongst the consultants who detailed a hundred and one different reasons why their private dining room should be preserved. How could they possibly discuss a patient's medical problems amongst themselves when the relatives might be sitting in close proximity? How would it appear if they were laughing and joking with a colleague over lunch, only to realise that, sitting at the next table, was the man whom they had just told his wife had incurable cancer?

Mr Harrison looked harassed but continued to press his case. He argued that it was wasteful of resources and an inefficient use of staff for the consultants to dine separately. Further he had heard complaints that it was elitist for the consultants to have waitress service in their own private room, whilst other members of staff had to queue at the counter in the self-service canteen. The consultants to a man rejected the proposal and in the end Mr Harrison backed down with the comment that he would have to make savings elsewhere to enable him to find alternative accommodation for the finance department. Paul wondered whether the consultant's budget for '*items of equipment*' might be at the back of his mind!

*****

Isolated from the outside world but fuming inside his Bentley, Leslie Potts tried to force his way through the heavy rush hour traffic. He looked at his watch with increasing frequency and frustration, knowing that he was going to be late for the meeting. The main agenda item was the government's attack on private practice; a subject on which he planned to impress his views forcibly upon his colleagues. It was an issue of great importance to him, an enormous threat to his standard of living. God knows how he would be able to repay his huge mortgage, enjoy expensive holidays or afford the children's school fees if he were no longer able to subsidise his NHS salary with lucrative private practice; and his wife would have to cut back on her spending too! He wouldn't enjoy having to tell her that!

Why did the traffic have to be so heavy when he was in such a rush? Why were there so many blasted cars on the road with imbecile drivers at the wheel?

Couldn't more of these wretched commuters use the bus or train and leave the roads free for people such as himself; people who really needed to drive a car? He sounded his horn angrily at a cyclist who pushed his way to the front of the queue. The cyclist then delayed him further by obstructing his path whilst mouthing an obscenity at him. He muttered in frustration at a pram pushing mother who chose to step onto a zebra crossing just as he was approaching and he swore at a policeman who was doing his best to ease traffic through a congested junction but who held up a white gloved hand in front of his limousine. '*Just because you can't afford a car like mine*', he said to himself under his breath.

He arrived at the gates of the hospital 30 minutes late, knowing that the meeting would be well under way by the time he reached the committee room. Driving passed the main car park, he groaned when he saw that every available space was taken. He realised that it must be visiting time. Unconcerned, he drove to the area set aside for consultants, only to find that someone had parked a battered old Morris Minor in his personal reserved spot. *'How dare they?'* he asked himself in a fury. For a moment he considered blocking them in but then thought better of it. If they were prepared to park 'illegally' they might be prepared to scratch the paintwork of his beloved car in revenge.

Dr Digby was in mid-sentence when the door was flung open and Mr Potts made his grand entrance.

"I'm sorry to be late," he boomed. "I got delayed in this blasted rush hour traffic and then found that some selfish blighter has parked in my reserved place. It really is time that we made the area more secure. Can I propose, Mr Chairman that we instruct management to install a barrier that can be locked, so that we can keep the riff-raff out! What would have happened had I been needed urgently in theatre? The patient could have bled to death whilst I was driving round in circles looking for a car parking spot."

The chairman, knowing Mr Potts of old, realised the smoothest and quickest way to resume the business of the evening was to placate the latecomer by ignoring the disruption he had caused and giving him a couple of minutes to cool off!

"Ah, Leslie, we were just discussing the need for further investment in the medical library but I'm pleased that you have been able to join us. We are all eager to hear of your recent encounter with Barbara Castle."

This was the item that was of most interest to Paul. With the increasing anger evident amongst the junior doctors over their excessive hours and workload, he was eager to learn how the consultants planned to deal with the threat that they faced over the loss of private practice. If the consultants were prepared to take industrial action, they could surely not object if some of the junior doctors followed suit.

Leslie Potts was soon in full flow, his fellow consultants listening with concern as he explained the present political situation.

"As you all know," he said, "the Labour Government has been elected on its manifesto commitment to phase out all the private beds from NHS hospitals and the Queen's Speech told us that they intend to abolish them almost immediately. This poses a serious threat which the BMA are fighting on our behalf. As your regional BMA representative, I recently attended a meeting with Barbara Castle. She's absolutely adamant that all pay beds will be removed but worse, we believe she's aiming to force us all to commit ourselves 100% to the NHS.

We told her that the existence of pay beds in NHS hospitals was enshrined in the original act, signed by Nye Bevin in 1946, but Barbara Castle disagrees.

Apparently, she has taken legal advice and insists that there never has been any such right. It seems that 'pay beds' exist solely at her discretion. She says that, had she wished, she could have abolished the private beds at a stroke when she was first appointed. That came as a shock and is a considerable setback. It means we have lost a very strong bargaining tool but we intend to press our case with every legitimate means at our disposal.

The BMA has also taken legal advice," Leslie continued. "We don't believe that she can force us to work exclusively for the NHS because it would infringe our employment rights. Just as you can't stop a joiner or a plumber from earning a little extra cash by taking a job in the evening or at the weekend to earn his beer money, you shouldn't be able to prevent a doctor doing some extra work when he has fulfilled his NHS duties. However if Mrs Castle succeeds in eliminating the private beds, we will have to do all our private work in non-NHS hospitals. A few of our major cities do have small independent hospitals but in the rest of the country, the only private beds are in NHS premises. That means that the vast majority of consultants would have no private beds at all. Furthermore Mrs Castle is also insisting that any beds outside of the NHS will have to be licensed by her; in other words she would be able to control their numbers. She would be able to block all applications for a licence is she so wished."

The chairman thanked Leslie Potts for outlining the situation, then invited questions and comments. They came thick and fast.

"It sounds as if she wants a communist system where the state controls everything," one consultant commented bitterly.

"It's a real threat to our independence," said another. "If weren't able to do private practice, we ought to be given a significant increase in our NHS pay as compensation; otherwise many of us will go and work in other countries where we can see private patients."

"I'm afraid any prospect of compensation is out of the question," Mr Potts replied. "Don't forget that there is a national embargo on pay rises at present. Mrs Castle made it clear that there can be no exceptions."

"That didn't stop the nurses getting a huge rise."

"True, but the nurses had the sympathy of the public – we don't."

"Was it explained to her that having pay beds on site makes us more effective as we spend less time travelling to other hospitals and therefore have more time for our NHS patients?"

"Yes, it was. We also pointed out their abolition would cost the government a lot of money since they are a source of revenue for the NHS. It's surprising that the Treasury haven't blocked it. Damn it, they're always telling us how short of money we are," Mr Potts commented. "I fear that Barbara Castle is deaf to all arguments. She even said that she would prefer consultants to work for 40 hours for the health service and then play golf, rather than work for 40 hours and then see private patients. How crazy is that? It seems that she's driven by socialist idealism, not by what is best for the NHS or for patients."

"It's outrageous," another consultant argued. "Surely it's the right of all members of the public to spend their money as they choose. And it will work to the disadvantage of patients," he added. "If someone waiting for surgery decides to have private treatment, it's one less patient on the NHS list. If someone waiting for a bus decides to take a taxi, everyone in the bus queue moves up a place."

"As I say," Mr Potts replied, "the wretched woman is deaf to reason."

"It may be in their blasted manifesto and in the Queen's Speech," an orthopaedic consultant said, "but it's not the law of the land."

"No, it isn't yet," Leslie Potts replied, "but they are the party in power. Unless we are able to stop it, all too soon it will be the law of the land and when it is we will have to obey it. That's why the BMA are suggesting that we introduce some sanctions to try to persuade the government to change its mind. Basically it amounts to restricting our work to activities that are defined in our contract; in other words, working to rule. If necessary the threat of mass resignations from the NHS will be implemented. So gentlemen, we have to decide what we are going to do about it here at the City General. I need to hear your views on industrial action so that I can feed them back to the BMA."

It quickly became clear that opinion was widely divided. Some consultants were furious at what they perceived as political interference, arguing that the entire consultant body should unite, follow the lead of consultants in other hospitals and only treat emergency cases. Others insisted that it should be left to individual consultants to decide what action, if any, they would take.

Dr Longfleet, the physician who had been involved with Mrs Twigg, whom Paul had considered to have been intimidated when facing Mr Potts, proved not to be so timid after all.

"I'm sure that any reasonable person looking at these proposals will agree that what is being suggested is entirely unfair but it does need to be recognised that the leadership of the BMA is biased in favour of those consultants who do private practice; indeed the members of their negotiating committee are almost all surgeons who engage in private work. We need to remember that 40% of the consultants in the country don't do any private work at all. The pay beds issue has no relevance for them.

If you look at the correspondence page of the British Medical Journal, you will see that there are many letters deploring the action currently being taken by consultants against patients; there's dismay at the damage being done to our reputation and concern that it is turning doctor against doctor."

Dr Longfleet then reminded his colleagues of the Hippocratic Oath he had taken when he entered the profession: "*With regard to healing the sick,*" he paraphrased, '*I will take care that they suffer no hurt or damage*'. This phrase has been altered over the years," he added, "but it still applies today. It means *'first do no harm'*." He eyed Mr Potts coldly. "Delaying a patient's investigation and treatment will obviously harm patients and I most definitely will not be involved in such tactics."

When pressed by his surgical colleague, he reluctantly conceded that he might be persuaded to stop doing administrative work, or possibly reduce his teaching commitment but he would certainly not contemplate anything more significant.

"Well, I shall certainly be making my view known," Mr Potts proclaimed loudly. "As from now, I shall only see emergency and cancer cases. I shall admit no routine cases to the ward. If the waiting list gets out of control, the responsibility will lie with Mrs Castle! I urge you all to follow my example."

Paul, sitting quietly but listening intently, noted that the most militant consultants were the surgeons, particularly those in specialties such as ENT and orthopaedics. They were the ones who enjoyed significant rewards from private practice; they were the hawks. The physicians and those who worked in the laboratory and x-ray department where there was little opportunity for private work were the doves.

For ninety minutes, the argument raged, self-interest to the fore. Eventually Dr Digby intervened. "Sir William," he said, "we haven't heard your views. Is there anything you would like to say before I draw this discussion to a close?"

The angry background muttering that had characterised the exchanges ceased when Sir William spoke, his voice quiet but clear.

"Personally, I find it very regrettable that doctors should be considering industrial action but I cannot deny that the government is acting in a high handed and unreasonable fashion. Mrs Castle doesn't appear to have considered the disadvantages of what she is proposing, particularly the financial implications. I understand that the exchequer would lose four million pounds a year if pay beds were abolished. I also wonder if she appreciates that thousands of consultants in the land forego 20% of their salary for the right to treat private patients, money that she would have to find if her proposal is adopted. It also seems to me that a responsible Minister of Health would not increase the pressure on NHS waiting lists by blocking the only alternative available to patients."

There was a murmur of approval in the room but Sir William held up a hand and silence again descended.

"I also feel that there is a good deal of hypocrisy in what is being suggested. Many labour MPs and a number of cabinet ministers were educated privately and I know that several have had surgery as private patients. Others use the NHS but expect to have the consultant of their choice and be treated in a side room on a date of their choosing. They are abusing the system by receiving 'personal' treatment, which effectively is private treatment, without it costing them a penny. So I agree that Mrs Castle's proposals are driven by ideology rather than by common sense and that they should be resisted. However I also believe that it is wrong to disadvantage patients, wrong to use their pain and suffering to further our cause. My view is that we should take action but that the action should be restricted to non cooperation in administrative and other non clinical matters."

This was not a view shared by all in the room but the respect others had for Sir William was such that they did not voice their disagreement.

The chairman, feeling that nothing would be gained by prolonging the debate, decided to draw the discussion to a close.

"It's clear," he summarised, "that there is no agreement or consensus on this difficult subject. It follows that no resolution can be agreed. Each and every one of us must decide as individuals and according to our conscience, what action, if any, we are prepared to take."

The consultants gathered up their papers and prepared to leave.

"Before you all go," the chair said above the chatter that now filled the room, "there is an item of '*any other business*' that Mr Harrison wishes to raise with you."

"Gentlemen," Mr Harrison said, "I know that it's getting late and that you've all had a long and tiring day so I won't keep you more than a moment but a problem has been brought to my attention by the laboratory staff. The multi-channel analyser that is used to analyse blood specimens has been causing problems. It's old; it can't be repaired and needs to be replaced. I'm afraid it's an expensive item; the cost of a new machine is in the region of £30k, but it is an essential item and something that will benefit everyone of you."

"Is that approved?" Dr Digby asked. "May I have a show of hands?"

Almost all hands were raised and the hubbub of conversation resumed.

"Is there any more '*any other business*' before we close?"

Paul timidly raised his hand.

"Yes, Mr Lambert."

"Sir, the junior doctors would like to know how they would stand if, in due course, they too were asked by the BMA to take some form of industrial action in their dispute with Mrs Castle. They want to be assured that they would not be disadvantaged or victimised in any way."

"The juniors will do what they always do. They will undertake precisely those duties prescribed by their individual consultant. No more and no less!" Mr Potts snapped as he marched out of the room.

The meeting broke up in disarray, without the chair formally declaring that the evening's business was concluded.

Sir William who had not spoken at any stage turned to Paul, a twinkle in his eye. "Well, Lambert, how did you enjoy your first meeting?"

"It was fascinating Sir. Tell me, will the multi-channel analyser come out of the same fund as the ECG machine?"

Sir William smiled. "It will. Mr Harrison will go home well pleased with his evening's work even if he didn't manage to throw us out of our dining room."

Chapter Twenty-Four

A list of the patients whose admissions were planned for the following week was circulated to the wards every Thursday afternoon. It gave the ward sisters an opportunity to plan the nurses' off duty and to make the best use of the available beds. On the male ward, Sister's eye swept over the details of the patients and their proposed surgical procedures. One name caught her attention. She groaned. Cedric King was to be re-admitted for repair of an incisional hernia. She turned to Victoria who chanced to be working in the office at the time.

"Did you know that Cedric King needed further surgery?" she asked.

"Yes, I did. He was seen in the clinic recently. When his wound finally healed, it was so weak that if offered no support to the guts inside his belly. His wound bulges forward in an alarming fashion. It looks like a nine month pregnancy. It causes the poor man a lot of pain. He has to wear a large metal-ribbed corset to control it. Sir William has listed him to have the rupture repaired."

"Poor man, be damned," Sister responded. "The man's a confounded nuisance. Do you think he'll be in for long?" she asked concern in her voice.

"I'm afraid so. The rupture is huge. He'll be in for ten days, maybe longer."

Sister swore under her breath. "He caused no end of trouble when he was on the ward last time – and he attracts the most undesirable visitors. Perhaps I'll stick him in the end side ward; then he'll be as far away from the other patients as possible!"

Paul too was dismayed when he heard the news. The terrible problems Cedric had experienced with his wound, and the trouble he was still having from it, all stemmed from his emergency operation; a procedure which Paul had performed. Cedric alleged that all his complications were entirely Paul's fault. Through his solicitor, he was accusing Paul of malpractice and suing him for negligence. In the circumstances, Paul didn't see how he could possibly be involved in Cedric's management and went to have a quiet word with Sir William, as he always did when he needed advice on a moral or ethical issue. He explained his dilemma and asked to be excused involvement in the case. To his surprise, his request was denied.

"No, Lambert," he said. "It's actually important that you are involved in his management. You see, I don't believe for a minute that Mr King blames you for his problems. In his heart, he probably appreciates that you saved his life. It's simply that by suing you, he hopes to win some compensation; not from you personally but from your medical insurance company. When he comes in, I suggest that you take a particular interest in him. If any practical procedures are required, do them yourself and when you prepare the consent form for his operation, specify that I shall be performing his surgery with you acting as my assistant."

Paul didn't understand the logic behind this scheme. Sir William smiled. "You see Lambert, if he really believes that you are a negligent doctor, he won't allow you anywhere near him. He certainly won't permit you to be involved in his treatment; but if he puts his signature to a form that states that you will be assisting at the operation, if he makes no objection when you take blood from him or put up his intravenous line, he undermines his own case. He can scarcely claim that you are a negligent doctor and then cheerfully allow you to treat him and operate on him for a second time.

Fortunately, Cedric's operation went smoothly, he avoided complications and made a good recovery but as Victoria had predicted, he remained in hospital for two weeks after his surgery, with his corset still in place, supporting the wound and giving it every opportunity to heal soundly. As Sister had anticipated, he was visited by a number of undesirable characters, who paid scant regard to the official visiting hours and, as before, often turning up late into the night. As the days passed, Paul began to feel more confident that Cedric's claim of negligence could be rebuffed. Sir William's plan had worked well. Paul had been involved in many aspects of his care and Cedric had not objected to Paul assisting at his operation. One day however, after Sir William had seen him on a routine ward round, Cedric called Paul back to his bedside. There was a menacing expression on his face.

"Doc, I need a word with you," he growled, his tone belligerent.

Paul presumed he was about to mention the negligence claim but when he spoke, it was on quite a different subject.

"Get that young male orderly to come and see me."

"You mean Charlie?" Paul asked.

"That's the one. He and I have some business to discuss." His voice was threatening.

"What sort of business?"

"Never you mind, that's nothing to do with you; but if he knows what's good for him, he'll make damn sure that he comes to see me today."

Charlie was the local hospital 'character' and it was impossible to be glum when he was around. Officially, he was the hospital barber but in practice he was the quick witted hospital comic and prankster. Cheeky and cheerful, he radiated sunshine where ever he went. It was Charlie's job to undertake the pre operative shaves on the male patients. Like most barbers, he chatted incessantly as he worked, making jokes, spreading gossip, discussing sport or telling tales about the hospital staff and the miracles that they achieved. He had never actually witnessed an operation in his life but claimed to have watched all the City General surgeons in action. He gave a glowing description of their technical ability, no matter how ham fisted or clumsy he considered them to be. He used an old-fashioned 'cut throat' razor and enjoyed watching the faces of his victims as he joked of Sweeney Todd whilst vigorously stropping his open blade in front of their eyes.

Feeling apprehensive and sensing that Charlie was in some sort of trouble, Paul asked the switchboard to page the young orderly but Charlie but didn't answer his bleep. That was by no means unusual, but a few casual enquiries led Paul to the yard at the back of the hospital. Charlie was having a quiet smoke, sitting on one of the large wicker laundry baskets. Paul made a casual remark about *'cancer sticks being bad for his health',* a comment which Charlie would normally have rebuffed with a smile and a joke. Charlie looked drawn and anxious and when he stood up, he was limping. There was also a bruise on the side of his face.

"You've been in the wars," Paul said cheerfully, "fighting over one of the nurses I suppose."

"I wish I had. No, Doc, I simply slipped and fell over. I rather overdid the booze last night."

When Paul explained that Cedric wished to see him, Charlie swore.

"Paul, I can't go and see him," he said anxiously. "You'll have to make some excuse for me. Tell him I'm not on duty, or that I've gone off sick."

Paul became suspicious that all was not well. "Is there a problem? Are you in some sort of trouble with Cedric?"

Charlie sat down again on the laundry skip. "Yes," he confessed, "I am. I owe him some money."

"Much?" Paul asked.

"Yes, quite a lot."

"And you can't pay him back?"

"I'm afraid not."

"Do you want to tell me about it?"

After a moment's hesitation, Charlie explained his problem. "You probably know that some of the men on the ward like to have a little flutter on the horses. For many years, I've taken their betting money to the bookies on the high street; but they don't know much about the races and they generally lose. Many of them have never placed a bet in their lives but they get bored on the ward and it creates an interest for them. I can't deny that I tend to encourage them a little. I bring the conversation round to the horses when I have the chance, then casually let them know that I shall be popping into the bookies later. I often buy the Racing Times and leave it for them to see in the day room. But betting is mug's game. By the time the taxman and the bookie have had their cut, the punters always lose. So recently, instead of placing the bets, I've simply pocketed the money then paid out if anybody won. Stupid I know, but over the years it's been quite profitable. Well, Cedric asked me to put a big bet on an outsider, I knew there was a risk if I didn't put the money on, but I became greedy and the wretched horse won at twelve to one. I owe him £65 and I simply don't have it. That's more than two week's wages for me."

"So, Cedric set his henchmen onto you?"

"Yes, I was followed when I went home from work last night. They know where I live. There will be worse to come it I can't pay." He looked appealingly at Paul.

"Look, I'm afraid I don't have that sort of ready cash Charlie. I could go and see if he was prepared to settle for a smaller amount."

Charlie looked desperate. "No, Paul, he wants the whole lot; but if you don't mind going to see him, perhaps you could ask if I can pay him back in instalments over a few months?"

"I'll go and see what I can do," Paul said but having been told by the police that Cedric was in the protection business, he didn't feel hopeful. Extracting money by extortion was right up Cedric's street and when Paul went back to Cedric's room, he found the villain in an uncompromising mood. Paul decided to be honest and he admitted that Charlie had not actually placed the bet. He suggested that Cedric might simply be prepared to take his stake money back and forget the matter, but Cedric simply laughed scornfully.

"He told me he would place the bet. If the fool didn't, that's his fault. He owes me sixty five quid and if he doesn't cough up, there will be interest to pay as well. You can tell him from me that if I don't have the cash by this time tomorrow, he'll get worse treatment than he's had so far."

"You arranged for him to be beaten up?"

"Maybe I did, maybe I didn't. Now you go and tell the idiot to bring me my money."

For the next couple of hours, Paul went about his duties on the ward much distracted. Cedric was obviously vicious and was prepared to use violence to force Charlie to pay. Even though he was stuck in his side ward, he had friends outside the hospital able to do his dirty work for him and unfortunately Charlie, through his own stupidity, had fallen foul of him. If it had been a smaller sum of money, Paul would gladly have lent it to Charlie but £65 was beyond his means.

Over supper that night in the doctor's residency, he discussed the problem with Victoria. They both thought that the matter should be handed over to the police but Victoria felt it inappropriate to involve the police in a hospital problem without Sir William's permission. So Paul rang his boss saying that he needed some advice as a matter of urgency. Sir William suggested that Paul might care to join him for a cup of coffee.

Sir William's home was only a hundred yards away. It had originally been the lodge to an old hall, which had long since had been demolished to make room for the hospital, so in less than five minutes Paul was ringing the front door bell. Again it was strange to see Sir William in his off duty clothes; this time slippers on his feet and a navy blue dressing gown over his city shirt and trousers. Although he was a bachelor, his home had a comfortable 'lived in' feel. He led Paul into his lounge with its well worn settee, easy chairs and tired carpet. There was a sheepskin rug in front of the hearth, where a coal fire blazed cheerfully. Paul thought Sir William might resent being disturbed in the evening, but he seemed genuinely pleased to have a visitor.

"I don't have many folk calling during the evening, Lambert, so it's good to see you. May I offer you a drink, perhaps a sherry or a whisky?"

"No, sir, I'd better not, I'm on duty."

"Well, if you don't mind I'll have a whisky and you can tell me what's on your mind." He poured himself a generous drink, added a splash of soda then settled comfortably into his arm chair and listened without interruption.

"I'm sorry to trouble you in the evening Sir, but something has cropped up at the hospital and I need some advice," Paul began. He then went on to tell the story of Charlie's scam and how it had backfired on him. He expressed concern as to what might happen to Charlie, if he were unable to pay the money that he owed.

"And you say that Charlie has been assaulted already?"

"Yes, he has."

Sir William sat pensively for a moment. "Okay Lambert, I'm pleased that you decided to share this problem with me. I don't think we'll involve the police just yet. I'll sleep on it overnight, but perhaps you would ask Charlie to come and see me first thing in the morning."

Charlie must have mentioned his predicament to others for by next morning, the hospital grapevine was hard at work, his dilemma being widely discussed. Charlie was a popular character and Paul learned that a collection had already been started in the hope that enough money could be raised to pay off his debt. However Charlie disappeared after he had seen Sir William giving rise to great anxiety and speculation. Rumours abounded. Some suggested that he must have been assaulted again; others felt that he was probably lying low. All the while, Cedric remained a patient on the ward. The staff found difficulty in continuing to treat him but somehow managed to maintain a professional if cool attitude towards him.

Two days later, however, Charlie raced into the office, a huge smile on his bruised face. He was beaming from ear to ear, bursting to tell everyone the news. The words poured out of his mouth.

"Sir William was amazing," he said, "an absolute star." He explained that Sir William had made him go to see Cedric to suggest that he offer to pay off the money on a weekly basis. However he had supplied him with a pocket Dictaphone to secrete in his coat. He had anticipated that Cedric would threaten Charlie with violence. Cedric did indeed boast that his boys had been responsible for the first attack on Charlie and threatened to arrange a much more vicious assault if the debt were not paid.

"And I got it all recorded on tape," Charlie said gleefully. The next day, armed with the tape recording, Sir William had visited Cedric's side ward and a negotiation had taken place. They had agreed that the tape recording would be locked away in Sir William's safe and Charlie's debt would be cancelled.

"I don't even have to pay the stake money back," Charlie said laughing. "Mind you there is just one snag; Sir William says that if I he catches me acting as a bookie's runner in the future, he'll post the tape to Cedric!

By the way, Paul; Sir William says he's got some news for you too. I didn't understand what it was about but he said he would tell you himself."

Sir William said nothing to Paul but a fortnight later he received another letter with a London postmark, again in an expensive envelope, once more bearing a first class stamp:

Dear Dr Lambert,

Re. Cedric King, aged 42

We write to inform you that we have now received a further instruction from our client to the effect that he no longer wishes to pursue his claim for negligence against you.

Yours sincerely,

James Purvis (on behalf of Quinell, Purvis and Weekes)

Chapter Twenty-Five

Sue Pickles, who administered the hospital's waiting list, greeted Paul with a frown on her face. "If this *'work to rule'* lasts much longer I shall need to have extra filing cabinets in the corridor," she grumbled as she waved a handful of index cards in the air. "Patients were waiting six months for their operations before this industrial action began; the list is now getting completely out of control. Does Mr Potts have no feelings for his patients at all?"

Paul was paying his weekly visit to the waiting list office. Although this was a tiny room in the bowels of the hospital, it performed a vital function, organising the admission of patients to the surgical wards. Paul's job was to select the patients who would come into Mr Potts' beds the following week, effectively scheduling the cases for future theatre lists. Victoria undertook the same job for Sir William. The task demanded an appreciation of the relative urgency of the patients who were waiting for surgery and an understanding of their expected length of stay. Sue though, was capable and experienced and could probably have done the job perfectly well even without Paul's input.

She pointed at two new filing cabinets that had been placed in the centre of the room. "Those extra cabinets are already nearly full. Doesn't Mr Potts realise that while people are kept waiting, they're suffering pain and disability. I have patients here who are unable to work because of their problems. If they wait eight or nine months for their operations and then have a period of convalescence, they will have been off work for a year or more. That creates real hardship for their families."

"I'm afraid that the boss has made his decision quite clear – only cancer patients and dire emergencies are to be admitted until the threat to private practice is lifted," Paul commented sadly.

"I wish Mr Potts needed an operation," Sue commented bitterly, "I'd get my husband to do it for him."

"And what does your husband do?"

"He's a slaughter man. He works in an abattoir!"

Paul smiled. "Come on Sue; show me what you have for me this week."

Sue was extremely efficient and had already selected the five patients that she felt should be admitted. Frankly, Paul's visits were something of a charade. Officially he was supposed to look through the numerous six by four cards; each recording a patient's personal and medical details, then ask Sue to arrange admission for those he selected. In practice, prior to his arrival, Sue chose the most pressing cases and Paul simply agreed with her judgement.

Paul looked at the cards, four were cancer patients but one was a man in his early-sixties who had gall stones.

"Hey, are you trying to get me into trouble? This patient hasn't got cancer."

Sue looked at him earnestly. "Paul, this patient's wife is at her wit's end. Her husband is in agony. I've even had his GP on the phone pleading on his behalf. My conscience simply won't let me leave his card on file."

Paul looked again at the card. The patient was called Sugden. The name rang a bell with him.

"Wait a minute. I remember this man. I saw him in casualty a week or so ago. He certainly was in a great deal of pain then."

"Well, can't you slip him in? Tell Mr Potts there's been a mistake. Blame it on me if you like."

"No, I daren't. That would simply cause an unholy scene on the ward."

"Then perhaps we could arrange a different sort of mistake. We could admit him into one of Sir William's beds 'by accident'. He's such a sweetie, I'm sure he wouldn't mind."

For a moment, Paul considered the possible consequences but knew Sue was right; Sir William wouldn't cause a fuss. He looked Sue in the eye and smiled. "Yes, let's do it. I'll square it with Victoria but you'd better just remind her when she next calls to see you. Make sure she knows to leave a space for him on one of Sir William's lists. Mr Sugden's gall bladder is likely to be badly inflamed; it may take longer than usual to remove it."

"That's great and if we get away with this one, I have some more patients that we can admit via the back door," Sue observed cheerfully, her only thought being the well being of the patients.

*****

"Hi Paul, we need a bit of advice. Do you have a moment?"

Paul looked up and saw the two housemen, Malcolm and Janet, standing at his side, a letter and some papers in their hands.

"Yes, I'm free," he replied, pleased to have a break from the small print of the huge textbook he was studying. "What seems to be the problem?"

"We've received these questionnaires from someone at the Health Authority. They're inquiring about the hours we work. You don't think there can be any harm in filling them in do you?"

"None at all," Paul replied, realising that what they were really asking was whether it might cause trouble with their consultants. "It's a fact finding initiative. It's has nothing to do with Sir William or Mr Potts. As junior hospital doctors, we're in dispute with the government over our ridiculous workload but there's no agreement on how many hours we actually work. Mrs Castle and our representatives make claim and counterclaim about it. The Treasury knows that any new deal is likely to be expensive - but it's impossible for them to know just how expensive it will be, until they know exactly how much overtime we do."

"This questionnaire only distinguishes between time spent '*in hospital*' and time spent '*on call at home*'," Malcolm said. "Does that imply that when we're in hospital the rate of pay will be the same whether we are actually working or just sitting watching the television?"

"These questions would seem to suggest that," Paul replied as he studied the form.

"Well, that's not fair! When it's my night on, I hardly ever finish on the ward before ten or eleven in the evening and I regularly get called from my bed. Yet there are some housemen, particularly those doing dermatology, who rarely get a call after six and never get disturbed through the night. All their patients are ambulant on the ward. Surely there should be a different rate of pay depending on the work load."

"That would seem fairer," Paul agreed, "but look, there's a space at the bottom for additional comments; you might want to mention it there. Now how many hours are you going to enter on this form?"

"It would be quicker to say how many hours we don't work," Janet commented bitterly.

Malcolm took a more positive approach. "We'll go through our weekly timetable day-by-day. There are two of us working as house men on Surgical

Five. We work different shifts on alternate weeks. I suggest we calculate the hours we do in a fortnight and then halve it."

"Right," Janet said. "Each fortnight I'm on duty all day and night on one Saturday and one Sunday; that's 48 hours. The following weekend I'm off duty. Of the remaining ten days, which are weekdays, I work five shifts of twenty four hours and five shifts of eight hours. At least it's supposed to be eight hours but it is often ten by the time the ward is tidy, but for the record we had better stick at eight."

Malcolm worked out the maths on a scrap of paper.

"That comes to 208 hours on duty in a fortnight, equating to 104 hours a week," he announced.

"That's incredible," said Janet.

"It's diabolical," added Malcolm.

"When your weekend on duty starts at 9 am on Friday and finishes at 5 pm on Monday, it's not just incredible or diabolical, it's unsafe," Paul commented. "I wouldn't want to be treated by a doctor who was coming to the end of an 80-hour shift."

"I'm afraid it's all going to be a complete waste of time," Janet observed. "No, one is going to believe it."

"But those are the hours you work, or at least they're the hours you are on duty. That's precisely what your contract requires of you."

"Does that mean that if we win a new contract we'll get paid for over a hundred hours a week?"

"Don't count your chickens too soon," Paul warned. "There's a national pay freeze in place at the moment; don't assume that your extra hours will be paid at your standard rate. Consider, if they were, do you think that things would continue as they are?"

"What do you mean?"

"Imagine that you are the hospital's finance officer. You suddenly have to pay the housemen for 100 hours instead of 40. Their pay goes up by 150%. You know that they spend some of their time playing snooker, watching TV or sleeping; what are you going to do to reduce the bill?"

Malcolm thought for quite some time before replying. "I suppose I would have one or two doctors on duty through the night but have them working nonstop. In other words, I'd have them come on duty at eight in the evening and work them solidly until eight in the morning, then give them the next day off. They would work a night shift just as the nurses do."

Janet followed the argument through to its logical conclusion. "That would mean that through the night they wouldn't just look after the patients on their own ward but on several wards, perhaps five or six; and they would be called to treat patients that they had never seen before."

"That's right," Paul agreed, "and next morning the doctor who had worked through the night would go home to bed like any other night shift worker. They wouldn't be on their consultant's ward round next day having continuing care of their own patients. If that happened, life in hospital would be very different for doctors as well as for patients."

Chapter Twenty-Six

A couple of days later, Paul was hard at work on the female ward, when he was interrupted by the irritating shrill call of his 'bleep'. All the doctors regarded the pagers that they were obliged to carry as a damned nuisance. They recognised their importance of course, knew it was essential that they could be contacted in case of emergency, but all too often the calls they received were unnecessary. Sometimes though, as on this occasion, it might be the consultant wishing to contact his junior, another reason why the 'bleep' could not be ignored!

"Lambert," Sir William said, "I have a little job for you. I'm in the outpatient clinic and I've an interesting chap here who needs to be admitted as a matter of urgency. He has a gland in his axilla. I rather fear it's something sinister."

"And his name, Sir?"

Paul heard Sir William's rich chuckle at the other end of the phone. "He's Polish and his name is quite unpronounceable; but everybody seems to call him 'Tom'. Shall I send him up to the ward?"

"Just give me a couple of minutes Sir, to check that we have an available bed. All being well, I'll ring the clinic to confirm in a minute or two."

Later that morning, having found an empty bed, Paul walked down the ward to see the new admission and to arrange some preliminary investigations. It was easy to understand why he was known as 'Tom'. According to his records, his full name was Aleksander Tomasz Szczepanski. The notes recorded that he was 57 years of age and had been born in Zerkow in Poland. His appearance was quite shocking, indeed distressing. Slightly built and short of stature, he would have been quite nondescript but for the appearance of his head and neck. His features were grossly deformed and it was clear that at some stage in his life, he had been most terribly burned on the left side of his face and neck.

His mouth was twisted and pulled over to one side and his left eye distorted to a narrow slit by severe scar tissue. The tip of his nose was missing, resulting in one nostril being twice the size of the other. He wore a close fitting grey woollen cap that was pulled low over his forehead and a sweater with a high roll neck. Later, when he undressed to allow a full examination, Paul saw that the ugly, livid scarring extended over most of his neck and scalp. All that remained of his left ear was a blunt stub.

Hoping that his expression did not reveal the distress he felt at seeing such terrible injuries, Paul attempted a light-hearted comment.

"You have been in the wars, haven't you?"

"Yes, Doctor, I have. I'm afraid I'm not a pretty sight."

The words were spoken with a strong East European accent.

"Hello," Paul said, holding out his hand. "My name is Paul Lambert. I've come to ask you a few questions and to take a look at the lump that you have."

He grasped Paul's hand readily in a firm grip. "Hello Doctor. I am Aleksander Szczepanski, but it is perhaps easier if you call me 'Tom'. That is what most people do." He spoke slowly, quietly and with dignity, his phrases punctuated with short pauses.

"If that really is alright with you, I will call you 'Tom' as well."

"I think that would be for the best."

Paul enquired about the swelling that had developed in his armpit and Tom explained that he had noticed it about two months earlier. Initially, he had thought little of it, because it had not caused him any pain. Subsequently, because it increased in size, he sought the advice of his general practitioner, who referred him to Sir William's clinic. There was little else of note in his story. When Paul came to examine him, he experienced no difficulty in locating the gland. It was about the size of a large acorn, situated just beneath the skin and was ominously hard and craggy

*****

Sir William reviewed Tom on his next ward round a couple of days later. The results of the blood tests and x-rays that Paul had arranged were now available.

"I'm sorry to say that the tests we have done so far, have not told us exactly what the problem is," Sir William said. Then, choosing his words carefully, he continued, "I think the best way to get to the root of your trouble would be to winkle out that little lump of yours and have a look at it under the microscope. I'm sure that that will help us to understand what is going on."

"And when will that be done, Doctor?"

"Hopefully tomorrow. Then it will take a few days for the experts in the laboratory to analyse the specimen. I suggest that you stay with us until then," replied Sir William. He already had a fair idea of the diagnosis and knew that a decision on further management would be required at that stage.

"That will be alright with me, thank you Doctor. Is it a big operation?"

"Not at all, in fact we can do it under local anaesthetic."

Sir William led his team on to the next patient. It was Michael Sugden, the patient whom Mr Potts would not admit until the private beds issue was resolved. With the connivance of Sue in the waiting list office, Victoria and Paul had manoeuvred him into one of Sir William's beds because of the intolerable pain he was experiencing. They wondered if Sir William would notice - and if he did, would he object? The consultant asked his houseman to present the patient's details to him.

Malcolm began, slightly nervously. "This elderly gentleman was admitted yesterday, Sir. For the last four months he has.....

"Did you say elderly?" Sir William asked innocently.

"Yes, Sir," Malcolm replied.

"And precisely how old is this *'elderly'* gentleman, Chapman?"

Malcolm glanced at the patient's notes. "He's 62, Sir. In fact he'll be 63 in two months time."

"I see; just two years younger than I am then."

Smiling broadly, Sir William put his arm on Mr Sugden's shoulder. "Hello old timer," he said, jovially, "it's good to meet you."

"And you, old fellow," Mr Sugden responded in kind, fully aware that the consultant was only teasing.

Malcolm was mortified; he turned bright red. "I'm so s -sorry, Sir," he stuttered. "I truly didn't mean any offence."

"And none taken, young man, none taken," Sir William replied, his eyes twinkling. He turned to the rest of his team. "What you consider to be *'young'* or *'old'* depends entirely on where you're standing. But perhaps we can agree that 62 is late-middle age! Mind you children always want to be older than they really are, don't they? How often do you hear a child say *'I'm nearly seven'*, when they're really only six and a half? And the very elderly, people older than 63," he added, with a sideways glance at Malcolm, "are often proud of their advanced years. They're also prepared to add a bit on! You will often hear an octogenarian say *'I'll be 85 next birthday, you know!'* Anyway, we had better move on. Chapman you were telling me about Mr Sugden."

Malcolm told the story of the patient's pain and then described what he had found during the examination that he had performed. He concluded by stating that gall stones had been demonstrated on x-ray. When he had finished, Sir William looked puzzled. "I don't remember seeing those x-rays. Perhaps I am getting old after all. May I see the notes please?"

Realising that their deceit, well-intentioned though it was, was about to be discovered, Victoria thought it best to be confess what they had done.

"In truth, Sir William, Mr Sugden was seen in the clinic by Mr Potts. He really ought to be in one of Mr Potts' beds."

"Then why is he in one of my beds?" Sir William's tone was one of puzzlement rather than anger.

"Well Sir, he was in such a lot of pain, that it seemed harsh to leave him on the waiting list."

Without it being made explicit, Sir William realised what had happened. He grinned, "I see. So there's been a rather fortunate little mistake, one might call it serendipity."

"I suppose you could call it that Sir," Victoria replied cautiously.

"Well, I think we can gloss over it. I don't mind the occasional mistake if it helps one of our patients - but it had better not happen too often. And perhaps it would be best if we don't advertise what has happened to our colleagues."

He turned back to Mr Sugden. "It seems that you have been admitted under my care by mistake but now you're here, we might as well carry on and remove that troublesome gall bladder of yours. I can do it tomorrow if you are happy with that?"

"Your staff really have been very careless," Mr Sugden replied, tongue in cheek, "it's most remiss of them but it's seems to have worked out for the best. I'm most grateful. Tomorrow will suit me fine."

Back in the office at the end of the round, Sir William, a mug of tea in his hand, put Tom's chest x-ray on the viewing box.

"All Tom's bloods tests are normal. What can you see on his x-ray?" he asked Malcolm.

The houseman had not seen many chest x-rays before, so Sir William put a normal x-ray on an adjacent screen so that he could compare them. Malcolm quickly spotted the abnormality; an ominous looking shadow in the lung. In the question and answer session that followed, Sir William suggested that the most likely diagnosis was a cancer of the lung. He went on explain that if the gland in the armpit was shown to consist of cancer cells which had spread from the lung then regrettably, the disease would be beyond the reach of any form of treatment. The outlook for Tom would be extremely poor.

Sir William thanked his team for their support, as he always did at the end of his round. As he was leaving though, he commented to Paul, "You should ask Tom how he was so badly burned and how he came to live in the UK. A lot of Poles walked half way across Europe to come here, you know. I feel sure he will have an interesting tale to tell."

Paul didn't know but resolved to find out.

*****

Experienced surgeons such as Sir William and Mr Potts seemed not to mind whether their patients were awake or asleep whilst performing surgery. Even Victoria would happily chat whilst operating under local anaesthetic. Paul though, preferred his patients to be fully anaesthetised. If the patient was conscious, he worried that they might experience pain or perhaps move at an unfortunate moment whilst he was working. This was a concern shared by many patients. Often though, as with Tom's gland, the nature of the procedure did not justify a general anaesthetic. In such cases, Paul usually asked one of the nurses to sit and chat to the patient which allowed him to give his full attention to the surgery. Another way of distracting patients was to invite them to listen to music. From the surgeon's point of view, music with a soft beat and a gentle lyric was most suitable; heavy rock was to be avoided! One patient insisted on hearing Frank Sinatra singing Mac the Knife but Sir William decreed that this was unsuitable and instructed that the music be turned off!

Sir William asked Paul to remove Tom's gland. He had undertaken similar procedures several times before and didn't anticipate any particular problems. The operation would probably take less than thirty minutes to complete. Tom seemed quite relaxed as he lay on the table with his arm out at right angles, supported by a board. The skin of the armpit was shaved, washed with an antiseptic solution and then towelled. Paul injected local anaesthetic into the area and then waited for a couple of minutes for the anaesthetic to take effect before making an incision with the scalpel. He found no difficulty in locating the lymph node in the fatty layer immediately beneath the skin. Fortunately, it was not close to any important structures and after dividing the blood vessel that supplied it with oxygen, it slipped out easily.

Paul looked at the gland carefully then took a fresh blade and cut it across. Having seen cancerous glands previously, he immediately feared the worst. It looked sinister. If the pathologist subsequently confirmed that the gland contained cancer cells that had spread from the lung, then the condition would be incurable. For Tom, this would be a death sentence. Without a word, he handed it to the scrub nurse, who placed it into a jar filled with preservative, ready for it to be transported to the laboratory for analysis.

"All finished now," he said to Tom. "I hope that wasn't too painful for you."

"Just a little uncomfortable Doctor; not the worst pain I've had in my life," Tom replied with a wry smile.

"The result should be available in about three days," Paul said. "As you know, Sir William would like you to stay in hospital until then, if that's alright with you."

"That's fine," replied Tom. "I'm quite happy on the ward."

"What a lovely man," said the nurse who had been sitting chatting to him. "He was so polite and dignified."

"What did you talk about?" Paul asked.

"You were there, weren't you listening?"

Paul confessed that he had been completely unaware of their conversation, engrossed as he was performing the surgery.

"He was telling me about village life in Poland when he was a child. It sounded idyllic. I wonder why he left."

"Did he tell you how he came to be so badly burned?" Paul asked.

"No, he didn't, and I didn't like to ask."

Chapter Twenty-Seven

Paul pushed his chair back from the table and gave a contented sigh.

"Thanks Kate, that was a lovely meal," he said.

"Hear, hear, to that," echoed Victoria and Sam her fiancé, as they all moved to the settee and easy chairs that were drawn up around the fire. Sam was a doctor at the neighbouring Maternity Hospital.

Paul felt at peace with the world. Thanks to Mr Potts' decision to limit admissions to emergency cases and patients with cancer, it had been much quieter than usual on the wards. There had been time to chat with patients, getting to know them better and to allay some of their fears and anxieties. During the day, he'd even been able to spend a couple of hours in the library. Then he had come home to a good meal, a couple of bottles of beer and was now enjoying the rest of the evening relaxing with friends. He gazed across the room at his young wife. He blessed the day that he had met her and marvelled at his good fortune. They had only been married for a year but it had proved to be the best twelve months of his life.

On the eve of the wedding, he had experienced doubts, worried about the permanence of marriage and the commitment to spending a lifetime together, as many men surely do, but he now relished that prospect. He wondered what it was about her that he so loved. There was the physical attraction, of course, but there was so much more; her warmth, her kindness, her generosity. And why she loved him as she so obviously did, he couldn't imagine. She could have had any man in the world. Suddenly, she caught his eye and she smiled the soft smile that he loved so much; and there was a certain sparkle in her eye that promised further pleasures when their guests had left.

He awoke from his reverie with a start. "Sorry Victoria, that's my job," he said realising that she was handing round the coffee.

During the meal they had discussed the latest film releases and their holiday plans but the conversation then turned to medical matters as so often happens when doctors and nurses socialise together.

"It's been a real pleasure working in the hospital today," Paul commented. "It would be lovely if we were able to work at this pace all the time; it's so satisfying to be able to do every job properly instead of rushing around like headless chickens."

"And that would be great for the patients too, at least for those that we treated," Victoria said. "But what about the poor folk who didn't get seen today, those who are still suffering at home, still waiting for their operations? The consultants should be ashamed of themselves using patients as pawns to further their own ends. They should have taken action that didn't increase the suffering of the sick."

"Such as?" demanded Sam.

"Any manner of things," Victoria responded. "They could have stopped doing administrative work, stopped teaching or stopped providing medical reports for insurance purposes."

"Action which the government would simply have ignored," Sam retorted. "If the consultants want to prevent the closure of the private beds, the action they take must have teeth."

"Teeth that bite patients can't be right," Kate commented. "I agree with Victoria. Patients wait for months to come into hospital already. This action by the consultants only makes things worse. Many are unable to work which means hardship for their families; others are waiting to be admitted for investigations. Some will prove to have cancer which will be getting more advanced with every passing day. How can you justify that?"

"Fortunately, Sir William isn't taking any action at all," Victoria commented, "which is a great help. Twice now we've admitted one of Mr Potts' patients under Sir William's care and he hasn't objected. He really is a gentleman. A bit old-fashioned maybe, but give me Sir William to Mr Potts any day." She turned to Sam. "Are your consultants taking any action?"

"Not with the maternity patients. You can't really stop the clock with pregnancy can you?" Sam replied with a smile. "But they're on a 'go slow' with the gynaecological cases. They're only putting three or four cases on each operating list, when normally we would have twice that number."

"Then it's clear that your consultants are harming patients just as Mr Potts is," Kate argued. "I think it's disgraceful. Would you take industrial action, Sam, for better pay and shorter hours, if the BMA called for it? I've heard that there has even been talk of an all out strike by the junior doctors."

"I'd love to see that, wouldn't you?" Sam said grinning broadly. "Can you imagine the consultants putting up the drips, doing the night calls and dealing with the drunks in casualty? Actually it's unlikely that we will be asked to go on strike, more likely that we would simply work our basic 40 hour week, but not work the extra 40 hours that we now have to do for peanuts."

Kate smiled sadly. "But it will still harm patients won't it?"

"But what else can we do to make Barbara Castle see sense?" Sam snapped angrily. "Joe Public seems to think we get paid 'time and a third' for the hours we work beyond forty, but we don't. We get paid at 30% of our standard rate. You nurses wouldn't stand for that! When you do overtime, you get paid at your standard rate or get time off in lieu. And you took industrial action didn't you, in order to get your whopping big pay rise?"

Kate responded forcibly. "No, we did not! Our action was limited to demonstrations and rallies. We didn't do anything to harm patients. We won the day by arousing the public's sympathy and support; and that's what the doctors should do."

Paul was reluctant to allow the discussion between friends to become overheated and sought to defuse the situation.

"I actually believe Barbara Castle is sympathetic to our situation," he said, "but she's hamstrung by the national incomes policy. I agree though that we will need to take some action if things are to improve; I'm just not sure what that action should be."

Further discussion was interrupted by the ring of the telephone. Paul lifted the receiver. It was the hospital's switchboard operator who rather apologetically asked Paul if the name Dr Sakalo meant anything to him. Paul thought the name was vaguely familiar but for the moment, he couldn't place it.

"He says he wants to talk to the representative of the junior doctors. I wasn't sure that there was a representative as such but then I remembered that you sat on the consultants' committee."

"OK, put him through," said Paul.

The moment that Dr Sakalo came on the line and Paul heard the strong Australian accent, he remembered who his caller was. It was Dr Wasily Sakalo, who was making a name for himself as the strident leader of the junior doctors in the region. In recent weeks Paul had seen his name regularly in the political columns of the British Medical Journal, the weekly magazine published by the BMA.

Dr Sakalo came straight to the point. "Paul," he said, "I believe you're leading the fight in your hospital for better pay and a new contract for the junior doctors. We need to get some significant industrial action going in your area and I need your help to get it organised."

"Just a minute," Paul said quietly, "I happen to chair their meetings but I'm not their union representative. My role is simply to listen to their concerns and act as a link with the consultants and management."

"It's exactly the same thing," retorted Dr Sakalo. "It's no good pussy footing around. If we want to get a proper wage for our ridiculously long hours, we must show some backbone and demonstrate to this Mrs Castle and her government that we mean business. You need to call a meeting of your doctors. Get the doctors at the Middleton Hospital to come as well; I'm told they're in your group. I'll come and tell them exactly what action they need to take. There won't be any need for you to speak. I'm available on either Tuesday or Thursday next week, so arrange it for one of those days. Probably best to do it about 7.30 in the evening, in the doctors' mess."

Paul thought quickly. He didn't like the forthright attitude of his caller, nor did he appreciate being told what to do by an outsider, but he did recognise that his colleagues needed to discuss the political situation. There were rumours that in other hospitals junior doctors were threatening to reduce their hours and only treat emergencies, but Paul didn't know how prevalent that view was. The political situation had been much discussed of course, but there hadn't been any suggestion that they might take industrial action at the City General. Communication amongst junior doctors nationally was poor and there was much misinformation. Frankly, most were too busy working to get involved in politics. Paul realised that it could be useful if someone who was well informed on the state of negotiations with the Health Minister came and gave an update. However, he was not at all sure that this particular individual, who had already made several wild statements in the press, was the right person to do it.

"All right," he said cautiously, realising that at the meeting he would have to stand up to this forceful character, "we will invite you to come. I will contact you in a couple of days to let you know when it will be convenient and, of course, I will chair the meeting."

He made a mental resolution that he would ensure that the meeting was not dominated by one person and that everybody had a chance to express their view.

"That call was about work, wasn't it, Paul?" Kate said indignantly. "It's supposed to be your night off. Just because we live in the hospital grounds doesn't mean the switchboard can ring you every time there's a problem on the ward!"

Paul smiled at the fierce tone of her voice. His mother would have been equally protective towards him!

"I think it's sensible to have a meeting," Sam said, when Paul had explained the nature of the call. "If there's to be some form of industrial action we shall be in uncharted waters. We would be doing something that junior doctors have never done before. It will be wise for all of us to act as one."

"If that's to be the case, there won't be any action here," Victoria said forcefully "since nothing is going to persuade me to participate."

"It could leave individuals very exposed if some doctors restricted their hours whilst others worked as normal," Sam observed.

"A junior would certainly be putting his career on the line, if he took action against his consultant's wishes," Paul added. "What would Sir William think of me if he was doing everything in his power to help patients and I deliberately obstructed him? My career in surgery would be at an end."

"But the consultants could hardly object," Sam retorted. "They're taking action themselves at this very moment."

"Yes, but not all of them," Victoria pointed out. "Mr Potts couldn't object, he might even encourage it, but Sir William most certainly would."

"I will call a meeting," Paul said. "It will be useful to learn what's going on nationally and to let the doctors here discuss the situation but I'm not sure that Dr Sakalo is the best person to address us. From statements he's made to the press recently, it sounds as if he's hell bent on an all out strike! He was quoted in the Daily Mail recently saying that when the strike starts patients will die - and that when they do Barbara Castle will be to blame!"

Later, after their guests had left and whilst Kate and Paul were clearing the dinner table, Kate remarked that Paul had kept very quiet when the possibility of industrial action by the junior doctors had been discussed. She was worried. "You wouldn't participate in anything of that sort would you?" she asked.

There was a pause before Paul replied. "I'm not sure," he said. "I would prefer not to but it may be the only way."

"Surely you wouldn't?" Kate responded surprised and shocked. "You mean you'd turn your back on patients that needed your help?"

"I wouldn't want to Kate, I really wouldn't; but the present situation isn't in the patients' best interests either. And unless some pressure is brought to bear, nothing is going to change."

"But Paul, you're a caring doctor, how could you even think of such a thing?"

"It's not as simple as you might imagine Kate. Some short-term disruption might be justified if it brought long-term benefit. The present situation is intolerable. Remember what happened last weekend. Just after midnight on Sunday night, I was in theatre with an old boy whose cancer was blocking his bowel. I'd been on duty solidly since nine on the Friday morning. I was shattered. Truly, Kate, there was a part of me that wanted to find that his belly was so riddled with cancer that the right course of action was simply to close him up and get to bed! As it happened we were able to remove the tumour but it took 'til three am. Goodness knows how many mistakes I made in the clinic on Monday morning! That's happening in hospitals all over the country and the politicians just don't want to do anything about it."

"Well, I don't agree," Kate retorted. "I'd be horrified if you took your spite out on patients."

"Kate, I'm not saying I would and I'm not saying I wouldn't. I'm just suggesting that it's not as simply as you might imagine."

But Kate was not convinced and the dishes were washed and put away in silence.

Chapter Twenty-Eight

It was noticeable that Tom did not mix well with his fellow patients. Many of the men on the ward were confined to bed, but those who were ambulant usually chatted in small groups, watched television or sat and read together in the smoky haze of the rest room. Tom was rarely with them. Paul wondered whether his isolation resulted from his different nationality, his appallingly disfigured face or possibly from his own personality and reticence.

One day, as he walked down the ward, he overheard laughter.

"Did you ever see such an ugly mug?" asked one patient.

"He looks like a Polish gargoyle, if you ask me;" responded another, "I've seen prettier faces on the monkeys at the zoo."

Paul ignored the remarks but later reproached himself for not intervening, realising that Tom's decision to keep his own company may have resulted from such cruel comments. Thereafter, as a matter of principle, he made a point of chatting to Tom whenever he was passing. It was usually no more than a superficial conversation about the weather or the hospital food but he hoped that it made Tom feel that he had a friend on the ward.

Life on the ward was generally less hectic in the evening than it was during the day. This was the time that Paul used to enjoy most when it was his turn to be resident through the night. By ten or eleven o'clock, a stillness and quietness had descended on the ward and a sense of peace and calm prevailed. The main lights would be switched off leaving most of the ward in darkness. One of the night nurses would be sitting at a small table, in the centre of the ward, reading or writing under a single overhead light at the nurses' station. Most of the patients would be lying quietly or sleeping, though one or two might still be reading using the night light on the wall above their bed-head. After a day spent dashing to and fro, working against the clock, Paul found it soothing to arrive and survey the scene from the ward doors. At this hour, it was possible to take a leisurely stroll round the ward, checking on each patient in turn, without feeling rushed; having time for a chat with any patient who was awake or anxious.

It was at such a time, whilst Tom remained on the ward waiting for the laboratory report on his gland, that Paul recalled Sir William's remark about there being 'an interesting story about the burns'. He plucked up the courage to ask.

"It happened a long time ago...." Tom began and then paused.

Paul prompted him to say more. "It happened in the war in Poland?"

"No, no. It happened in England."

"You mean in the blitz, in London or Liverpool?"

"No, I was in the air force. I had a crash."

"You mean in the RAF?" Paul said surprised. He couldn't imagine how a Pole could come to fly with the RAF and felt somewhat ashamed of his ignorance. Slowly he persuaded Tom to tell the whole story.

"I was born in a small village near Zerkow. My father was the headmaster of the local school which my sister and I attended. She was two years younger than me. I left school when I was 15 and when old enough, joined the Polish Air Force. I was young and adventurous and probably a little foolish. I learned to fly and in 1936, joined a squadron flying fighter planes. Then in 1939, our whole world changed; Germany attacked Poland with overwhelming force."

He spoke slowly, quietly and as the theatre nurse had remarked, with great dignity. There were long pauses as he shared with Paul the events that had devastated his life; the memories still raw a quarter of a century later. Paul found himself staring at Tom's mouth as he told his story. One side was rigid and immobile with scar tissue, whilst the other side contorted into strange shapes as he sought to enunciate his words clearly. Paul forced himself to look into Tom's eyes for fear of being considered rude.

"It was a David versus Goliath contest," Tom continued, "Germany was far too strong. The attack took us completely by surprise, there was no warning and many of our planes were destroyed before they had time to leave the ground. Others, including my own, got into the air. We managed to shoot one or two enemy planes down but in reality we never stood a chance. In the end, a few of us managed to fly to Romania. I wanted to fight on but our planes were stolen by the Romanians."

"But how on earth did you get from Romania to England, with Germany in between?" Paul asked.

Tom's lips twisting into an awkward smile. "Very slowly," he replied. "I went through Yugoslavia, then into Italy and eventually reached France."

"And how long did the journey take?" Paul asked.

"Five or six months," Tom replied. "I walked a lot of the way. At one stage I stole a bicycle and cycled a bit and completed the journey by train. When I got to England, I thought I should be welcomed into the RAF with open arms. I had combat experience; I had already shot down a German bomber, but they didn't want me. Eventually, they saw sense and created a Polish Squadron." Again there was his crooked smile. "I was in 302 squadron flying Hurricanes. We fought alongside the RAF. We were young and reckless. I suppose we were all a bit crazy. We had success too. We shot down plenty of enemy aircraft. I did too, but one day my luck ran out and I crashed. I spent the next two years in and out of hospital."

One might imagine that he would speak of pride in his achievements, but the words were spoken with sadness. The events still lay heavy on his mind.

"You took part in the Battle of Britain then?"

"Yes, I did. That's when I had my accident."

"I confess that I didn't know that Polish airmen fought in the Battle of Britain." Paul admitted.

"I sometimes feel people here don't want to know about Poland's contribution to the defeat of Germany." There was now a hint of bitterness in his voice.

Paul waited, sensing that he wanted to say more. Then when he continued, his voice was no more than a whisper.

"Few people realise how badly Poland suffered. My homeland was invaded from two sides; by Germany from the West and by Russia from the East. The people suffered horrendously.

"You must have been about 24 at the time," Paul asked. "Were you married?"

Again, Tom paused and Paul wondered if his question had been too personal. But he continued. "Yes, I was, to Zofia. She and I came from the same town, Zerkow. Zofia was a teacher at my father's school. That's where we met. We married just before the war began, but I lost her. I was away in the air force when the Germans swept through. They captured her. They were picking up most of the educated people; teachers, lawyers, priests and doctors. I learned later that she had been taken away with others in a truck. They all simply disappeared as did thousands of others. I still don't know what happened to Zofia though I presume she must have been killed."

It was a horrendous story.

"You went looking for your wife?"

"Yes, yes, of course. But I had left Poland in 1939 and it wasn't possible to go back at the end of the war. When the war was over," he explained, "we Poles expected to be free to return home. After all, we had fought alongside the British from 1940 onwards but Poland was annexed by the Soviet Union. Mr Churchill and the Americans allowed Poland to be ruled by Stalin. It was many years before I was able to return in an attempt to find Zofia. I went back to Zerkow but learned very little; simply that she had been taken away along with my father and my sister. But nobody knew where they had gone, no messages were ever received and none of them ever returned. Presumably Zofia was killed along with many others. But how, or where or what happened to her I shall never know. I just pray that she did not suffer too much before she died."

"Did you and Zofia have any children?"

"No. We had only been married for six months when Poland was invaded. I had a letter from Zofia just before the war started. She said she had missed a monthly period and to this day I still wonder if perhaps....." His voice gave out and tears filled his eyes. Quietly Paul rose and pulled the screens around the bed. He gave Tom a few moments to recover.

"I'm sorry," Tom said. "It's been a long time since I spoke like this of those terrible days."

"And so you returned to England?"

"I thought about staying in Poland but there was no future for me there; my fellow Poles were second class citizens in their own country. So yes, I returned to England, but found that Poles were not welcome here either." Again there was bitterness in his voice. "It took me a long time to find a job. My appearance put people off of course, and there were British servicemen coming home who were also looking for jobs. I've been a night watchman ever since, on my own, and out of sight."

Paul could hear laughter coming from the day room where other patients were playing cards, despite the lateness of the hour.

"And apart here as well it seems."

"Maybe, but I've grown used to my own company."

"Look," Paul said, "I know there are only three playing; it would be far easier with four. Do you want to join them?"

"That would be nice," he replied.

"Well, come on then. Let me introduce you."

"No," he said firmly. "If they want me to join them, they will ask."

He clearly had his pride and was not prepared to beg. For the last thirty minutes or so, Paul had been asking him questions, not because it was necessary as part of Tom's medical history, but out of interest and for his own education. It struck him, and not for the first time, that medical staff ought to know much more of the background of their patients; not just those with interesting life stories but all of them, especially the elderly in nursing homes and residential accommodation. Doctors and nurses enquire about their patient's medical symptoms; maybe ask how many cigarettes they smoke or how much beer they drink, but they really know very little of the lives they have led in the past or to which they will return when discharged from hospital. Too often they were just known as Ben or Betty in bed No 11 or 12. How much better it would be, and how much more respect they might receive, if they wore a name badge saying *'Ben, retired teacher', 'Betty, retired telephonist', or 'Tom, Battle of Britain Fighter Pilot'.*

Tom had told his story quietly but now he looked Paul in the eye and spoke forcibly. "Are you married, Dr Lambert?"

Normally, Paul would have ducked such a question from a patient, preferring to keep his personal life private, but this man had opened his heart to him and deserved honesty in return.

"Yes, I am."

"Does your wife work in the hospital - one of the nurses perhaps?"

"Yes, she's one of the nurses; she's called Kate."

"On this ward?"

"No, she used to work on this ward. This is where she was when we first met but now she works on the female ward.

For a second, Tom put his hand on Paul's in a simple gesture of friendship.

"Well, Doctor Lambert, you make sure that you look after her and live for the present. You can never tell what the future might hold or when happiness may be snatched away from you."

His words, spoken with such feeling, struck a chord deep within Paul. When he and Kate had been courting, a silly misunderstanding had come between them. He had let her slip away and for over a year had lost contact with her. Paul realised how lucky he was to have found Kate and had resolved to take great care to make certain that such a thing never happened again. But as Tom's story illustrated, life could throw up nasty surprises that could upset the best laid plans.

A couple of days later, during a quiet moment on Paul's next night on duty, he went to have another chat with Tom, only to find that he wasn't by his bed. Nor was he in the group of patients who were chatting and playing cards to while away the long evening. He asked if they knew where he was.

He was answered by a bearded man with a strong Mancunian accent. "You mean the ugly Polak, Doc? No I don't know where he is, and I can't say I am particularly fussed."

Slightly shocked, Paul glanced to see what reaction his remarks had engendered in the rest of the group.

The only one who seemed to show any surprise commented. "He tends to keep to himself, Doctor. Sometimes, he leaves the ward and has a wander around the hospital. At other times, he sits and reads in the day room. You may find him there."

"Perhaps he would like a bit of company and enjoy a game of cards," Paul ventured.

The bearded man replied. "He wouldn't be welcome here. We don't owe the Poles anything. They're an ungrateful lot."

Paul asked him to explain.

"Well Doc, I served in the war. Served for four years, I did. There wouldn't have been a war but for Poland. The Germans rolled them over in a couple of weeks. They just turned and ran. And when it was all over, what did they do?

They poured into our country looking for sympathy and taking jobs away from true Brits."

Paul knew that it was not appropriate for him as a doctor to have a dispute with his patients or indeed to educate them. He was also conscious that the Polish war experience had been a closed book to him until Tom had so recently opened his eyes but he didn't feel able to allow such a remark to pass by unchallenged.

"I don't think your facts are completely correct," he suggested.

"Maybe they are, maybe they aren't, but I don't want to see his ugly face here. It would stop me concentrating on my cards!"

"Where did you serve in the war?" Paul asked pointedly, wondering if it was appropriate to reveal how Tom came by his appalling injuries.

"I was in the Royal Army Catering Corp," he replied. "I wanted to see active service but failed the medical. I've got flat feet."

It was as well that Paul's pager sounded at that moment, for had he not been required to return to the office to answer it, he might well have said something that he would have regretted!

Chapter Twenty-Nine

It was evident from the moment that Dr Sakalo addressed the meeting, that he was hell bent on industrial action. He was loud, brash and rapidly itemized a list of injustices that juniors had suffered over the years.

"Eight years ago," he roared, "junior doctors were paid no overtime payments at all, and then what were we offered?" he asked sarcastically. "A tiny amount of extra money for any doctor who worked more than 80 hours a week! Now you only have to work 40 hours before you get overtime. But how much do they paid you? Time and a half? Double time at weekends?" His voice rose to a crescendo. "No, they give you 30% of your base rate for working in the hospital and just 10% for being 'on call' at home! Not time and 30%, just 30% of the standard rate for slaving away through the night on the wards, in casualty and in theatre.

I'm part of the group that have been negotiating a better deal for junior hospital doctors and I can tell you that only militant action will win us a fair wage for the ridiculously long hours we work. Did you know that under the new arrangements that Castle is offering, many of us will actually be worse off than we are at present? She says there isn't any extra money because of their precious pay policy. So she expects us to accept a deal in which the money available will simply be a redistribution of the existing pot. Some of us will get a little more but Castle is actually brazen enough to admit that a third of us will actually lose money! If it weren't so outrageous, it would be funny. They don't value us. They take us for granted. They think they can treat us like slaves, pretending that they're training us and holding out the carrot that maybe one or two of us will one day become consultants. It's utterly preposterous and it's got to stop; and the only way to stop it, is for all of us to unite and take industrial action.

At long last, we've got some momentum going. Thanks to the action that some doctors are taking, we've finally got the ear of Mrs Castle. We're forcing her to listen. We now have the chance to do something about it. But we mustn't let this opportunity slip by. Castle is banking on the whole thing fizzling out. We must not let that happen. You mustn't let it happen. The action must be increased. At present, some doctors are working only their standard 40 hours. It's proving to be a very effective ploy. The disruption in some hospitals has been huge. It's meant that only emergency cases are being seen. The next step is to adopt that policy in all hospitals, including this one, and if that fails we'll shut down some hospitals altogether.

"What about the man with his heart attack or the lad with appendicitis?" Victoria asked from the floor.

"If any patient comes to harm, the responsibility will rest firmly on Castle's shoulders," Dr Sakalo declared.

Paul intervened. "Dr Sakalo. Before there is any talk of industrial action, the doctors here need to be informed of the negotiations that are taking place with the Secretary of State. It wouldn't be justifiable to take action, if an agreement is in the offing."

Dr Sakalo took the hint. "As you know, in January of this year, our National representatives met Castle in London," he said. The continuing use of the surname without a forename or title grated with Paul but he knew better than to comment.

Dr Sakalo continued. "She agreed verbally that we should have a contract based on a 40 hour working week. Then she conveniently forgot to tell our employers and they are working on the assumption that the standard week is 44 hours. It seems that clever Castle forgot to put the '40 hours' in writing! Our employers are calling it *'free qualifying time'*, in other words we're expected to work those four hours for nothing.

To make matters worse, our representatives foolishly agreed with Castle that we would provide free cover in *'emergency and unforeseen situations'*, but we're being taken for a ride. We're being cheated. The authorities have adopted a calculated policy of not filling vacancies. By doing so, they are deliberately creating *'emergency situations'* and expecting us to work unpaid. Well, it's got to stop. The time has come for militant action. The plan is to get every doctor to restrict work to a basic 40 hour week. Dealing with emergency cases will use up all of those hours, so it means we'll do no routine work at all. No outpatient clinics, no elective surgery, no routine ward rounds. The action will start.....'"

Once more, Dr Sakalo was in his stride and would have gone on, but Paul decided it was time to hear the views of his colleagues. He intervened and addressed the assembled doctors himself.

"I don't want this to become a one man show," he said rather pointedly. "It's important that we have an opportunity to discuss this matter amongst ourselves, so please can we have comments and questions from the floor."

When opening the subject for debate, Paul had little idea how his colleagues would react. They all grumbled, of course, about the low pay and the chronic tiredness that resulted from long hours; but would they consider taking action which jeopardised patient care? One of the medical house officers spoke first. He spoke quietly but with authority. "My brother," he said," is a doctor in London. He has been involved in meetings with Mrs Castle and her officials. His account of those meetings is at variance with what we have heard tonight. He states, indeed he is quite certain, that Mrs Castle is extremely sympathetic to our cause. She agrees that the hours that we work are quite intolerable and she is genuinely on our side. The difficulty is....."

But Dr Sakalo was already on his feet interrupting. "Castle is a political professional, an expert negotiator. By comparison, the junior doctors representing us are rank amateurs. They may be good doctors but what experience do they have of industrial negotiation? They are being completely deceived. They....."

The houseman had remained standing. He looked his opponent in the eye and held up one hand. "Thank you," he said icily. "I did not interrupt you when you were speaking and I expect you to extend the same courtesy to me. My brother is no fool. He is quite certain that although Mrs Castle feels great antagonism towards the consultants, we have her sympathy. The sticking point is the national policy for pay restraint. The government has an agreement with the TUC and can't afford to be seen to be making any exceptions. If they allow an exception in our case, it will be impossible to deny a pay rise to others."

There was an immediate response from one of the other housemen. "That's all very well," he argued, "but no one else works the hours that we do. NUPE led the hospital porters and kitchen staff into industrial action three or four years ago and they only work a 40 hour week. And they get a proper overtime rate as well. When I'm working my eightieth hour as a doctor, I'm paid at an hourly rate that amounts to only a quarter of a porter's overtime wage. Remember too that the nurses got a mammoth pay rise last year. I agree with Dr Sakalo, the only way forward is to take industrial action. We need to show them that we mean business."

Other competing views were expressed. "But if we restrict our hours of work, perhaps only working for 40 hours a week or only treating emergencies, patients are bound to suffer. What about the old granny struggling at home with a painful hip? She's going to have to wait much longer for her surgery. And what about those patients referred by their family doctors to the clinic who actually turn out to have cancers? Do we really want that on our conscience?"

The counter view was immediately expressed. "And when I'm operating on a Sunday night, fixing your little old granny's broken hip, totally exhausted because I've been on duty nonstop for 60 hours, is that in her best interests?"

Then Malcolm raised a different concern. "My boss," he said, meaning Sir William "is very old-fashioned, he's a traditionalist. He's fiercely critical of his consultant colleagues who are taking action at the moment. He keeps telling me how lucky I am to get paid at all! He's hardly likely to give me a good reference, if I go on strike."

But another junior immediately responded. "But the consultants are showing us the way. Some of them have only been seeing emergencies for several months in pursuit of their right to do private practice. It doesn't seem to worry them."

"No, it doesn't, but they're not the consultants that I will have to approach for a reference, are they? I'm only working in the hospital for another couple of months and then I'm going into general practice. There's no way that I am going to blot my copybook."

One doctor, a trainee surgeon, argued he needed to be on duty for long periods to obtain the practical experience required before he could be considered for a consultant post. "I have technical skills to acquire; I can only get them if I work long hours. If my hours were cut by half, my training would take twice as long. I'd certainly like to be paid more, but I don't want my hours cut."

Then Malcolm raised a different issue.

"The real question," he said, "is whether we wish to belong to a profession or to a trade. Everyone is talking about a standard week then overtime payments. We might as well be factory workers or labourers! The real issue is not the level of remuneration for 'overtime' work; it's whether we want to have a professional contract for the care we give to our patients or whether we wish to become hourly paid workers."

This comment though fell on deaf ears; remuneration continued to dominate the discussion. Several were angry at Dr Sakalo for his 'Blame Castle if patients die' statement to the press. Many felt that they had the support of the public and that it would be premature to take any form of industrial action whilst negotiations were ongoing.

And so it went on, the arguments raging to and fro. Then Victoria spoke. "We've argued about this at great length but I've only heard one mention of the effect that industrial action will have on our patients. We're doctors for heaven's sake, professional people who studied medicine because we want to help our fellow man. What about the Geneva Convention, 'The health of my patients will be my first consideration'? What about the Hippocratic oath 'First do no harm'? Personally, I refuse to take any action that increases suffering. If others wish to take a different line, so be it, but whatever happens, individual doctors must be left to make their own decision."

Paul felt that all the differing views in the room had been expressed and thought that this was a suitable sentiment on which to close the meeting.

"As you can see," he said, "there are as many different opinions as there are people in this room. However, within the next two weeks a ballot of all junior hospital doctors in the country is to be held. Hopefully that will clarify matters. It's not clear at this stage, precisely what the question or questions on the ballot paper will be, but I'm sure we will be asked whether we are prepared to take industrial action. Each and every one of us must answer as they see fit but, as Victoria has suggested, even if the ballot shows a majority in favour of industrial action, no one must be forced to participate. We're not members of a union; we must be free to decide as individuals whether to work normally or to limit our work in some way."

He turned to the guest speaker. "Is there anything you wish to say before I close the meeting?"

Dr Sakalo needed no second invitation. "Be sure to vote for industrial action; and when the ballot shows an overwhelming majority in favour, as it will, I expect all of you to participate. If we want to improve our working conditions, we're going to have to fight for it."

Chapter Thirty

As instructed by the secretary, Paul knocked on the office door. "Come in," a voice immediately replied, "it's not locked."

"Good morning, Mr Harrison," Paul began.

As he entered, he glanced around the office of the hospital's most senior manager, not knowing quite what to expect. Rumour had it that the managers looked after themselves in style, with modern comfortable furnishings and expensive fittings, but this office, although large, was not dissimilar to many others that Paul had seen in the hospital. The walls were plaster board, painted off-white, though largely covered with a collage of lists, charts and timetables, as well as a selection of children's paintings and drawings. There was a framed photograph on the desk of two youngsters, a boy and a girl, both probably still at primary school, presumably the artists responsible for the pictures.

Paul gauged the senior manager to be in his late-thirties or early-forties, somewhat younger than he had expected. He was casually dressed in corduroy trousers and a checked shirt; his jacket thrown over the back of his chair. Many would consider him good-looking with his strong, square face and prominent jaw, crowned by a mop of unruly light brown hair. He looked weary though, with deep furrows on his forehead and the shadows under his eyes suggested sleepless nights. Not altogether surprising, Paul thought, given the unrest amongst the staff and the backlog of cases that was building up for both inpatient and outpatient treatment, as a result of the sanctions being taken by the consultants.

"You must be Mr Lambert," Mr Harrison said. "I was told you wanted to see me."

"That's right," Paul said, "for my sins, I represent the junior doctors. It means that they have elected me to speak on their behalf. I need to talk to you about the discontent they feel with their current contracts."

"I trust this isn't going to be more bad news," Mr Harrison chipped in. "Doctors are supposed to be members of a caring profession and at the moment, nothing could be further from the truth."

Paul decided to ignore the interruption. "A Dr Sakalo came to speak with the junior doctors a couple of nights ago; he's a rather forthright Australian. You may have heard of him; he's been in the news recently being highly critical of Mrs Castle. He was trying to persuade the doctors here to take industrial action in support of their claim for better pay."

"And what did they decide?" Mr Harrison asked, in a resigned voice.

"There was no consensus. Many didn't like his bossy, belligerent attitude. He virtually demanded that we should all restrict ourselves to a forty hour week. It was a long and stormy meeting and many different views were expressed. In the end, it was agreed that any decision about industrial action should be left to individual doctors but it seems likely that some will restrict their work load, perhaps by not undertaking elective work."

"That's all I need. Many consultants are already doing exactly that. So what effect is that likely to have, do you think?"

"I'm afraid it's very difficult to say. The effect on the medical wards will probably be negligible since all the juniors have agreed that they won't do anything that affects emergencies and, of course, at least ninety percent of medical admissions come though casualty. I suspect that the effect on surgical wards will be greater. It will all depend on the number of doctors who feel strongly enough about their workload to be involved. But if a doctor who has been working an eighty hour week only works for forty hours, the effect could be considerable."

"Everyone knows that the so called eighty hour week is a myth; that it doesn't really happen!" Mr Harrison declared.

The manager's words were said scornfully and with emphasis. They irritated Paul. He knew exactly how many hours they put in, how hard they worked and he saw how chronic tiredness sapped their morale. He wasn't prepared to let the comment pass.

"You're mistaken," he replied coldly. "Many juniors do work eighty hours; the housemen on our unit average over one hundred hours a week."

"That's utter nonsense. I know for a fact that the eighty hours is a falsification designed purely to elicit sympathy from the public."

"May I ask how you can be so sure?" Paul asked, holding back his anger with some difficulty.

"I know because managers have analysed the overtime claims of all the doctors in the region for the last six months. One or two may work eighty hours but the vast majority don't. The average works out at little over fifty hours."

"And you honestly believe that?"

"Yes, I do."

"In that case, you have been grossly misinformed and you're completely out of touch with what goes on in your own hospital," Paul declared furiously.

"Now you listen to me, Mr Lambert. The analysis has been done. You may want to go on strike, it may be you plan to cause chaos in the hospital and put patients' lives at risk but that doesn't justify you coming in here and telling me that black is white."

Paul's anger boiled over. "No, you listen," he shouted. "Let me tell you two reasons why your analysis is not worth the paper its written on. Firstly, many consultants refuse to sign the overtime forms submitted to them. Mr Potts won't for example. He believes that doctors should have a professional contract and not become hourly workers. Secondly, many junior doctors dare not even ask their consultant to sign because they know their consultant doesn't agree with overtime payments. No-one is prepared to ask Sir William to sign a form because he keeps reminding us that when he was a houseman, the post was honorary. He wasn't paid at all. In each case, your records will show that the junior doctor works forty hours, when in some cases they are working over a hundred."

"Nobody in this hospital works over a hundred hours a week. Now you're being ridiculous!"

"No, they don't 'work' for a hundred hours but many, at least twenty, are 'on duty' for that length of time each week. And when it's their emergency weekend, they are 'on call' continuously for eighty hours, from Friday morning 'til Monday evening. Frankly, that's dangerous for the doctor and the patient."

"I simply don't believe that. It's a blatant lie."

"Right," said Paul, "if you don't believe me, go to your personnel department and look at the contract of any of the housemen. You will see that in every fortnight they are 'on call' for 208 hours, that's 104 hours a week. And if you still don't believe me, I suggest that you shadow one of them for a day or two – that would open your eyes."

Paul was furious that the senior manager was so ignorant of the workload of the staff he employed. It was particularly galling because only once had he ever seen Mr Harrison in the hospital after six in the evening, which was at the consultant's meeting."

Paul realised that he had been shouting. "Look, I'm sorry," he said, "I didn't mean to raise my voice but I'm astounded that you don't know how hard the juniors work."

"Apology accepted," replied Mr Harrison coldly. "Since you are so adamant, I will check their contracts but before you take any action you need to stop and think of the damage you're going to do to the reputation of the hospital and to the patients you are paid to care for."

"Personally, I'm far from certain that industrial action involving patients is the right thing to do but I'm not here to speak for myself; I'm here as a messenger. You needed to be informed of the situation so that you can make whatever arrangements you feel to be appropriate. Now if you'll excuse me, I have some jobs on the ward to attend to."

Paul left feeling ashamed that he had lost his temper but considered it was justified, given the manager's ignorance.

Paul never discovered whether Mr Harrison did or did not look at the details of the housemen's contract or whether he bowed to the inevitable when the result of the junior doctors' ballot showed that 60% were prepared to take industrial action; but ten days later, he circulated a carefully worded notice to the effect that all elective admissions were cancelled forthwith. Quietly, Paul heaved a sigh of relief that it was no longer necessary for him to make his own decision on the matter.

Chapter Thirty-One

As Christmas 1975 approached, there was a distinct lack of festive joy at the Treasury. Denis Healey, the Chancellor, was becoming increasingly alarmed at the burgeoning national debt and after a long and frank discussion with Prime Minister Harold Wilson, he decided that there was no alternative but to increase the squeeze on government expenditure. At a distinctly unseasonal meeting of the Cabinet, Denis informed his ministerial colleagues that he would be reviewing each of their departmental budgets in turn. No longer was he asking them to hold spending at current levels, he was expecting them to make savings.

"There will be no exceptions," he warned. "Everyone will be required to make a contribution."

Barbara Castle was alarmed when she heard the news. The negotiations with both the consultants and the junior doctors were at a delicate stage and she needed all the financial lubrication she could get. She had no sympathy whatsoever for the consultants, she would fight them to the bitter end. Their prime objective was to change the government's policy on pay beds and she would not allow that to happen. But she felt obliged to do something for the juniors. Their case for a better deal was unanswerable.

Denis then outlined the cuts that he expected from each minister. Barbara was quick to claim that health was a special case.

"I'm sorry to demand these savings, Barbara," Denis replied, "but cuts are required across the board. We can't make any exceptions. I want you to make an annual saving of 100 million pounds."

"That's quite impossible, completely out of the question. A cut of that level would seriously affect front line services."

Most of her cabinet colleagues were resigned to the inevitable but Barbara fought back vigorously.

"You have to look behind the figures," she argued. "You have to consider the effect on services. I can offer some savings from the social services budget but none from the health budget."

"We're not just picking on you, Barbara," Denis commented. "We can't make exceptions. All departments are required to make cuts."

There were murmurs of "Hear, hear," from ministers who feared that Barbara's feisty manner might enable her to escape the harsh medicine that they were being forced to swallow. Barbara noted the disapproval of her colleagues with apprehension. Somehow or other she needed them back on board. If she became isolated her cause was lost.

Michael Foot intervened. "Barbara my heart agrees with you. I hate to see any reduction in our welfare programme but the country simply hasn't the money to continue the current level of spending."

"Well, let me explain what a cut of that magnitude would mean," Barbara said, looking round the table at each of her colleagues in turn. She had done her homework and began to itemize the effect such a draconian reduction in the health budget would have in each of their constituencies.

"For a start, it would mean the cancellation of the hospital building programme. That would, of course, include the new hospital planned in Leeds." She looked meaningfully at Denis whose constituency was Leeds East. "There would also be nursing staff redundancies; surely the number of people unemployed is already unacceptably high."

Harold Wilson intervened. He recognised that nurses had a special place in the affection of the public and that a cut in their numbers would not only be hugely unpopular but would undermine the goodwill that had accrued from their recent pay rise.

"Barbara, I'm certain that in a department as large as yours, there must be some slack. Perhaps the number of civil servants or managers in administrative posts could be cut instead."

"That certainly would be possible," Barbara agreed, "but that will not produce the savings you suggest."

The argument raged to and fro, at times becoming acrimonious, but in the end, when the Prime Minister closed the discussion, Barbara was forced to give up 42 million pounds instead of the 100 million Denis had initially demanded. Her colleagues insisted that she had got off lightly but she was bitterly disappointed. The decision added significantly to her problems. Though relieved that no clinical jobs would be lost, as a hard-line socialist her ambition was to expand the scope of the NHS, not to curtail it; and she didn't see how she could settle her bitter dispute with the consultants if there was no money to act as a sweetener.

*****

After the meeting, Harold Wilson retired to his private office. The morning's papers were waiting for him. He spread them out on his desk and was alarmed to find that, for the third time in a week, the 'work to rule' in the Health Service and the effect it was having on patient care, was headline news. Inevitably, the Daily Mail and Daily Telegraph blamed the Labour Government for the impasse with the consultants, and both carried heart rending stories of patients inconvenienced and imperilled by their industrial action. Emmwood, the cartoonist in The Mail, showed Barbara Castle as a wizened old harridan celebrating the death of the NHS. The report in The Times was more balanced, chiding the consultants for using patients as pawns in their fight to protect the pay beds but Mrs Castle did not escape criticism for her stubbornness, inflexibility and her uncompromising pursuit of socialist ideology.

Harold Wilson knew that whilst all his ministers agreed that a speedy settlement was urgently required, there was no consensus on the way to resolve the issue. The NHS was a proud Labour achievement; perhaps the most significant social advance there had been since the war. It should be our greatest strength, the PM thought, a vote winner, yet it was in chaos even though the Labour Party was in government.

How the hell can this dispute be settled, he asked himself. Barbara was certainly correct when she declared that had the financial situation been different, the consultants might have been 'bought off', given a pay rise to compensate them for the loss of private practice, but the nation's finances didn't allow that. One alternative would be to let Barbara have the extra money she needed, steal it from other departments but if he did that the pay policy would be in tatters and the entire Cabinet would be at his throat. His days as prime minister would certainly be numbered.

Another possibility was to let the consultants have their way and allow the pay beds to remain, at least until the economic situation improved but that meant back pedalling on a manifesto commitment and welshing on the pledge given in the Queen's Speech. If he went down that road, Barbara would certainly resign which would upset the left wing of the party. And the unions, especially the health unions, would be furious. Disruption by the consultants would be replaced by disruption by NUPE and CoHSE's ancillary workers.

Neither alternative was acceptable. He had to find a third way. For ten minutes, he sat at his desk, puffing thoughtfully on his pipe, wondering how best to proceed. Then he reached for the phone.

Chapter Thirty-Two

Three days later, the pathology report from the gland removed from Tom's armpit became available. Paul read it apprehensively:

Name: Aleksander Szczepanski.

Dob: 18-10-16   Hosp no: 37846

Consultant: Sir WW

Ward: S5M

Clinical information: Lymph gland from L. axilla   No other details given!

Macroscopic appearance: The specimen comprises a previously bisected lymph gland 2cms in diameter. The cut surface has an irregular grey appearance.

Microscopic appearance: The lymphoid tissue is almost entirely replaced by malignant cells showing abnormally large and irregular nuclei and multiple mitoses.

Histological diagnosis: Lymph gland infiltrated by undifferentiated cancer cells, compatible with secondary spread from the lung. It would have been helpful if fuller clinical information had been supplied.

Signed

Dr G Farmer, Consultant Pathologist.

Paul groaned. It was exactly what had been expected but it was still sad to have the diagnosis confirmed. Had the tumour been confined to the lung, then surgical removal might have offered the chance of a cure, albeit a small one but the presence of cancer cells in the armpit, indicated that the growth had spread far beyond the reach of any treatment. Regrettably, Tom had only a few months to live.

Paul also knew that the next time Sir William was on the ward, he would be taken quietly on one side and offered a word of advice about supplying the pathology department with appropriate information - and he wasn't mistaken!

"If we are to get the best from the laboratory," Sir William began, "we must give them all the help we can. It's the same when you are requesting x-rays; the more clinical information you supply, the more accurate will be the diagnosis."

Paul knew there was no excuse, he had heard his boss give this advice to his juniors often enough. All he could do was to apologise. At least, he consoled himself, the reprimand had been constructive and delivered in private. Mr Potts would have torn a strip off him in public.

Alone with Sir William, Paul took the opportunity to seek advice on another issue which had long troubled him. Breaking bad news to a patient was one of the worst parts of a doctor's job and no matter how many times Paul had been required to do it, he dreaded it.

"Sir," he began, "as a student at medical school, I didn't receive any training on how to tell a patient that their condition was incurable; that they were going to die. Obviously someone has to tell Tom and I really don't know the best way to go about it."

Sir William put a hand on Paul's shoulder. "I agree it isn't an easy task but it's one we doctors have to face up to. Shall we go and have a word with Tom now? You have a chat with him and I'll just sit and listen."

Together they walked to Tom's bed. As usual he was on his own, reading a newspaper. He seemed pleased to see them.

"Oh, Doctors, I'm glad you've come. I seem to have developed another lump and wondered if you would take a look at it for me."

"It's a bit public here," Sir William said. "There's an empty side room at the end of the ward. We'll go there and I'm sure that Mr Lambert will have a look at it for you."

When the door was closed, Tom took off his pyjama top. He pointed to a nodule which was about the size of a small pea on the front of his chest. It was pink and firm. Adjacent to it were two smaller nodules that he had not noticed.

"Does it hurt?" Paul asked.

"No. Not at all."

"And you think it's new?"

"Yes, I'm fairly sure of it. I have a shower each day. I think I should have noticed it, had it been there before."

Paul's examination of Tom's trunk revealed several similar nodules on his back. The appearances were classical. There was little doubt that these were also deposits of tumour. As well as the involvement of the gland in the armpit, the lung cancer had now spread to the skin. It was clearly rampant and of a very aggressive type.

"What do you think it is?" asked Tom.

"I rather suspect it's connected to the gland in your armpit," Paul replied.

"Does that mean it will need to be removed," asked Tom.

"No, I don't think that will be necessary," Paul replied, aware that since the diagnosis was already known, there was little point in removing one of these skin nodules for analysis. Let me try and explain what's going on. We have the results of the gland sample now."

A look of concern crossed Tom's face but he said nothing as he buttoned up his pyjama jacket. Paul, aware that Tom had coped with terrible tragedies in his life, thought that he would appreciate an honest and direct approach.

"I'm afraid the news that we have from the laboratory is not good." Paul paused, watching Tom closely, but his expression was unchanged. He ploughed on.

"When you first came into hospital you had a chest x-ray. I confess that we didn't tell you at the time, but that showed a problem; there was a shadow on your lung. We thought there might be a connection between the shadow and the lump in your armpit and unfortunately that has proved to be correct. I'm afraid it means that you have cancer; it started in your lung and some of the cancer cells have now spread to the armpit. The little nodule that has just appeared on your skin is probably part of the same problem."

There was a long silence while he digested this news.

"That's not good, is it Doctor?"

"No, Tom, I'm afraid it's not."

"But I don't have a problem with my chest, just a bit of a cough. Perhaps it has been a bit worse recently, but I just put that down to the cigarettes."

Bloody cigarettes, Paul thought; if people only realised how dangerous they were! Tom had smoked when he was in the RAF where cigarettes were cheap and readily available. He had continued to smoke ever since. That presumably was the cause of the problem. They were seeing far too many men with lung cancer, men who got hooked on cigarettes whilst in the forces, without knowing what harm they did, or how addictive they were.

"A cancer in the lung does often present with breathing problems, a cough, or some blood in the phlegm, but it's by no means unusual for it only to come to light when it has spread, in your case Tom, to the gland under your arm."

Tom remained calm and in control while Paul confessed, as gently as he could, that there was no treatment which could halt the process. For a time, Tom and the tumour would live side by side but in the end it was to be expected that the cancer would win. When he had finished he asked if Tom had any questions.

Quietly, he replied, "Doctor, you've given me a lot to consider. Perhaps we can have another chat in a day or two, when I've had a chance to think."

As they left the side ward, Sir William said, "Lambert, you show Tom back to his bed then come and join me in my room."

Sir William's room was a cosy affair; there was a 'lived in' feel to it. It had a couple of easy chairs and some personal photographs on the desk. On the walls were the group photos of all the doctors Sir William had helped to train.

"How did you feel that went, Lambert?" he asked when Paul joined him.

"Well enough," Paul replied, "but I always feel so terribly inadequate. I desperately feel the need to help, yet there is nothing I can do."

"Anyone who's human," Sir William said, "feels exactly the same. We all find it difficult to have an honest conversation with patients who are dying, although I suspect that nurses may be better in this respect than doctors. But it's wrong to think that there's nothing you can do to help. Just being there helps, supporting them and alleviating their symptoms also helps."

"I'm glad Tom didn't ask how long he had to live," Paul commented. "I know how rapidly his tumour is spreading; those skin nodules weren't there when he came in a week ago. I guess he'll be gone in a matter of weeks but I wouldn't have liked to tell him that."

"Few doctors are totally honest when asked that awful question," Sir William observed. "But I'm afraid that if the question is asked, it ought to be answered honestly. How can we address a patient's anxieties if we don't know what they are? Too often on a ward round the exchange between the medical staff and the patient is superficial and inconsequential. A doctor may open a conversation with a terminally ill patient by saying *'You're looking a bit better today.'*

'Thank you, Doctor, but I can't sleep at night and I'm troubled with a nasty pain in my side.'

It's tempting for the doctor to sidestep the real issue by commenting, *'Don't you worry. We'll soon sort that out with a sleeping tablet and a painkiller. Can you see to that Sister please?'* Then the doctor may move to the next bed, leaving the patient and their unspoken questions and anxieties, unanswered.

It's not just doctors who shy away from honest exchanges," Sir William continued, "patients' relatives do as well and that's something which they may subsequently regret. Too often, things remain unsaid, small differences are left unresolved, which may result in great anguish for those left behind. After their loved one has died, there is endless time to agonise over words left unspoken and small grievances left unsettled, only to realise that it is too late. The moment has gone and they are left deeply regretting that they didn't take the opportunity to resolve their differences whilst they had the chance."

Chapter Thirty-Three

Barbara Castle was furious; she was bursting with rage and indignation. The Prime Minister, alarmed at the damage being done to his party's reputation as guardians of the NHS, had gone behind her back and appointed Lord Goodman to take over the negotiations on pay beds with the BMA. He hadn't even had the decency to inform her of his intention!

The civil servants in her department were not wholly surprised. The negotiations had stalled, both parties held entrenched positions, the consultants' 'work to contract' was increasing waiting lists and the press were blaming Barbara's intransigence. To add to her distress, when she made further inquiries, she discovered that Lord Goodman had already arranged to meet the doctor's leaders! It was the greatest snub that she had experienced in her entire political career and she was deeply hurt. Damn it; wasn't she was fighting to uphold socialist principles? Wasn't she was battling to defend government policy against those who would undermine it? But the implications were clear. The Prime Minister was prepared to meet the consultants halfway and in doing so sacrifice the values of the Labour Party. It was also glaringly obvious to her, that her position in the cabinet was threatened.

The significance of the Prime Minister's action was equally clear to Dr Stevenson, the BMA's leader and he was delighted. Harold Wilson had obviously decided that the dispute needed to be settled quickly and was prepared to make significant concessions. The balance of power had swung significantly in his favour. It gave him the confidence and determination to push hard for a favourable deal.

Lord Goodman, a lawyer and personal friend of the Prime Minister, embarked on some shuttle diplomacy. Working behind the scenes, he saw each side privately in turn and avoided all contact with the media. Dr Stevenson emphasised to him that losing the revenue that accrued from pay beds would be an additional expense at a time when the country was already in economic difficulties. He also stressed that to require doctors to work exclusively for the NHS was inequitable since no such limitation was imposed on nurses, teachers or others employed by the state and that if the government were to become a monopoly employer, many doctors would simply pack their bags and work overseas. He left Lord Goodman in no doubt that the consultants would settle for nothing less than the right to continue to treat private patients.

Having spoken with both sides, Lord Goodman proposed a compromise; the consultants would accept Barbara's right to pass legislation to remove the private beds. In return, the government would guarantee that the pay beds would be retained until alternative provision was available in non NHS hospitals. Then, having given both parties time to reflect on this proposal, he brought them together in the privacy of his home, hoping that an agreement could be hammered out.

So, for what promised to be the last time, Barbara faced the BMA's negotiating team. She hated having to make compromises but knew that her position was weak. Left to her own devices she would have fought them to the bitter end but Harold Wilson had undermined her authority.

Lord Goodman began by asking Barbara if she was able to agree to his proposal.

"All right," she conceded reluctantly. "The government will proceed with its legislation to remove all the pay beds but we agree to allow time for alternative facilities to become available."

"We agree to that as well," Dr Stevenson confirmed, then turned to face the Minister.

"Mrs Castle," he said, "we insist that the alternative beds, those that are to be developed outside the NHS, must be of a satisfactory standard. The wording of our agreement must make that clear."

"Oh, very well," Barbara snapped, 'let the phrase be '*the reasonable availability of alternative facilities* '."

"I think you misunderstand our concern Mrs Castle," Dr Stevenson replied smoothly. The beds in the new independent hospitals must have the full range of diagnostic and therapeutic facilities; equivalent to those available in the NHS. Otherwise we would not be able to provide adequate care for all our patients, including those needing intensive care; we would not be swopping like for like. The phrase must be *the availability of reasonable alternative facilities.*"

It became a battle of wills but Dr Stevenson, recognising his opponent's weakness, gave no ground. After much wrangling, a compromise was reached which would be '*the reasonable availability of reasonable alternative facilities* '! It was a classic fudge!! Dr Stevenson though was delighted. The future of private practice had been secured. Initially, it would continue within the NHS, but in due course it would be practised within modern purpose built facilities.

When the meeting appeared to be over, Barbara told the doctors that her office would draw up an agreement for both parties to sign. The next day, the draft was forwarded to the BMA and Barbara confidently expected the consultants would immediately call off their industrial action, that a joint communiqué would be issued and the bad press she had endured would be at an end. She was to be disappointed.

The draft was immediately returned by courier. The doctors were adamant that the agreement should be presented, not as a *'negotiated settlement'* but as an offer from her to the BMA. They wished to be perceived as having been victorious in their battle with the government.

Barbara replied suggested that the document be presented as a *'joint statement'*.

The draft came back again; the BMA now insisting the proposal be submitted, not from her, but in the form of an offer to them from the Prime Minister.

Further prolonged and bad tempered exchanges involving the Prime Minister's office took place before a letter was drafted for Harold Wilson to sign, saying that the settlement was *'commended for approval'*. This form of words meant that the BMA's 'work to rule' remained in place whilst they consulted with their members. It was to be several more weeks before normal working was resumed.

By this time, Barbara was mentally and physically exhausted. She knew that she had lost the confidence and support of the Prime Minister and many of her colleagues in the Cabinet. She had been forced to compromise on her socialist principles. Her only consolation was the thought that the way was now clear for her to be able to close the pay beds, although regrettably there would be a considerable delay before this could be implemented. What she didn't know was that within a few months she would be sacked.

Chapter Thirty-Four

"Sir Willam," Victoria began, "do you feel that Tom should be treated with one of the new cytotoxic drugs? I read recently that they may help patients with Tom's problem; his life might be extended for several weeks?"

"A doctor's priority," Sir William replied, "is not to keep the patient alive as long as possible but to think about the quality of their life; to consider what makes their life worth living. At the moment, Tom is weak, he's tired but he has no pain. He's able to walk around and enjoy his food. If we start him on chemotherapy, he'll spend what little time remains vomiting. The same principle applies to heroic surgery for advanced tumours. It may make the surgeon feel that he is doing something to help but in reality, he is inflicting pain and additional suffering upon someone who is destined to die. It's better to help the patient to accept that their life is drawing to a close and to concentrate on relieving pain and anxiety. There really ought to be an eleventh commandment you know 'Thou shalt not strive officiously to keep alive.'"

"Then we must think about the support Tom needs for his remaining days," Victoria said. "It's clear that he's going to deteriorate rapidly. Ideally he would be nursed at home in the midst of a caring family, but Tom has no living relatives and his next of kin apparently is a neighbour."

"Do you think that the neighbour will be able to help?" Sir William asked.

"I think it's unlikely. Apparently, he's little more than a key holder whilst Tom is in hospital. It looks as if Tom is destined to spend his final days with us."

Sir William frowned. "It does look like that but it's far from ideal. Surgical wards are not quiet and restful places; the pace of life is fast, the turnover of patients rapid and the ward is always busy. Also, with thirty or more people sleeping in what effectively is a large dormitory, there's noise at night; inevitably some patients snore or are restless. I suggest Tom is given the chance to go home now, provided he feels able to do so, but understands he may return to us when the time comes." He turned to Sister, "I'm sure we could find a side room for him where it will be relatively quiet, can't we Sister?"

"I'm sure we can. Tom is quite a favourite with the staff," she replied.

As expected, Tom declined quickly. He asked Sister what he should do if he hadn't made a will. He confided to her that, not only did he have no family, but apart from one or two people with whom he was acquainted through his work, there was no-one whom he regarded as a close friend. Knowing that dying intestate could cause difficulties, Sister referred the problem to Sir William who, aware of Tom's war service, suggested he consider leaving his estate to the Royal British Legion to help support ex-service men.

Fortunately, Tom remained free of pain but rapidly grew weaker, such that there was never any prospect of him caring for himself at home. He was not confined to the ward and was occasionally able to visit the hospital shop, though the distance he was able to walk reduced daily. He accepted the inevitability of his fate with quiet dignity and, unlike many patients, was not afraid to ask how his illness was likely to progress. His various questions were answered with total honesty. It was a surprise therefore when Victoria found him in tears one evening as she happened to be passing.

Quietly, she pulled the screens round his bed. "Hey Tom, this isn't like you."

"I'm sorry. I'm letting myself down," he said, pulling a handkerchief from under the pillow and wiping his eyes.

"Is there a problem? Are you in pain?"

"No, Doctor, it's just silly thoughts going through my head. I'll be alright in a minute."

"Is there anything I can do to help?" Victoria asked kindly, "I've got time for a chat."

"I'm suddenly overwhelmed with sadness," Tom confessed.

"We all have to die sometime," Victoria said gently. "The clock ticks for everyone."

"I know. But you see, I'm not sad that I'm going to die, I'm not afraid of dying. I know you kind people will be here to help me. I'm sad that no one will remember me. I've lost all those who were dear to me long ago. When I'm gone, no one will even know that I've been here."

Victoria was lost for words. She felt her eyes watering. Here was a man whose entire family had been snatched away from him, who had searched in vain for years to find out what had become of them and then, having accepted that they must all be dead, but not knowing how they had died or whether they had suffered before they died, had lived in the shadows, isolated by his dreadful disfigurement. Slowly she composed herself and put her hand on Tom's.

"Perhaps only a few will remember you as an individual, as Aleksander Szczepanski," she said softly, "but millions will be grateful to you for the service that you rendered to the world in the war. Every time they stand in silence on Remembrance Sunday, they will be honouring you and your comrades. And you've made a great impression on all the staff here. You can be sure we will remember you."

Tom allowed himself a weak smile. "It seems funny to hear you call me Aleksander," he said, "after all these years being known as 'Tom'. My wife used to call me Aleks. You've no idea how much I have missed her over the years. My life would have been so different had she been at my side."

Victoria felt herself welling up again; she did not trust herself to speak. Tom gave her hand a squeeze and added "perhaps it won't be too long before I see her again."

*****

Two days later, Paul was working his way steadily through the surgical cubicles in the accident department when the casualty sister dashed in.

"Paul, do you know a man called Szczepanski; a man with scars on his face from old burns?"

"Certainly I do. He's one of our patients on the ward. Why do you ask?"

"He's been found collapsed on the main corridor of the hospital. Apparently, he was having an epileptic fit so he was brought here. He's wearing pyjamas and a dressing gown and his hospital bracelet states that he's a Surgical Five patient."

"And you say he was fitting? He doesn't have a history of epilepsy."

"Yes. Apparently, he was seen having a major fit and he's now unconscious. Dr Makin is looking after him. He thought you might be able to give him some background information."

Paul joined Bill Makin in the medical cubicle and found that Tom was indeed deeply unconscious. Bill had been considering all the various causes of fits and coma. When told that Tom was terminally ill with a lung cancer that had already spread to the skin and lymph glands, he readily accepted that Tom's latest problems were due to tumour deposits now having spread to the brain. Tom was transferred back to the surgical ward where he was nursed in a side room. He was given large doses of sedatives to prevent further epileptic fits, remained deeply unconscious and the staff felt that it was a blessing when he slipped away the next morning.

Chapter Thirty-Five

"I've worked dammed hard recently," Barbara announced, "I'm going to have some belated fun. Cancel all my engagements for the rest of the day and let no-one disturb me."

"No-one, not even the Prime Minister?" her Private Secretary asked.

"No-one. Not even the Queen and most certainly not the Prime Minister!"

It was the week before Christmas and she planned a break in her busy schedule. Once again, she was going to Transport House, the home of the TUC, to attend their Christmas party. It was one of her favourite events, her annual treat. She relished the chance to socialise with old friends and reminisce with trades union officials about previous political battles fought and won. She savoured the prospect of 'being with her own', letting her hair down and watching the hilarious political cabaret that was always performed. No doubt some wag would put on the red wig and *'take her off'* just as they had last year.

So with a drink in one hand and a plate of salami snacks in the other, she ran upstairs to sit in the balcony to watch the performance. She wasn't disappointed. The show, as always, was highly entertaining. There were comedy sketches, irreverent songs, digs at the Prime Minister and his cabinet, pointed criticism of the Tory opposition and, to her delight; she was the butt of several good jokes. It was the perfect tonic after her exhausting week. Thoroughly relaxed a couple of hours later, she decided it was time to go home and catch up on her sleep. She made her excuses and made for the exit. Then disaster struck. As she descended the stairs, she missed her footing. Maybe it was the subdued lighting, maybe her new bifocal spectacles or even the alcohol she had consumed;

possibly it was a combination of all three but she flew through the air, crashed down half a dozen steps and landed on her face.

She found herself in agony, counting stars, spread eagled on the floor. For a moment she lay where she was, stunned. Her instinct was not to make a fuss. She tried to struggle to her feet but found herself unable to do so; her leg wouldn't take her weight. It was bleeding and extremely painful. Two labour MPs, Shirley Williams and Eric Heffer were first on the scene and she needed them both to half carry, half drag her to the car. They drove rapidly to the Houses of Parliament and, despite Barbara's pain and distress, managed somehow to get her up the stairs to her room.

Shirley Williams took charge in a competent, motherly way. Gently she took off Barbara's stocking. She looked at the leg and, even without any medical knowledge, realised that it was a nasty injury. Midway from knee to ankle, the skin was lacerated and there was a huge swelling due to bruising. She feared the leg might be broken. She made Barbara as comfortable as she could, elevating the leg and offering hot drinks and a blanket, all the while cooing sympathetically. Then she instructed Barbara to remain seated whilst she dashed off to see if by chance there happened to be a doctor in the House.

"A couple of our MP's are doctors," she said, "I'm sure I shall manage to find one of them."

Barbara waited in agony for what appeared to be an age before there was a polite knock at the door and the conservative MP, Dr Gerald Vaughan appeared. He smiled apologetically.

"I'm sorry it's me, Barbara," he said, "but there's no one else available."

Barbara groaned, not only was Gerry Vaughan a Tory, he was also her political shadow! She would have welcomed any other doctor in the world but him! "I'm grateful to you for coming," she managed to say.

As Shirley Williams watched anxiously from the side lines, Gerry Vaughan washed his hands assiduously, and then diligently examined Barbara's leg.

"You've had a nasty fall Barbara; it's quite an injury you have there. It must be very painful."

Barbara stifled a profanity. "I know that," she said, through teeth clenched not merely because of her painful injury!

"If it was anyone else but you, Barbara, I'd send you for an immediate x-ray."

"I know exactly what you mean!" Barbara hissed in reply. "With all the emergency departments still shut down by industrial action, every one of your wretched colleagues will be waiting to play medical politics with my personal pain. I wouldn't go for an x-ray even if I was dying," she added. "Can you imagine the headlines in tomorrow's papers if I go to hospital? I can see them now. *Industrial action not a problem for Health Minister. No waiting for Mrs Castle. Barbara gets special treatment whilst others queue.*"

In view of Barbara's determination not to go to hospital, she was driven home where she retired to bed with pain killers. For the next 48 hours, she stayed there, immobile and in severe pain. Ted, her husband looked after her as best he could, all the while worrying what additional damage might be caused if indeed the leg was broken and the injury left untreated. Her GP visited. He also advised that it would be wise to have an x-ray, but once again Barbara refused. Her husband cursed her stubbornness but knew that once her mind was made up, it would take a miracle to change it.

Later in the day, the press got to hear of Barbara's dilemma. How they found out she never discovered. Presumably someone at Transport House had witnessed her fall and informed them.

"Newspaper men have a natural instinct for sniffing out embarrassing situations," she complained, "but they're nowhere to be found when there's good news to relate!"

The house was besieged. Pressmen and cameramen camped outside her door. They tried to speak with her on the telephone. Her GP was bombarded with questions but he stonewalled brilliantly and gave nothing away. Inevitably they wanted to know why Barbara wasn't having an x-ray.

"I'm in a 'catch 22' situation," she moaned. "Whatever I say, whatever I decide, I'm damned. I just can't win. If I go to have an x-ray, I'll be accused of taking advantage of my position; seeking preferential treatment in an 'emergency only' situation. On the other hand, if I don't have one, the doctors will complain that I have no confidence in their profession.

Her secretary called and was obviously worried. "Look," he said, "it really isn't sensible for you to be pig headed about having an x-ray. Your GP is concerned, we're concerned and your husband is concerned. We would all be much happier if you had one. You're in pain; you have a nasty injury, you owe it to yourself to have one. If you were any other person, you would have been x-rayed two days ago. That leg of yours might well be broken. If it is, you're not doing yourself any favours by lying here. Let me ring round and see which hospitals are working normally? You could attend as an outpatient if you prefer not to go to casualty."

Finally, defeated by the continuing pain, lack of sleep and a barrage of advice, Barbara conceded that it would be sensible to have an x-ray. Much relieved, her secretary went to investigate where treatment might be arranged. He discovered that the Whittington Hospital was operating normally and that there was an orthopaedic outpatient clinic that afternoon. He hurried back with the good news.

"I've taken the liberty of arranging an appointment for you at 3.30 pm. With a bit of luck, you won't have to wait too long."

"Surely I ought to go to casualty."

"I don't think that would be wise," he replied. "Casualty departments are very public places. You're bound to be recognised. Better to go to the outpatient clinic and just slip in and out unnoticed. I've no doubt your GP will write you a referral letter."

Reluctantly, Barbara agreed. Later, the GP arrived, pleased to get away from his surgery without being interrogated. He too had been besieged by the press.

"Don't worry. They won't get anything out of me," he said, conspiratorially. "I'll ring the consultant to tell him you're coming."

But with years of experience in public life, Barbara realised it would be foolish to ask for any special treatment. "No, please don't do that; simply write me a doctor's letter in the usual way. I'll go along just as any other patient would, without anyone knowing that I'm coming."

At three o'clock, having dressed very gingerly, she was assisted downstairs to the car by her husband. Fortunately, they were able to slip away without being noticed by the press. At the hospital, following the GP's instructions, they turned through the gates and into the car park. But Barbara immediately groaned. "Look! Someone is expecting us. They've been forewarned."

A uniformed figure waved and beckoned them to follow him. He led them to the front door of the casualty department. As the car stopped, a middle aged man in a smart suit converged on them.

"Welcome, Mrs Castle, I'm the area administrator. I'm sorry to hear that you've had an accident but I'm sure that we'll be able to sort things out for you."

Two seconds later, Matron's stout figure emerged, resplendent in white cap, maroon cape and pristine starched apron. She was accompanied by a porter, a red hospital blanket and a wheelchair. Within seconds, the Secretary of State for Health was being wheeled smartly into the hospital.

Barbara was dismayed. "How did you know I was coming?" she wailed. "I specifically didn't want anyone to know."

In the absence of any reply, she assumed it was either her GP or her secretary. She sped through the hospital corridors to a small well furnished consulting room in an annex, set apart from the main outpatients building. A sister and a nurse sprang to attention as she entered and assisted her onto a couch. Immediately the door opened and the orthopaedic consultant, Mr Payton, marched in, a white coat covering his smart grey city suit. Barbara knew that this was not the ordinary NHS outpatient department. To her chagrin, she realised that she had been ushered into a private consulting suit. But it had all happened so quickly that in her injured state, despite her lifelong socialist views, she didn't feel strong enough to object.

Then, quite abruptly, emotion got the better of her. Her leg was still extremely painful despite dosing on painkillers and she had managed little sleep for the previous two nights. She was in a strange environment, being treated against her wishes. Suddenly, feeling frail and helpless, she burst into tears.

"Look, I specifically said I didn't want anyone to know I was coming," she cried. "I want to be treated the same as anybody else. I don't want to be treated in a private suite. Look, I've brought a doctor's letter just like any other patient. I just want to go to the ordinary outpatient department. I want to queue, I don't care how long I wait; one hour, two hours, however long it takes. See, I've brought something with me to read."

The nursing sister tried to reassure her. "There's no need to get upset Mrs Castle," she said but then made matters ten times worse by adding, "I'll get you some tissues and perhaps you would like a coffee and some biscuits."

"I don't want tissues. I don't want any coffee. I don't want special treatment; I just want to be treated as an ordinary patient," Barbara sobbed.

Mr Payton was clearly embarrassed. "We merely thought, Minister, that a busy person like yourself, would not want to be held up in the outpatient clinic, but as it happens the clinic is nearly over and you wouldn't have had to wait very long in any case. We weren't trying to give you any special treatment, just trying to be helpful."

Slowly, Barbara gained control of her tears and insisted, "But that's not true, is it? This is special treatment. I know you mean it for the best, but none of you have any idea how I'm persecuted by the press. They've been trying to break into my home to photograph me in bed. They never stop ringing, so I can't get any rest. They camp on the street, watching the front door day and night. They even follow my GP to see if he visits me. They hate me. They invent stories to show me in a bad light. Only today, the Daily Mail told their readers that I was drunk when I fell, and I swear that I wasn't."

"But there's absolutely no reason why the press should learn of this visit," the consultant replied smoothly. "Medical confidentiality will ensure that."

"Mr Payton," she pleaded, "you simply do not know or understand the press. They would bribe every patient in the building to discover that I'd been here and to find out if I'd received preferential treatment. I must be treated as an ordinary patient."

"Very well, if you insist," Mr Payton replied. "Sister, you had better register Mrs Castle into the outpatient department in the normal way."

Once more, Mrs Castle was loaded onto a wheelchair, taken along the hospital corridors and registered as an NHS patient at the outpatient reception desk. Along the way she was recognised by several members of the public and hospital staff, who stopped to stare at this famous figure whose picture they had seen so frequently in recent weeks in their morning newspapers and on their television screens. Her wheelchair did not stop in the large outpatient waiting area but was driven straight into an examination cubicle. This room was much barer than the earlier one. There were neither flowers on the desk, nor pictures on the wall but it was perfectly adequate.

"I don't think you will have to wait very long," Sister said, a smile on her face. True to her word, she returned with Mr Payton two minutes later. He examined the leg carefully, noting the laceration and severe bruising.

"I doubt that the leg is broken, nonetheless I think an x-ray would be a wise precaution. I'd do the same for anybody else, so this is not special treatment." He spoke the words to reassure his patient, though he was conscious that to overlook a fracture in a Minister of the Crown, particularly the Health Minister would be a career threatening mistake!

Barbara was whisked through the x-ray department and was reviewed by Mr Payton less than 15 minutes later. Fortunately, the x-ray did not reveal a break. The leg was then expertly bandaged, stronger pain killers were dispensed and she returned home without further mishap. The entire hospital visit had taken less than an hour.

Subsequent events were to prove that Barbara's concerns about the media's intelligence network were amply confirmed. Their sniffer dogs had already got hold of the story. Whether there was mole amongst the hospital staff prepared to ring a news desk and earn a quick fiver or whether the story came from a hospital patient or visitor Barbara would never know.

For the next 24 hours, her husband had to fend off endless press enquiries. '*Did Barbara have to wait or did she walk straight in? Did she see the consultant or a junior member of staff?*' With a sense of deep foreboding, she waited to find out what the national newspapers would say the next day. Her apprehension was fully justified. The Daily Express carried the headline, '*Emergency my foot*'. The Daily Telegraph trumpeted '*She was seen by a consultant surgeon, a privilege for which NHS patients have to wait months!*'

Chapter Thirty-Six

Early in the New Year, whilst Barbara's bruised and lacerated leg was slowly healing, the consultants who had been taking industrial action gradually drifted back to work. They acknowledged that the Government were entitled to enact legislation to abolish the NHS pay beds but were satisfied that Lord Goodman's agreement, guaranteeing that the beds would not disappear until *'reasonable'* alternative beds were available, secured a healthy future for private medicine.

Having settled with the nurses and consultants, Barbara Castle still faced the thorny issue of the junior hospital doctor's ludicrously long hours – and once again the pressure on her was building. The number of hospitals affect by the juniors overtime ban that had started in London had dramatically increased. The Midlands and the North West were now the regions worst affected. The Royal Infirmary in her own Blackburn constituency was particularly badly hit, as were hospitals in neighbouring Lancashire towns and in Manchester. The Chairmen of several Regional Health Authorities travelled to Westminster to impress upon her the urgency of the situation and the risk to patients. Once more, her competency was being questioned, not only by MPs in the House of Commons but also by members of the Cabinet and, all the while, she was being vilified by sections of the press.

Gloomily, she sat in her office and reflected on the situation. She realised that she was stuck between a rock and a hard place. She accepted that the hours of the juniors were intolerable. She had seen for herself that in many hospitals a pair of doctors were required by their contracts to provide continuous cover for the patients on their ward. Even if they were never on duty at the same time, each covering 12 hours in every 24, that amounted to 84 hours a week. That was not only unacceptable; it was unsafe for patients and doctors alike. But, she was trapped. The government's pay policy stipulated that only money that had actually been paid previously in salaries was available and in the past, many juniors had not claimed pay for the hours they worked. There was simply no room for manoeuvre, no possibility of a compromise.

She remembered all too clearly that when the consultants' dispute on pay beds had stalled, the Prime Minister had gone over her head and asked Lord Goodman to negotiate a settlement. She was determined that her authority would not be undermined again. She could see only one way out of the impasse. Somehow or other, she would have to settle with the juniors and make it appear that the pay policy had not been breached - even if that involved using smoke and mirrors.

Responsibility for the policy lay with Michael Foot and she knew how fearful he was that if one group of workers broke the pay code, the entire policy would fall apart with terrible consequences for the nation's economic situation. She arranged to meet him over a sandwich lunch.

"We have to accept," she said, "the salary of the junior doctors is based on a 40 hour week. There really is no alternative. That's the norm throughout the land."

"So how much will they be paid for the hours they work beyond forty?" Michael asked.

"That's something which will be decided by the body that makes recommendations on doctor's pay," Barbara replied, ducking the question. "Remember that although ostensibly they are an independent body, they are obliged to take notice of our pay policy."

"Barbara," Michael began looking concerned, "We know that many work long hours. There are stories of some working for 80 hours a week, possibly longer. I presume that's an exaggeration designed to gain public sympathy but if it is true that some haven't been claiming their overtime pay for various reasons, we really have very little idea how much this will cost. We are in danger of making an agreement without knowing whether or not it will breach pay policy. As guardian of the policy, I can't possibly agree to that."

"Don't you worry, Michael," Barbara replied reassuringly, not admitting that she knew the stories of long hours were certainly not an exaggeration, "there is a safeguard. The final cost will depend on the level of payment that is agreed for the standard rate. If that rate is low, the overall package will be affordable. An independent audit to verify the hours they actually work is being carried out, and as you say, the doctors are certain to have overstated the figures. I'm sure it will all fall nicely within the government's agreement with the unions."

Perhaps realising that patients might die as a result of the industrial action being taken, perhaps aware that Labour's reputation as guardian of the NHS was in tatters, perhaps appreciating that there was no other way to resolve the issue, Michael did not pursue the matter. Nor did he seek further clarification, though he may well have realised that Barbara was being economical with the truth.

Barbara did not like to mislead her old friend in this way. Privately she knew that this would be a very expensive settlement. She had already agreed that the juniors' basic week should be 40 hours instead of 44. She had also agreed that doctors on 'standby' at home should in future be paid at the same rate as those on duty in hospital. She had no idea what the independent audit on hours would reveal but accepted that the junior doctors were currently working a vast amount of unpaid overtime. She also knew that it was unthinkable to suggest that the basic rate of pay be reduced in order to free up money to reward those working excessive hours. If that were to happen, many doctors in x-ray and pathology departments, who worked a forty hour week, would have to take a pay cut of 20% or 30% which simply wouldn't be tolerated.

Pleased that Michael Foot had accepted her reassurance that the pay policy was not at risk, she coyly made a statement to Parliament the next day to that effect. The House was almost empty to hear her speak, no awkward questions were asked and she was even congratulated for resolving a problem that at one stage had seemed insoluble. She heaved an enormous sigh of relief. It would be a couple of months before the final cost became known. At that stage she might have some explaining to do but for the moment, she could relax.

Although Cabinet and Parliament may have been deceived, the press certainly weren't. When the news was released, much to the surprise and delight of the junior doctors, a telling cartoon appeared in the Sun newspaper. Barbara Castle was caricatured remarking to Harold Wilson, *'Oh silly me, I must have got my sums wrong about the doctors pay. I shall tell the cabinet I can't count.'*

To which the Prime Minister replies, *'I have already told them she doesn't count.'*

Chapter Thirty-Seven

Since Tom had no known living relatives either in England or in Poland, it was the neighbour, who had been listed as Tom's next of kin, who was phoned by Sister and asked to collect his belongings. The neighbour politely declined.

"I'm not his next of kin," he said. "I don't know why I've been listed as such. I used to see him coming and going from time to time but I scarcely knew him. I was surprised when he asked me to take his key when he went into hospital. It wouldn't be appropriate for me to handle his belongings. Besides I don't suppose there's anything in the place apart from some dirty washing."

Sister spoke with the senior administrator to seek guidance, as it was not a situation she had encountered before. She was advised to collect Tom's belongings, document them and then keep them under lock and key until further notice. She thought it wise to have her actions witnessed, so she took Paul with her when she went to empty Tom's locker. They found some dirty socks, underpants and handkerchiefs, a couple of books, a watch and a few coins but, in addition, there was a brown envelope addressed to Sir William and a tiny box made of particularly stiff, white cardboard. The box contained a bronze medal in the shape of a cross. The cross was two inches wide; it's horizontal bar represented aircraft wings, whilst the vertical bar depicted aeroplane propellers. Hanging from the medal was a ribbon with purple and white diagonal stripes. It was accompanied by a slip of card on which was typed *'Distinguished Flying Cross. Awarded to Aleksander Tomasz Szczepanski'*

"May I borrow that for a moment?" Paul asked.

He took the medal and walked down the ward. The bearded Mancunian was lounging in the patient's rest room, smoking and watching television.

"I thought you might be interested to see this," he said, fixing him with his eye and showing him the medal.

"What is it, Doc?"

"It's the Distinguished Flying Cross," he said. "It was awarded to Tom, the ugly Polak. I guess you didn't realise he served in the RAF and fought in the Battle of Britain. He got those terrible burns when he crashed defending this country."

"Well, bugger me," commented the Mancunian, "would you believe it?"

Sir William brought Tom's letter with him when he came for his next ward round. "I thought you would be interested to know what Tom wrote," he said. He read the letter out loud:

Dear Doctor,

Please thank your doctors and nurses for their kindness to me. I do not think I shall have time to write a proper will, so respectfully ask you to decide these matters for me. Do give my things to old soldiers if you think that best.

May God bless you all,

Aleksander Szczepanski   'Tom'

There was silence as everyone reflected on Tom's courage and the quiet dignity he had shown throughout his illness. His homeland had been overrun in war, his wife captured and killed. Then after an arduous journey across Europe he had joined the Polish arm of the Royal Air force. He had served with great bravery and distinction before being so terribly injured. Yet when the war was won, he found that his own country was subjugated and when he settled in England, had never been made welcome by those who ought to have been grateful to him. He had been forced to work as a night watchman, out of sight and out of mind.

A month later, there was great excitement and general rejoicing as the junior doctors assembled for Sir William's ward round. The independent body had considered the result of the audit of the hours they worked and their new contract had been priced. Paul and his colleagues now knew exactly what the settlement meant for them as individuals.

For Janet and Malcolm, the two house officers, it meant a 30% rise. The hours they worked beyond 40 now formed part of their contract and would be remunerated. For Paul and Victoria it meant a smaller rise but one that was very welcome nonetheless! Immediately Paul's thoughts turned to the possibility of a move out of their hospital flat into a home of their own. Kate would love that and they could now think about starting a family. All four were delighted that the government had also agreed to work with the BMA to reduce their excessive hours. If that could be achieved, the remaining time they spent as junior doctors would be so much less onerous.

Plans were underway to organise a party in the doctor's residency to celebrate when, on the stroke of ten o'clock, Sir William entered the office; a smile on his face and a parcel under his arm. He looked round at the sea of happy faces.

"You've obviously heard the news," he said, "and I'm delighted for you. You all work extremely hard and the award is well deserved. I appreciate how much you do for my patients and feel fortunate that I have such a wonderful team working alongside me. I have found it distressing that some doctors should withdraw their care from their patients in my retirement year but I'm delighted that you all continued to put patients first.

"Now," he continued, "I have some news of my own to share with you."

He started to unwrap the parcel.

"Victoria, you said that Tom's great sadness was that he felt that no-one would remember him when he was gone, that no-one would ever know he existed."

He revealed a polished oak plaque into which Tom's medal had been inlaid. Beneath the medal, on a small brass plate, were inscribed the words:

In memory of 'Tom' Szczepanski DFC

who served with distinction in the Polish arm of the Royal Air Force

"I am pleased to say the hospital has agreed that the side ward he occupied should be dedicated to him. Now, our patients are waiting for us, I think we should get on with the business of the day."

"Sir William, may I offer you a cup of coffee and a biscuit before you start your round?" Sister asked politely.

"Thank you Sister, that's very kind but I think we ought to see our patients first," the senior consultant replied.

Victoria met Paul's eye and smiled. It was comforting to hear Sir William utter his familiar response to Sister. Perhaps after all the recent political strife, they could now get back to doing what they really wanted to do – looking after their patients.

Postscript

On 17th September 1974, the Government accepted the Halsbury report. Nurses were granted an average pay increase of 30%, backdated to 23rd May, together with improvements in overtime and holidays. An interim award was made for professions supplementary to medicine such as physiotherapists and radiographers. Most nurses, but not all were delighted; the award was skewed in favour of senior experienced nurses, the award to student nurses being less than 10%. The rate of inflation in the following 12 months was 24% which negated much of the benefit. The overall cost of the pay rise was £170 million.

The Junior Hospital Doctors dispute ended with a contract based on a 40 hour week. Extra payment for additional hours (be they hours spent on duty in the hospital or on call at home) became a part of the contract and could no longer be denied by an unsympathetic consultant. Initially, the Government had suggested that only£1.5 million pounds was available to introduce the new contract. Subsequently it was found to cost £30 million. Mrs Castle had persuaded parliament that the pay rise would not breach the Government's pay policy – in fact it drove a coach and horses through it.

The Consultants retained the right to undertake private practice within both NHS and private hospitals. 1000 of the 4100 'pay beds' were immediately removed, (their average occupancy had been 50%). Phasing out of the remaining beds was dependent on the *'reasonable availability of reasonable alternative facilities'* in the private sector as judged by a Health Service Board. This board was subsequently abolished by Mrs Thatcher. The long-term result of the bitter battle fought between the BMA and the Labour Government has been the development of the significant private health sector that exists today. The majority of private patients are now treated in modern independent purpose-built hospitals.

James Callaghan succeeded Harold Wilson in April 1976 and immediately dismissed Mrs Castle from the cabinet. She did not stand for re-election as an MP but subsequently served as a Member of the European Parliament for ten years.

These disputes had a significant effect on patients.

In 1975, the number of patients treated in hospital was 4% lower than in 1974.

The number of patients waiting for admission rose by 12% to the highest level since the NHS began.

Out-patient attendances were down by 7%.

Message from the author

Writing this novel has allowed me the pleasure of reminiscing about days gone by. I hope that you've enjoyed reading it. Should you have any questions or comments about it, or wish to be informed when the sequel is published, I should be pleased to hear from you. I can be reached via the 'contact' tab on the website www.petersykes.org

Sources

Archives of the Royal College of Nursing

Archives of the British Medical Association

Records of the Confederation of Health Service Employees

Hansard

'The Castle Diaries 1964 – 1976' Barbara Castle

'Fighting all the way' Barbara Castle

'The Red Queen' Authorised biography of Barbara Castle. Anne Perkins

'The Junior Doctors Pay Dispute 1975 – 1976 Susan Treloar

'A history of the Royal College of Nursing 1916 – 1990' Susan McGann, Anne Crowther and Rona Dougall

Lord David Owen Personal Communication